Street Cat Blues

Alison O'Leary

CROOKED
CAT

Discover us online:
www.crookedcatbooks.com

Join us on facebook:
www.facebook.com/crookedcat

Tweet a photo of yourself holding
this book to **@crookedcatbooks**
and something nice will happen.

For John

About the Author

Alison was born in London and spent her teenaged years in Hertfordshire where she spent large amounts of time reading Agatha Christie novels and avoiding school. Failing to gain any qualifications in Science whatsoever, the dream of being a forensic scientist collided with reality when a careers teacher suggested that she might like to work in a department store. Later studying Law, she decided to teach rather than go into practice and has spent many years working as a college lecturer teaching mainly Criminal Law to adults and young people.

Alison lives on the south coast with her husband John and cat Archie. When not writing, she enjoys crosswords, reading crime fiction, walking by the sea, and drinking wine. Not necessarily in that order.

www.alisonoleary.co.uk

Acknowledgements

A huge thank you to the real Aubrey, the cat who inspired this book and who never knowingly passed up a food opportunity. A king among cats, he enjoyed life to the full and was never less than generous with his affection. Love and appreciation also to Jo Beaven for his patience, wit and wisdom and to Carol Nash for the love, food and wine. Gratitude also to Lesley and Fred Cox for just being lovely and to Tanya Beaven and Laura and Dave Hunt likewise. For always being a mate, grateful thanks go to Alan Cushway and David Corbridge and similarly to Pat Greenwood for cheering me on from the side lines. Thanks also to Kathryn Price and Dinah Ceeley from Cornerstones Literary Consultancy for expert guidance and advice and always believing in me, Steph and Laurence Patterson for giving me the chance, all my fellow Crooked Cat authors for being brilliant and generous, and last, but by no means least, my dear friend and fellow crime writer Sarah Bohane for understanding everything.

Street Cat Blues

Chapter One

"What happened? Was he done in like the others, or what?"

Across the road, a small knot of people were staring at old Mr Telling's house. Even Ozzie the postman had paused from his customary breakneck hurtle down the street and was leaning on his bike watching the scene. A police car and ambulance stood waiting. Aubrey watched for a second and then slipped beneath the nearest parked car and inched his way along its length to get a closer look.

The grease and dirt coating the undercarriage nudged against his fur and he paused for a moment, trying to hold his breath against the petrol fumes. He moved further forward to get a better view, as the legs and ankles of the little crowd jostled across his line of vision. He narrowed his eyes as Mr Telling's front door opened and two burly men emerged carrying a large zippered bag. Their rough hands handled the bag as tenderly as if the thing inside it was still a living, breathing thing, a sentient being that might cry out in shock or pain if suddenly jolted. Behind them, walking at a measured pace, head bowed and hands clasped together, marched a pair of short, fat legs ending in a pair of sparkly, flip-flopped feet. Aubrey held his breath and watched through slitted eyes. His old enemy, Maria. He might have known it.

"That'll do now, madam, thank you, although we may need to talk to you again later."

The young police officer spoke gently but firmly, barring Maria's way to the waiting ambulance. She opened her mouth to protest and then closed it again, watching in silence along with Aubrey and the rest of the crowd as the ambulance swung out into the road with the police car following.

"What happened?"

Maria turned to the waiting audience.

"Was it you that found him?"

Aubrey watched her as she regarded them in silence for a moment, her sharp, dark eyes alight with self-importance. She tipped back on her heels and thrust out her chest. The buttons on her thin cotton blouse strained against the pressure as she lowered her voice and moved forward. The waiting neighbours drew in and gathered in a semi-circle around her.

"Yes, it is me," she whispered. "I am the person who find him."

Maria lowered her voice still further and slid her gaze to right and left, as though watching for a sniper in the crowd before continuing.

"This morning all is normal. I get off bus. I walk down road. I sing. La la. I let myself in with key. I am doing the houseworks. But suddenly I stop and think, but where is Mr Telling?" She stared round at the crowd, eyes widened and eyebrows raised. "He is not here. But then I think, he must be here. Always he is here."

One or two of the heads in the crowd nodded in agreement.

"That's right. He never went out. Well, hardly ever. Only down The Laurels."

"And so," continued Maria, "I think if Mr Telling is not out then he must be in." She nodded and looked around her as she spoke, clearly impressed with her own powers of deduction. Several of the less mentally agile among the crowd nodded along with her. "And so, I put down duster and I go upstairs. Perhaps he is ill, I am thinking, perhaps he is ill and he is in bed. If Mr Telling is ill, I will get doctor. I am not paid to do this but this I will do."

From beneath the car Aubrey snorted. Put her feet up and help herself to his sherry more likely. Or go snouting through the papers that Mr Telling kept in a battered old biscuit tin in the cupboard under the stairs. She was always poking her stubby little fingers into things when she thought that nobody was looking.

"But he is not upstairs and so I go back down and look in other room." She paused for dramatic effect and then continued on a rising note, her voice spiralling upwards. "And

4

then I find him. Me." She stabbed herself in the chest with a fat finger. "He is stretched out on floor. At first," she continued, warming to her story, "I think that he has fainted but then I am seeing that there is no breath. But I do not panic. No."

"Yes, but what happened? Was it a heart attack or what?"

A new voice this time. The crowd were becoming impatient.

Maria raised her hand and waited for silence before continuing.

"I lean over and I say Mr Telling, Mr Telling, wake up! But he does not wake up! And then I lean over more and I see blood! Blood on floor! Blood on mantelpiece! Blood on hair! And then I think Mr Telling he has fall. He has fall backwards and he has hit his head. Like this!"

Aubrey watched as she raised her arms and lurched her podgy little feet stiffly forward in dramatic effect, her glittery flip-flops winking in the pale sunshine that had started to break through.

"So it was an accident then?"

The crowd began to disperse around the edges; the excitement was clearly over. Aubrey waited until the last one had left and then he, too, slid out from beneath the car and headed for home. His heart beat fast as he jumped the garden wall. In all honesty, he hadn't been particularly upset when Miss Bradford and Mrs Lomax had been killed, and Miss Jenkins he had positively disliked, but now it was Mr Telling, dear kind gentle Mr Telling, and that was another matter altogether.

Chapter Two

Aubrey slipped through the cat flap and made his way upstairs. Jumping onto the pile of ironing which lay on the bed in the spare room, he licked his paw and flicked it across his left ear. He needed to get things straight in his mind, and a quick wash always helped. Maria had said that Mr Telling had fallen over backwards and had died as a result. That couldn't be right, for a start. Aubrey knew for a fact that when people fell over, they fell forwards, not backwards. It was something to do with how they were made. He'd actually seen one of them do it once.

It had been at the height of summer the previous year, temperatures had been soaring and a young woman carrying heavy shopping had stopped suddenly in the middle of the pavement. Stretched along the warm roof of a parked car from where he had been an interested observer, Aubrey had watched as she had sort of folded at the knees and fallen forward in a little crumpled heap. But the point was that she had fallen forwards, not backwards. So, if Mr Telling had fallen backwards, then he must have been pushed. And if he'd been pushed, then there must have been someone in the house with him. But who could that have been? Mr Telling lived by himself, and the few visitors that he had were usually of the feline variety who regularly called in on the off-chance of a drop of milk or the lickings from an empty yoghurt pot.

Mr Telling's own cat had long since died, but the cat flap was still operational and there weren't many strays that slipped through and were sent away with an empty paw. Truth to tell, Mr Telling had been down on Aubrey's own reserve list, so to speak, just in case it didn't work out with Molly and Jeremy. Not that he was complaining. So far so good, but you could never tell with these things. It was all very well being picked out at a rescue centre and taken home with a new set of owners, but any cat with half a brain cell always had not only a Plan B but a Plan C, D, and E as well. Kindly, friendly, and unfussy, Mr Telling had been the ideal human. If Aubrey had ever been in need of an alternative address in a hurry, Mr Telling's place would have been his first port of call.

He licked his paw again ready to wash the other ear, but then stiffened as the unmistakeable click clack sound of the cat flap echoed from below. Leaping from the bed, he raced down towards the kitchen. He wasn't hungry but he was damned if he was going to let some strange cat near his food. He flexed his claws ready to spring and narrowed his eyes as a small orange-coloured snout struggled its way through the flap, followed by the rest of a little furry body. Aubrey relaxed. It was only Moses.

"All right, Aubrey?"

Aubrey nodded. So called because he'd been found by his owner abandoned in a plastic carrier bag down by the canal, Moses had a high little squeak of a voice and bright excitable eyes that exactly matched the rest of him. Aubrey watched as he landed and shook himself, his tiny paws skittering on the polished tiles.

"Vincent sent me," said Moses, his eyes shining.

"Did he?" said Aubrey. "What for?"

Moses looked back at him, his expression blank, and then gave a longing glance towards Aubrey's dish.

"You wanting that?"

"Help yourself."

He watched as Moses dipped his head and tucked into the food, spraying half of it up the wall in his eagerness to get it into his mouth. For such a small cat he couldn't half put some food away, and yet he never seemed to get any bigger. Funny that. Aubrey wondered what Vincent wanted. Nothing in particular, probably. Just a catch-up. And even if it was something, there was no point in telling Moses; he would have forgotten it by the time he got to the end of the street. But Aubrey should have thought of Vincent in the first place. Vincent always knew what was going on. If anybody had any information about what had happened at Mr Telling's place, it would be Vincent.

7

The cool breeze fluttered the ends of his fur as he made his way across the gardens. Behind him and struggling to keep up, he could hear the scamper of Moses' little legs. A faint rustling sound drew him to a halt. It was coming from near the bushes. His green-gold eyes swept the landscape. It was all right if it was only, say, a hedgehog, but it might be a badger and with badgers you could never tell. They weren't the sort of creatures that you ever wanted to cross. They could turn nasty if you came up against one in the wrong mood, as he knew from experience. He put one paw tentatively forward and then jumped sideways as a soft, lithe shape brushed against him.

"God, Vinnie, don't do that. You startled me."

Vincent grinned, his green eyes gleaming. His gold-coloured neck tag glittered against his rich, dark fur.

"Aubsie, me old mate. How's tricks? Don't seem to have seen you in a while. Thought I'd send Moses, see if you was all right. Was wondering how you were getting on. What you been up to?"

Aubrey shrugged.

"Not much. Same old same old."

The two cats fell into step and strolled round the side of the house towards the bins. Moses trotted along behind them. Funny, thought Aubrey, how old habits die hard. Sleek and well fed, the pair of them, and yet they still couldn't resist the lure of a good bin. Aubrey waited while Vincent sprang up and inserted a muscular paw under the lid of the nearest bin, pulling it towards him and jumping clear just as it hit the ground.

"Vin, I was wondering, did you hear anything about what happened at Mr Telling's place today?"

"Number sixty-two? Talk is that he fell over and hit his head." Vincent paused and looked at him sideways. "Why? You thinking something different?"

Aubrey nodded.

"It doesn't seem right, Vin. Mr Telling wasn't the sort of bloke to just go around falling over."

"I'll put the word out. The twins might know something."

Aubrey felt a quick shiver run through his fur. A pair of

Siamese, rumour had it that Rupert and Roger were running every racket this side of the railway bridge. The further away they were from Aubrey, the better he liked it. The mere mention of their names made him feel tense. Even Vincent didn't cross them. But there was no denying, if any cats had their paws on the pulse it was them.

"Thanks, Vin."

For a moment, both cats were silent as they surveyed the contents of the bin strewn on the ground in front of them. Vincent pulled out a tangle of chop bones and tossed one to Moses.

"Course, what with all the fuss about the others, you might not be the only one thinking it was no accident," said Vincent. "And you know what that means."

Aubrey nodded gloomily. When Miss Jenkins, the retired school teacher, had been found with her head caved in, it had been bad enough. There had been press and police swarming all over the place, you couldn't move for running into one of them. And when Miss Bradford was discovered strangled in her kitchen, followed shortly afterwards by Mrs Lomax in a similar state, the emotional temperature had hit an all-time high. It had all been very unsettling for the cat community, especially with the increase in traffic zooming up and down the roads. You took your life in your paws every time you went out.

"Looks like your bloke was only the first," continued Vincent.

"My bloke?"

"The one you used to live with before you come here. The one who got himself done in at the back of his shop over on the parade."

Aubrey stared at him. He hadn't thought of Raj in relation to the others. It had been over a year ago, and there hadn't been nearly the same amount of fuss for a start. In fact, there had hardly been any. Raj's murder had simply been put down to a robbery that went wrong. It had barely made the inside page of the local paper. But maybe Vincent was right. Maybe Raj had been the first in what was turning out to be many. A tiny knot of anxiety lodged itself in Aubrey's stomach and he let go of the piece of fish batter that he had just pulled from its wrapping.

"Lots of changes going on round these parts, Aubsie," continued Vincent. "Not all of them bad. This place is practically unrecognisable from what it used to be." Vincent paused for a moment and stared around him. "I mean, take this street. Never seen so many builders. Practically can't move for skips. And another thing." He chewed reflectively for a moment. "Less dogs. Time was when every other house had one. Not now. Nowadays, what everyone wants is cats. Less trouble. Cleaner. Nicer to look at, obviously. This place is on the way up, stand on me. Once they stop killing each other, that is."

Aubrey thought for a moment. Vincent was right. He couldn't remember the last time he'd actually seen a dog out on the street. Not that he was complaining. He didn't actively dislike dogs; he just didn't want to get too close to one. Vincent dropped the chop bone he had been chewing and licked appreciatively at his paw.

"Anyway, about time I was off. Got a bit of business to sort. Just wanted to check that you was all right." He glanced over to where Moses had fallen asleep in an empty flower pot. "Come on, Moses, shift yourself. Can't stay here all day."

"Vin?"

"What?"

"You won't forget about Mr Telling, will you? He was a good mate."

Aubrey watched as Vincent slid away, his shape merging with the bushes. For a moment, he stayed perfectly still, thinking again about what Vincent had said about Raj. Was Vincent right? Had Raj been the first victim? It was possible; he fitted the profile. Like the others, he had been over sixty and living alone. Also like the others, he had no family. Well, none that ever visited. And like the others, his death had been sudden, violent, and unnatural.

The memory of that last evening, never far from the front of Aubrey's mind, trickled back. He had known that something

10

was wrong. He had sensed it as soon as he had jumped through the narrow little pantry window that Raj always left open for him. At first, he hadn't been able to work out what it was, and he had stood for a moment sniffing the air. Then he had realised. There was no smell of food. Raj had long since given up caring what he ate, and more often than not had simply taken stuff that was past its sell-by date off the shelves and shoved it into a pan, often with not altogether pleasing results. But on that night, there had been nothing cooking. There had been no obnoxious mess bubbling in a pan, no cabbagey smell drifting its way down the hall. Aubrey had nudged his way round the door to the sitting room, and that was where he had found him. Lying on his side on the threadbare carpet, Raj lay cold and still. A tiny frown was etched on his kindly face, and his right hand still clutched at the crusting gash in his side from which the blood had ceased to flow. Around him lay the smashed and desecrated debris of his life.

He had lain there – Aubrey knew, because he had been back every day to check – for four days before anyone had discovered him. Four whole days before a single person in the whole of the district had bothered to find out why a shop that had been open for the best part of fourteen hours a day for the last ten years, was now shut. Not one person had knocked on the door. Not one person had looked through the window. In the end, it had been the postman trying to deliver a parcel from Raj's cousin in India, who had raised the alarm.

He set off for home, glancing as he did so over to the east and the parade of shops where Raj's News and Groceries had once been. Never busy at the best of times, it now stood dark and empty, the window boarded up and rubbish piled in front of the door. Poor Raj. He had worried almost constantly about the day's takings. Or rather, the lack of them. And now it was as if he had never been. Aubrey could hear his voice even now, the gentle tones lapping against him as they sat in the back room together and watched recorded episodes of *EastEnders*.

"You see, the thing is, cat, always it was crap. Crap shop to start with, and now it is even crapper. Everyone want Tesco. Even I want Tesco, innit."

And Aubrey had to agree with him. Everybody did want Tesco. Tesco was big, cheap, and stayed open all night, and in comparison Raj's News and Groceries was, well, crap.

"Of course, cat, all would have been better if Bitch had not gone."

Aubrey knew all about Bitch. She was Raj's wife, and mother to his three children. According to Raj, he had given Bitch everything, but that hadn't stopped her upping and leaving when he was working the night shift at the brush factory to make ends meet.

He felt his throat thicken and the familiar flicker of discomfort wriggle through him. By the time he had arrived home that night, Raj had clearly been dead for several hours. There was nothing that he could have done. But maybe if he had come home a bit earlier, maybe if he had spent a bit less time larking about on the canal bank, he might at least have had the time to say goodbye. He might have had the chance to give Raj one last lick, and feel the gentle palm of his hand as he stroked his head.

Reaching home, he ran back along the side of the house and leapt over the front gate. The crowd outside Mr Telling's house had dispersed and the street was deserted. He paused for a moment. There was nothing to stop him having a look round. There was bound to be a way in, there almost always was. Anyway, in common with most empty houses, it was odds on that nobody had thought to close up the cat flap. He quickened his pace towards number sixty-two.

Chapter Three

Aubrey paused and glanced about him before slipping through the cat flap and into Mr Telling's kitchen. He hesitated for a moment, listening, and then padded his way across the floor, conscious of the faint tapping of his claws against the tiles. He was fairly sure that nobody had seen him come in and that there was nobody already inside, but you could never be certain. If he knew that the house was empty, then so did everybody else.

He shivered and felt his fur tingle. It was strange, but there was a real difference between a house that was merely empty because everybody was out, and a house that was empty because nobody lived in it. It was something to do with the coolness of the temperature, the oppressive silence, and the absolute stillness. It was as if not even the air moved. He had experienced it after Raj had died, and it was exactly the same feeling here.

In Molly and Jeremy's house there was always a bubble of expectancy, a certain knowledge that it was only a matter of time before the emptiness was broken by the rattle of a key in the lock, the sound of the kettle being filled, or the rustle of a footfall from overhead. Here, somehow you just knew that nobody was going to run down the stairs or walk through a door. There would be no burble of a radio from another room, and the dishes that were stacked on the draining board would stay there gathering dust long after the tea towel that had been hung on its hook was dry. Here, not even a ghost stirred.

He made his way through to the back room, the room in which Mr Telling had spent most of his time. As far as he could tell, everything looked the same. There was nothing out of place, nothing to arouse suspicion of any sort. All was exactly as it had been the last time he'd sat in here. Mr Telling was always a neat and tidy sort of person and, apart from frequently losing his spectacles, he had always known where everything was. He had been a man of order and routine, qualities that Aubrey totally approved of. In common with most other cats, there was nothing that he hated and feared so much as unpredictability. That had been the one good thing about his stretch in Sunny Banks Rescue Centre; everything had run according to the clock.

He darted glances around him. Everything was as he had expected it to be. Even the newspaper was still lying on the arm of the chair, the page folded down to the quick crossword. Aubrey half-smiled to himself. The old man had loved any sort of crossword or puzzle, and had always completed the quick ones in about three minutes, using them as a kind of limbering up exercise before having a go at what he'd called the real one. He'd won prizes sometimes, too, the most recent being an electronic dictionary which he had never used but nevertheless had put on display on the bookshelf.

Aubrey squeezed his way round the door which had been left ajar and made his way down the hall towards the front room. Standing back, he leapt up and forced his full weight down on the door handle, grunting as he felt the plastic ball mechanism give way and the door open. He hovered on the threshold for a moment, gathering his breath. So, this was where it had happened. This was the room in which Mr Telling had died.

He felt a catch at the back of his throat. He hoped that it hadn't hurt too much, and that the old man hadn't had time to be frightened or confused. It was bad enough that it had happened, without thinking about him panicking or struggling with no-one to help him. Aubrey pushed the thought away and rose up and walked over to the fireplace, trying to calculate in his mind how the accident might have happened. He ran his eye slowly over the mantelpiece.

Mr Telling hadn't been very tall and the mantelpiece was high – a big, greyish, creamy marble affair, exactly like the one in Molly and Jeremy's house. Aubrey stared at it for a moment. Mr Telling must have tipped over backwards and cracked the back of his skull against the marble as he went down. As if to prove his thoughts, Aubrey could see now a dark spattering all along one side. They'd have to clean that up before they sold it, he thought. Nobody would fancy buying a place where the death of the previous owner was quite so clearly marked.

Whose house was it now, he wondered? Did Mr Telling have any family? He had never seen any and he had never heard the telephone ring here unlike at Molly and Jeremy's place where it never seemed to stop. Whenever Aubrey had been at Mr Telling's house, it had always been just him, the old man, and whatever strays he had been currently looking after. The only other voices he had heard had come from the radio. Aubrey had never thought about it before but, really, it was quite odd. For example, it had been Mr Telling's birthday last month. Aubrey knew that because Mr Telling had given him half a tin of tuna to help him celebrate. But there hadn't been any birthday cards on display like Molly and Jeremy had when it was their birthdays, and even when it was Aubrey's birthday, which they had decided for some mysterious reason was May 9th. The only things on display in Mr Telling's sitting room were his books, his electronic dictionary, a clock, and a small china cat.

In this room, there was an empty porcelain vase and two small photographs in frames, but Aubrey could tell from the people in them that the photographs were quite old. Even the fact that they were in frames at all aged them. At Molly and Jeremy's house, most of the pictures – apart from one of their wedding and one of Jeremy's parents – were kept in some sort of revolving screen. He had been quite disconcerted the first time he had noticed it.

He looked up at the silver-plated frames now, absorbing the details. The pictures were in black and white. The first showed two couples set against a backdrop of what looked like the seaside. The women in them stood ramrod straight, staring into the camera, their chubby little knees pressed together and their big starched petticoats just visible beneath their skirts. Their arms were wrapped loosely around each other's waists. Unlike

15

Molly, whose hair was soft and wavy and framed her face, these two had stiff, flicky hairstyles that sort of stood out and made them look as if their heads had been concreted. You could cut your paw on hair like that. One of the men standing next to them held a cigarette pinched between forefinger and thumb, and both men were wearing narrow-shouldered suits with straight trousers and pointed shoes.

Aubrey looked across at the other photograph – a portrait of a grinning young man in uniform, his cap pushed to the back of his head and his eyes merry. He stared at the picture, his head on one side. This one was definitely Mr Telling. Even after all these years, you could still tell that it was him.

He stiffened at the faint clicking sound of the back door opening. Someone was coming in. His eyes darted rapidly around the sparsely furnished room. There were more places to hide in the other room and it was nearer to the cat flap. He ran back down the hall and slipped round the door to the back room. Starting to squeeze himself beneath the sofa, nose first, he stopped and backed out again. It was no good, it was too tight. He couldn't even get his head under. There was only one other obvious place. Leaping over the back of the sofa, he landed four-square on the window sill and crouched down behind the curtain. He held himself tense, listening to his breathing start to steady, and thankful for the thick lining that disguised his bulk. All he had to do was wait his moment. As soon as whoever it was had done whatever it was they had come to do and left the room, he'd streak across it and be out of the cat flap and over the wall. Provided whoever it was that had just come in didn't shut the door to the kitchen. The kitchen was the room with the cat flap. And the door to the kitchen had a different kind of handle to the other doors in the house. A kind that he couldn't open.

Chapter Four

Aubrey strained his ears to hear what was going on and felt his heart start to thump against his ribs. He'd only just got behind the curtain in time. The sill was narrow and there was barely room to move. He wouldn't be able to keep still for too long, he knew. Apart from anything else, a layer of thin dust coated the lining of the curtains, and it was already causing a tickle at the back of his throat. This was a cat's worst nightmare, being cornered somewhere with no way of escape. It was right up there with being stuck in a room with a tin of cat food and nobody to open it.

He swallowed hard. Whatever happened, he daren't make a noise. Whoever was in the house would find him and haul him out. Even if it was someone who didn't hate cats, they might think that he was a stray and decide to rescue him. Some cat lovers were almost as bad as cat haters with their do-gooding. It would be like it had been after Raj had died; before he knew where he was, he'd be banged up in the rescue centre again.

He squeezed his eyes shut and tried not to panic. There was nothing on him to say where he lived. What if he got taken back to Sunny Banks Rescue Centre? Molly and Jeremy would think that he had just disappeared, cats often did, and there would be nothing that he could do about it. It wouldn't be like he could get a message to them or anything. And even if he got chosen again, he might not be so lucky in his new owners the next time. A cat in a rescue centre is at the mercy of whoever decides to pick it. There was nothing to stop any psycho turning up and pretending to be a cat lover and that was that. Robert was your mother's brother. Dead as a door knocker. Or worse.

For the first time he cursed his own stubbornness in refusing to wear a collar. Molly and Jeremy had bought him at

17

least three, but each time they had patiently fastened one around his neck he had simply waited until they were out of sight and then chewed it off. Eventually, they had given up. But, as he now realised with a sinking heart, if he had a collar it would be obvious that he lived somewhere. It would be clear that people would be out looking for him. It would be clear that he wasn't a stray.

He opened his eyes again and flicked his ears. Someone had entered the room and was walking across the carpet. Carefully, he nudged his face gently against the edge of the curtain. A person with very keen sight might just have spotted one cat's eye staring back. Across his line of vision, a pair of short, fat legs ending in grubby, glittery, flip-flopped feet walked past. The toenails were painted aubergine, the paint chipped in places, and one of the toes was wearing a silver coloured ring. He raised his eyes and held his breath. Maria. If she found him, he'd be dead meat. She had hated him from the first time that she had set eyes on him, ever since she had discovered him sleeping under one of the beds upstairs. She had sworn at him in a language that he didn't recognise, and then she had whacked him across the back with the vacuum cleaner nozzle as he had raced towards the door to escape her.

He breathed out slowly and watched her through narrowed eyes as she crossed and re-crossed the floor. She seemed to be carrying things through to the kitchen. Why was she doing that? And what was she doing here anyway? Mr Telling was dead, so he was hardly in need of the services of a cleaner any more. But whatever she was doing, she obviously wasn't doing any cleaning. There was none of the usual bustle of the vacuum cleaner being taken from the cupboard under the stairs, or the hiss of polish being sprayed from a can.

Aubrey kept perfectly still and watched as she pulled open the drawers and cupboard doors of the sideboard. Her hand reached across to something that was out of his line of vision, and then came the unmistakeable sound of glass clinking against bottle. She was helping herself to Mr Telling's sherry. A sudden crackle and burst of noise leapt into the room, a disjointed cacophony that struck a hostile note in the usual tranquillity of the atmosphere. She had turned the radio on and was tuning it to a music station. Aubrey listened as she hummed merrily along to the song, watching her plump backside swaying rhythmically in time to the beat, pausing only to take another swig from the glass that she was holding.

A sudden stab of fear clutched at his heart as the catch on the back door clicked again. Someone else was coming into the house. Maria must have left the back door unlocked. That was all he needed. For a house that was supposed to be empty, this place was getting horribly crowded. He tensed and waited. Whoever it was would have to go sometime. They both would, and then he could escape. But what if they didn't go? What if this newcomer stayed in the house for hours? Or even worse, had come to live there? It was no good, he couldn't afford to just sit and hope. Even if they did both leave immediately, they might shut the kitchen door on their way out. It could be days before anyone else came into the house, days in which he would have had time to starve to death. He didn't think that Mr Telling's house had any mice, but even if it did, he would need more than the odd mouse to keep him going. He braced himself. There was only one thing for it, he would have to make a bold dash. It was risky but it had to be better than dying slowly of starvation.

He flexed his back and got ready to slip out at the first opportunity. He was a big cat but he could be pretty fast when he wanted to be. The element of surprise, he thought, that was the answer. He would spring out and start steaming round the room. He'd seen some of the other cats do it when they'd been banged up in Sunny Banks. Driven to the edge by the enforced incarceration, they had been totally stir crazy. When the screws had brought the food bowls in, they had leapt right out of their cages and headed straight up the walls, often knocking the trays of food right out of the screws' hands. The rest of the cats had watched in silent admiration, mentally cheering them on.

Aubrey's mind raced ahead. He would rush out from behind the curtain in a sudden mad dash of frenetic energy. He would come at them, teeth bared and ears back, and then, while they were still startled, he'd charge across the room and up the walls. Before they had time to realise what was happening and while they were still disorientated, he would race past them and out of the cat flap before they had time to draw breath.

He crouched low, ready to spring. A pair of trainer-clad feet walked past him and stopped in the middle of the room. Aubrey hesitated and then inched back further behind the curtain. He'd lost the moment. He should have followed his instinct and jumped out before he had time to think about it. He could have been halfway home by now. In any event, he wouldn't still be stuck behind this curtain. He stared miserably at a small splash of green paint caught along one heel of the trainers as the man stood with his back to the window. For a moment, the silence hung on the air and then Maria spoke.

"You startle me. I am clearing up."

"Really?"

The man's voice was low and slightly nasal, a note of faint amusement evident in its tone. He couldn't see his face but he sounded quite young, thought Aubrey. Not old, anyway.

"Yes," Maria continued. "I am doing the houseworks. But, poor old man, poor old Mr Telling, always at this time we have sherry together and so I do it for him. I say, what would he like, and so this is what I do."

"Is that right."

It was a statement rather than a question; the tone was flat and ironic, disbelieving, as well it might be, thought Aubrey. As Mr Telling had told him more than once, he only tolerated Maria because she was all that social services could send him. If he had been steady enough on his feet to do his own housework, he wouldn't have let Maria within a mile of the place.

"Aa... choo!" The man's sneeze reverberated around the room. "Aa...choo!" Again, even louder.

"Have you got a cat in here?" The man's voice was sharp with suspicion.

"No cat." Maria sounded indignant. She paused and thought for a moment, and then she said, "Old man, he sometime let in strays. One he let come in more often, big fat stray with stripes."

Fat? Bloody cheek. Aubrey bridled, in so far as it was possible to bridle in so confined a space. He was all muscle. What was it that the vet had called him when the screw at Sunny Banks had taken him for his pre-release check-up? Solid, that was it. Solid. Like a proper cat should be, not like that soppy little nerk Carstairs that lived in the house next door to Molly and Jeremy's. Carstairs was so thin he could practically slip between rain drops. Anyway, she could talk. Blobby old bitch. If her arse got any bigger, it would be in danger of stalking her.

"Next time I catch him," continued Maria casually, "I kill him."

There was a pause and then the man said, "How did you get in?"

"I have key." Maria sounded indignant.

The man crossed the room and stared at Mr Telling's electronic dictionary, his back still turned to Aubrey. He watched as the man leaned down and switched off the radio before reaching into his jacket and drawing out a packet of cigarettes. For a moment, there was silence as he flicked his thumb across a small plastic lighter. A curl of acrid smoke wafted across the room. Aubrey stuffed his paw across his nose and mouth to block them. One of the things that he had prayed for in new owners was that they should be non-smokers, and it was a prayer that had been answered. Cigarettes affected his chest, and it was the one thing that he had disliked about living with Raj. He pushed his paw harder against his mouth. If he sneezed or coughed now, the game was up. They'd have him out of there faster than you could say cat flap.

Maria spoke again. Her tone sounded slightly shrill now and her voice was coming faster. She had evidently decided, having been caught on the premises and drinking Mr Telling's sherry, that attack was the best way forward.

"I know what you are doing here. Yes, you cannot fool me. You are from Council. You are spy." She paused to gulp down a large mouthful of sherry. "You have come to spy and poke nose and to see what I do. Well, I tell you this, Mr Council Poke Nose, I do good job. Bloody good job. Everybody say." She took another mouthful of sherry and smacked her lips with an unpleasant sucking sound. "Every single body."

"I'm sure that you do." The man's voice sounded slightly mocking.

There was another pause. Aubrey watched as Maria poured herself another drink. She was obviously of the school that believed she might as well be hung for a sheep as a lamb. She had turned her back to him now so he couldn't see her face, but he could visualise it well enough. Ever since it had presented itself, hanging bat-like upside down as she had peered under the bed at him that day, it had imprinted on his memory. It resembled nothing so much as a piece of rancid and uncooked dough, but with the kind of sharp black eyes that you might expect to see in the face of something that was feeling a bit peckish and was thinking about putting you on the lunch menu. What with that, the scraped back hair, and the kind of earrings that looked like they should have had parrots swinging from them, she was the stuff of nightmares.

For several moments neither of them spoke, and then at last Maria said, "I think I have seen you before."

"Have you? I don't think so."

"Yes," she continued, speaking slowly now. "It is not mistake. I see you last week. I recognise. I remember now."

"It's nice to have a good memory." The man's voice was light, pleasant even. He paused for a moment, as though weighing out his words, and then continued. "Not always a good thing, though." His tone was still light but it was edged now with something else, something that Aubrey couldn't quite identify.

"Yes, you are here before." Maria spoke softly, her voice barely above a whisper so that Aubrey had to strain to hear it. "I see you near house."

"You're quite sure about that, are you?"

"I fetch saucer for ash."

Aubrey watched her leave the room. Why, he wondered, had she gone into the kitchen? She was unlikely to be concerned about a bit of cigarette ash on the carpet. She must have something out there that she didn't want him to see. She returned and placed one of Mr Telling's best bone china saucers on the edge of the mantelpiece.

"So, this time that you imagined you saw me..."

There was no mistaking the threat now. The man's voice was just as quiet, just as even, but the menace was clear. Maria continued, her tone still low but defiant now, and determined.

"No, it is not imagine. It is you. It is definite. You walk past house. Two times. Three times. And you stare at window."

"And when was it exactly, this time that you thought you saw me?"

"The week he die, the last time that I come here when Mr Telling is still alive. I see you outside house when I leave and go to get bus." There was a pause, and then she added, "I see you yesterday, too." She paused again. "I see you standing on corner. I recognise."

"Ah."

Again, the silence stretched between them, the tension was so palpable that it could almost be touched. When she spoke again, Maria's voice was even softer and this time more calculating.

"I think that I am the only person who see you."

Aubrey still couldn't see her face, she still had her back to him, but he could imagine the expression well enough. It was the same expression he'd observed when he'd seen her pick up a pound coin from the floor and slip it into her overall pocket.

"I see." The man's tone was thoughtful.

"I am poor woman." Maria spoke slowly now, as though weighing the effect of her words on her listener, ready to draw back in an instant if necessary. "Very poor woman. Little money. I leave Brazil because no money. I come to this country to make good life, better life. I work hard. Work, work. More work. And yet still I have very small money. And I have my little boy to look after. He is name Carlos. He is fourteen. He need new jeans, new trainers. Nice trainers," she added after a moment's pause.

The man was silent as though thinking, and then he said,

"Did the old man have any family, anybody that he ever spoke about?"

Aubrey watched the faint shrug of her plump shoulders and the slight fluttering of her hands.

"He have no wife."

"Children?"

"He have one son. He live in Australia but no-one know where. Also he have brother, but brother die."

More snooping, Aubrey thought.

"So, only a son as next of kin?"

"Next of?"

"Next of, oh never mind. What's happening about the funeral?"

"Funeral is next week. Son cannot be found so Council arrange. They have person to take care when no family."

"And the house?"

Maria shrugged again.

"I do not know. I am not told."

"So, nobody's coming round to empty it, no family or anything?"

"Council perhaps?"

Aubrey tensed as the man suddenly thrust his hand towards her.

"Give me the key."

The woman spluttered. "I cannot. Today I must give key to Council for funeral arrangement. I just call in first to make sure all is nice."

And help yourself to whatever was going, thought Aubrey. That was almost certainly what she had hidden in the kitchen, he suddenly realised – pickings from Mr Telling's house. And he doubted if it was just food.

"The key," the man repeated.

There was a moment's pause and then the man said, "Thank you."

"The Council, they will ask for it." Maria's tone was sulky, petulant. "What will I say?"

"Say you lost it."

Aubrey watched as the man turned to go.

24

"My little boy… my Carlos."

The man stopped and turned back.

"Yes?"

"He need computer for his homework. His school, it is lousy. Sir Frank Wainwright's, it is rubbish school. Too many children. Not enough teacher. No computer. My Carlos he need computer, small computer, no wires."

"Does he?"

The man's voice was thoughtful.

"He need new computer, small computer, to sit on lap, to do homeworks. He must do all homeworks to pass exams. Also he need books. Sir Frank's, they have not enough books. All children, they must share." She paused and swallowed. "These things, they are costing money."

Her meaning was clear now but she was also, Aubrey thought, verging on the edge of hysteria. Maybe it was the sherry, but he thought that it was more likely that she was beginning to regret what she had started. Nicking the odd bit of food and pocketing small change was one thing, but this was in a different league altogether. This man, whoever he was, didn't sound like the sort of person to mess with.

"Here, write your address and phone number on this." The man reached into his jacket pocket and pulled out a small notebook. "And keep your ears open. I need to know what day the funeral is arranged for." His tone was clipped now, clearly he'd had enough.

Again, there was a faint rustle and then silence as Maria and Aubrey were left alone in the room.

Chapter Five

Aubrey shivered slightly and squeezed his eyes shut. Would Maria never leave? He listened as she continued to mutter to herself, the words clicking against her teeth and drifting in and out of English and some other language. Only one word in three made any sense. Not that it mattered. The tone of barely suppressed excitement was intelligible in any language. His ears flicked instinctively as the letterbox rattled, and he tensed himself ready to dash, but he hesitated too long. Maria was out to the hall and back again almost before he had time to stretch a paw.

He was, he had to admit, shaken by her statement that she intended to kill him if she caught him. While with some people it might have been taken as a throwaway remark, he had the distinct impression that with Maria it was no more than a bald statement of fact. He waited, his despair mounting by the second as she helped herself to more sherry and then settled herself back in Mr Telling's chair. She was still muttering away, but now she started to repeat herself so that some of the same words seemed to come round on a continuous loop.

Aubrey held his breath and then let it out very slowly, bit by bit. Whatever happened, if he was going to survive this he had to hold his nerve and he mustn't make the slightest sound. Talk about nine lives. If Maria had her way, he would lose at least four of them straight off and the other five would follow very shortly after. This was even worse than being banged up in Sunny Banks. While the screws at the rescue centre might have been distinctly lacking in charm, at least they weren't planning to strangle him with their bare hands.

He was aware suddenly of a change. The manic muttering had stopped and was replaced by a low repetitive rumble.

Maria was snoring. He watched as her mouth fell slack, and the now empty glass slipped from her hand and rolled to the floor. Half a bottle of sherry coupled with a blatant attempt at blackmail had obviously been too much for her. He inched his way slowly around the curtain and jumped lightly to the floor. He paused for a second and then, feeling his way one paw at a time and keeping low to the ground, he crept silently past the sleeping figure and towards the kitchen door. Relief flooded through him. The door had been left ajar.

Aubrey watched from under a chair as Jeremy slid the bolt across the top of the kitchen door. After a moment's hesitation, he bent down and slid the bottom one across, too. Through the open doorway Aubrey heard a faint clink and rattle. Molly was putting the chain on the front door. She came through to the kitchen. Jeremy turned and stared at her for a moment.

"You know, none of this seems real somehow. Things like this don't happen in places where people like us live. It's like living out a scene in one of those nineteen-fifties horror films."

Molly nodded and walked over to the window. She stared out into the darkness, her shoulders rigid with tension and her small face tense.

"Except, you know what always happened in those horror films? Once the main characters started locking all the doors, you knew the murderer was hiding somewhere inside the house."

Jeremy reached over her shoulder and pulled down the blind.

"Well, he's been bloody quiet if he is. I've been home for nearly two hours and we haven't had a peep out of him. Don't worry, Moll. All this," he turned and waved his arm up and down in front of the bolted kitchen door, 'is just a precaution."

"But, Jeremy, he's out there somewhere." Molly's voice was tight with anxiety, the note of strain evident. "He's out there somewhere right now and it feels like he's getting closer. He could be anyone. He might even be a she. He might even be someone that we know, like those stories that you read in the papers."

"What stories in the papers?"

"Oh, you know the sort of thing, 'he was always such a nice man; we lived next door to him for years; he was very good to his mother'. That sort of thing. And then they dig up ten bodies in the cellar."

"These houses haven't got cellars."

"Don't be so literal. You know what I mean."

"Well, I don't think we've got too much to worry about with either of our neighbours. Anna's always far too busy and I can't see Gerald lifting a hand to anyone. A puff of wind would blow him over."

Aubrey nodded silently in agreement. He couldn't see Anna, who was a single parent with three kids and a full-time job, finding the time to murder anyone, even if she had the inclination. And as for Gerald, the bloke that Carstairs lived with; well, he agreed with Jeremy. He'd never seen man and beast look so alike. Carstairs was thin, weedy, and limp, and so was his owner. In a fight between Gerald and Miss Jenkins, Aubrey knew who he would have put his money on. Old Jenkins would have made mincemeat of him.

Molly twisted her hands in a small wringing gesture.

"It's all very well you saying that, but the police obviously haven't got a clue. And it's always the person you least expect."

Jeremy smiled.

"Well, on that basis, I take it back. It's obviously Gerald."

Molly smiled reluctantly back at him.

"Well, all right, probably not Gerald. But this person, Jeremy, this person who's doing these things, he could be in our garden right now, for all we know. He could be watching everything that we're doing, creeping around among the bushes, and looking straight in at us."

"Not unless he's got x-ray vision and can see through blinds." Jeremy took her gently by the shoulders and turned her to face him. "Come on, Moll. There's nothing to get upset about. Apart from anything else, we don't fit the profile. We're not over sixty and, besides which, we don't live on our own. There are two of us here. Three if you count Aubrey."

28

Aubrey looked up at him appreciatively. Thanks, mate. It was always nice to be included, and if it came to it they could count on him, for sure. But Jeremy was forgetting one thing. This bloke, whoever he was, was clearly totally and utterly round the twist. You couldn't apply the same logic. Rubbing out the elderly might be his fancy this week. Who was to say what he might develop a taste for next week? And anyway, he might be targeting the elderly simply because they were easy prey. Limbering up, so to speak, ready for a bigger challenge.

"And now Mr Telling," said Molly, her voice tearful. "Of all people. I still can't believe it. He was such a nice old man. What did Mr Telling ever do to anybody?"

"What did any of them ever do?" said Jeremy.

Actually, thought Aubrey, quite a lot. If you were a cat, that is. He didn't have anything on Lomax and Bradshaw, but old Jenkins had been a well-known cat-hater. She had been a tall, thin, vinegar-lipped bitch of an old woman, who had kept a water pistol ready loaded and a little pile of stones on her window sill to throw at cats when they made the mistake of crossing her garden. Her aim had been horribly accurate.

"Anyway," continued Jeremy, "we don't know for sure yet about Mr Telling. It may still turn out to be an accident."

He reached down and scooped Aubrey up under his arm.

"Come on, let's go and sit by the fire."

Aubrey glanced sideways up at Jeremy and then looked away again, feigning reluctance. Jeremy tickled him gently behind his ears and Aubrey bit back a purr. It wouldn't do to start too soon. He folded his paws in under him and assumed an air of studied resignation as Jeremy flopped down on the sofa. For a moment they sat and watched as the flames licked up and the coals rustled down.

"What sort of day?" asked Molly.

"No worse than usual." Jeremy sat back and reflected for a moment. Aubrey closed his eyes in satisfaction as Jeremy's hand smoothed the thick tabby fur across his back. There was something very comforting about Jeremy's hands. Square and clean with short clipped nails, there was something about them that just made you feel safe.

"One more day in the parallel universe known as Sir Frank Wainwright's," Jeremy continued. "All the kids are still talking about the murders, of course. It's difficult to stop them."

"Did any of them know any of the victims?"

"No, but they all claim to know somebody who did. If Year Ten are to be believed, old Mrs Lomax was grandmother to half the district. She must have been a little population explosion all of her own. And then Henry went home sick halfway through the morning, leaving me to cover Year Nine maths. I don't know who was more confused by the end of the lesson, me or Year Nine. And then we finished on a high by one of my tutor group very nearly managing to get himself suspended for fighting in the cloakrooms."

"Who was it?"

"That new kid I told you about, Carlos, the one that lives in the flats over at The Meadows. I didn't manage to find out what it was all about, although I suspect that evil little sod Jed Caparo of being at the bottom of it. He usually is."

"Is he still carrying that rat around in his blazer pocket?"

Jeremy nodded gloomily.

"I don't know what it is about Caparo. He's a horrible little runt, but he only has to raise an eyebrow and all the other lads come running. Including, it now seems, Carlos." He paused. "I really thought we had Caparo last term with that fire in the art rooms, but I should have known he'd have an alibi."

"It was genuine, though, wasn't it?"

"Yeah." Jeremy sighed. "Even Caparo can't be in two places at once."

Aubrey shifted position slightly. He'd seen Caparo once. He was a small, white, greasy-faced boy with pock-marked skin and narrow, grey, flinty eyes. He had been hanging around the staff car park at Sir Frank's when Molly had picked Jeremy up once after taking Aubrey to the vet when he'd torn his ear in a fight. Jeremy had told Caparo to clear off.

Molly hesitated for a moment and then said, "There's something that I've been meaning to mention to you."

"What?"

"Rachel and Clive are coming back. In fact, I think that

they're probably back already."

Aubrey felt his heart sink and his mood of quiet contentment drain slowly away. Tall, thin, knobbly, and cat-hating, with long arms that dangled loosely by his sides, Clive was everything that a sensible cat would take considerable pains to avoid. Clive didn't talk to people, he addressed them. And he was always right. In Aubrey's opinion, the only things that were worse than Clive were Clive's wife and children.

"What?" Jeremy suddenly sat up straight, almost dislodging Aubrey from his lap. "I thought that they were safely tucked up in Africa? No, don't tell me, Africa couldn't stand them either."

Molly smiled. "No, it's a family thing. The old lady that was killed, the first one, Miss Jenkins. Apparently, she's Clive's aunt. Or she was, I should say."

Aubrey wasn't surprised. When he thought about it, there was a distinct family likeness.

Jeremy groaned.

"So why do Rachel and Clive have to come back here? Why can't they stay in Africa? The old girl's dead. I mean, I don't want to sound callous and all that, but it's not like they can do anything about it."

"Miss Jenkins didn't have any other family. Clive was her only nephew. He and Rachel have to arrange the funeral and see to her affairs."

"Just a fleeting visit then?" Jeremy's expression was hopeful.

"Afraid not." Molly gave a rueful smile. "Clive is the main beneficiary under her will. We're holding it at Donaghue's; I had a sneak look at it today. Apart from a few charitable bequests, Clive gets the lot. Which, of course, includes her house. And quite a bit of money, too," she added.

"He would," said Jeremy bitterly. "Only Clive could profit from what looks like a serial killer on the loose. If you dropped him in a bucket of shit, he'd come up with the winning lottery ticket stuck to his forehead."

"Anyway, one of the partners was talking about it in the office today. Clive and Rachel are going to rent somewhere until the will and everything is sorted out."

Jeremy flopped back on the sofa again. Aubrey flopped with him.

"What a pity that missionaries don't get eaten any more."

"Christian teachers."

"What?"

"They didn't go as missionaries. They went as Christian teachers."

"Oh yes, I forgot," said Jeremy. "Christian teachers get paid more. Well, whatever they went as, no doubt they'll be just as hideous when they come back. And Sir Frank's is so short of staff that they'll almost certainly welcome Clive back with open arms. The fact that he's a God-bothering, sanctimonious twerp, who can't teach his way out of a paper bag and knows when to jump ship, will be conveniently forgotten."

For several minutes, neither of them spoke and then Molly said, "I thought I saw Dave today."

Aubrey's heart sank still further. First Clive and now Dave. It was getting so a cat couldn't even have a bit of peace and quiet in his own home. He sighed and tucked his head under his paw. The mere mention of Dave the builder was enough to ruin his day. That time last week when Dave had trodden on his tail had been no accident. Oh yes, he'd been all apologies to Jeremy, but Aubrey had seen the sudden smirk flash across his face when he had leapt in the air with fright. And then there was that ugly little mutt that travelled about with him in his van. Rascal was a short, wiry animal of indeterminate breed, part terrier and part lunatic, but with the emphasis on the latter. Jeremy had told Dave not to let it in the house, but Jeremy wasn't always there.

"I thought he was going away to see his mother again," said Jeremy.

Molly looked thoughtful for a moment.

"I know. That's what he said. But I'm sure that it was him. He was just up the road from Mr Telling's house, sitting in his van. He was talking on his mobile and watching the house in his wing mirror."

Aubrey suppressed another sigh. Dave, big bum builder

unextraordinaire, might have told Molly and Jeremy that he was off to spend some time in Devon with his elderly mother, but Aubrey knew for a fact that he had gone no further than half a mile away where he had been working on the health centre renovation.

Chapter Six

Aubrey flicked an eye open at the familiar scrape of the key in the lock. It was much too early for Molly or Jeremy to be home, which meant only one thing. Dave blubberman builder was on the loose. He sprang off the bed where he'd been lying trying to work out what to do next about Mr Telling, and ran lightly down the stairs. It was raining out there but he didn't want to get caught in the house if Dave had Rascal with him. The last time that had happened, he'd been stuck on top of the wardrobe for hours, it being one of the few occasions that Dave had actually stayed to do any work. He slipped through the kitchen door moments ahead of Dave, and jumped out through the cat flap.

"You'd better be straight with me, Rick."

Dave's voice boomed out across the garden as he pulled open the kitchen door and peered out into the rain, mobile in one hand and roll-up in the other.

"The Grim Reaper's been round here again. Some old bloke called Telling. The place is crawling with the odd lot. They'll be back asking questions at The Laurels, if they haven't been already."

Aubrey could smell the stench of Dave's roll-up even from behind the big terracotta flowerpot where he was sitting. Smoking was another thing that Jeremy had asked Dave not to do in the house.

"From where I'm standing," Dave continued, flicking his fag end out across the lawn, "it looks like me what's taking all the risk."

There was a small pause and then, "Yeah, well, don't give me all that. Don't forget that if it wasn't for me you would never have got the job in the first place."

Another pause and then, "Check out the greenhouse today.

It must be nearly ready. And as for the other thing, we can't just ignore it, don't be ludicrous. It's going to start to smell pretty soon, if it doesn't already. We've got to get it moved. We should have sorted it properly at the time, instead of just leaving it there."

Dave paused and rubbed a fat hand across his eyes.

"I'll be over later."

He snapped his phone shut and ducked back into the kitchen. He stood and surveyed the kitchen for a moment and then pulled open a drawer. Aubrey jumped up onto the window ledge and watched as Dave pushed some papers aside and extracted a small red notebook. Pausing only to help himself from the biscuit tin, he sat down and began to leaf through the notebook, mouth open and short stubby finger following the columns of figures. Did Molly and Jeremy know, Aubrey wondered, that Dave routinely went through their account book? Did they realise that, in fact, he had a better idea of their finances than they did themselves? They obviously didn't, anymore than they knew that when they thought that he was there working on the new bathroom or re-lining the chimneys, as he was supposed to be doing, he usually wasn't.

On most days, as soon as their backs were turned, he was off on other jobs or away visiting his mysterious mother that nobody had ever actually seen. Dave 'Does It All' Builder would, in Aubrey's opinion, be much more accurately called Dave 'Does Sod All' Builder. His best trick was returning to the house just before Molly and Jeremy got home from work and bursting into a hive of furious activity. So far, he'd only been caught out once, when Jeremy had arrived home unexpectedly early after the school boiler had burst and had found the place suspiciously empty of builders. But Dave had talked his way out of it, blustering his way in and talking nineteen to the dozen before Jeremy had a chance to get a word in edgeways.

"God, I'm knackered. Not putting the kettle on are you, mate? Cheers. I been over to Wembley to that architectural salvage place, see if I could find the right bathroom fittings. Waste of time. No good." And he'd sighed and flopped his big bum down on a kitchen chair as if he'd just run a half marathon, instead of driving two miles back from the primary school where he'd been doing a roofing job for the council.

"Might as well give you this while I'm here, mate." And he'd handed Jeremy another of his grossly inflated invoices. The logo printed at the top was an illustration of a handsome-looking builder in a hard hat, holding a trowel in one hand and something that looked remarkably like a dried turd in the other. Anything less like Dave would be hard to imagine. Apart from the dried turd, of course.

" All right, Aubrey?"

Aubrey half-turned on the ledge and looked down.

Moses beamed up at him. "There's stuff going off at the flats, over at The Meadows. All the guys are going down there. Vincent sent me, he said to tell you."

"What sort of stuff?"

Moses looked blankly back at him. Aubrey sighed. Clearly the question had been too demanding. Oh well. Moses couldn't help being dimmer than a spent light bulb.

Aubrey tried again. "What... Oh, never mind."

He thought for a moment. He didn't really fancy going over to the Meadows. Apart from the fact that it was still raining, he would much rather stay here and keep an eye on what Dave was up to. On the other hand, if all the lads were up at the flats, whatever it was that was going on, he didn't want to be the only one not there. It would be sure to be noticed and he didn't want to alienate anyone now, not just when everything was turning out so nicely.

It was mostly due to Vincent that things had gone so well, he had to admit. It was never easy moving onto a new patch, and it had been a real stroke of luck that Vincent had taken to him from the first. A word from Vinnie went a long way on this particular manor, and it was a word that could so easily have gone the wrong way. After all, Aubrey was a big male cat, and any cat less sure of himself than Vincent might not only have objected to his presence in the street but might also have taken steps to make sure that he left it. It wouldn't have been hard. Aubrey could hold his own with the best of them when it was one-to-one or even one-to-two, but he wouldn't give much for his chances against three or four. Vincent would only have to give the word and that would be that.

He looked over the top of Moses' head and stared into the middle distance while the little cat waited patiently at his feet. For a cat that was barely more than two years old, Aubrey had known more than his fair share of addresses. At less than six months he had been abandoned by his mother and living under a hedge with his brother and sister. One night, he had gone wandering off in search of food. Two hours later and soaked through to the skin by the storm that had whipped up out of nowhere, he had looked in vain for the hedge that he thought of as home, but at five months old one hedge had looked very much like another. In the end, he had simply sat down on the pavement, exhausted, the rain beating down on his head and the sweep of passing car headlights blinding him every few seconds. It had been Raj, peering out at the rain from his shop window, who had dashed outside to pick him up and bring him into the warmth.

For a while, life had been good. He and Raj had settled down into a nice cosy life together. But then Raj had been killed and he'd been out on his own again. It had been ok; he had survived, and had even started to enjoy life. But he'd become complacent and had been caught rustling round the bins at the back of the shops once too often. Before he knew where he was, he'd been rescued. Found before he was lost. It had all happened really quickly, and before he'd had time to think, he had been bundled into a cardboard box, pushed into the back of a car, and then slung in the Big House.

That day when Molly and Jeremy had come to Sunny Banks Rescue Centre and walked over to his cage, he had tried not to look too desperate. He had been there far longer than any of the other cats and nobody had so much as glanced his way. He had overheard one of the screws telling a visitor that they never destroyed any animal, but he wasn't convinced. Some of the screws had a very nasty look in their eye, and for every day longer that he remained he had begun to steel himself against the prospect of being taken for the last ride.

He couldn't compete with the kittens, he knew that. All that waggy-tailed, round-eyed fluffiness gave them instant appeal, but his heart had yearned for Molly and Jeremy to see something in him that none of the other visitors to the rescue centre had seen. He needn't have worried. It had been his lucky day. Molly and Jeremy had not been looking for a kitten. They hadn't even been looking for a particularly young cat. They had, he had heard them telling the head screw, a positive preference for a slightly older cat, because an older cat would be calmer and able to be left while they were at work. Aubrey had resisted the urge to fling himself against the bars. If they wanted left, he could do left. He'd been left all his life.

He looked back down at Moses who was still waiting patiently for an answer. He couldn't risk anything now, not just when it was all turning out so nicely. There was nothing else for it, he'd have to take a trot down to the flats. Just to show his face.

Chapter Seven

Aubrey shivered and felt his fur flutter slightly. A cold wind was blowing across the forecourt of the flats, lifting the empty crisp packets and old newspapers and sending them scuttering before it. A greasy chip wrapper danced towards him and he batted it irritably away. He wasn't quite sure what all the fuss was about. There were lots of people standing around but so far nothing much had happened, apart from a lot of shouting and coming and going. There were several police cars parked at odd angles with their blue lights turned on, but the officers inside them were just sitting there. He could see one of them eating a sandwich. They didn't seem to be actually doing anything. Aubrey couldn't see that any of it was his business anyway. This was all human stuff, it was nothing to do with cats.

Across the way on top of the wall, he could see the twins, their heads lifted expectantly and their thin, lithe bodies silhouetted against the sky. He made a mental note to keep out of their way. Vincent might swear that they were good lads, but there were some cats around the neighbourhood that took a rather different view, the sort of cats that had some of their body parts missing. Talking of Vinnie, he thought, he hadn't seen him yet, but Moses had said that he was definitely here.

He looked around him, considering. As far as he could see, there was nothing to keep him here but he'd better make a point of finding Vincent and showing his face before he left, partly to find out if he'd heard anything more about Mr Telling but also to make sure that he'd been seen. Around him, the lights from the parked police cars continued to slowly revolve, throwing sudden flashes of cold, blue light through the grey curtain of rain.

He stepped back behind the bins and looked down at Moses

who was already there. He'd fallen asleep. Aubrey smiled to himself. Only Moses could sleep through all this chaos. He had the attention span of a retarded gnat and his capacity for sleep was second only to his capacity to eat. Still, he looked so peaceful. It would be a pity to wake him.

"Fuck off!"

Aubrey looked up, startled. On the fourth floor balcony, a small, sallow-faced youth stood screaming down into the crowd that had started to gather round, the hood from his oversized jacket falling across his face and shrouding it in a mad monk effect. Two more boys stood one on either side of him. Even from where he was standing, Aubrey could see that the one on the left looked absolutely terrified. The other one looked merely bored.

"Come on down, Caparo. Be sensible. Come on down and bring the other lads with you."

A tall, uniformed police officer had got out of his car and was looking up at the balcony. Aubrey watched as he spoke into a loud hailer, his voice hitting the height and then echoing and bouncing back down off the cracked tarmac.

"Fuck off," yelled the boy again, although, Aubrey thought, on a slightly less convincing note this time. The police officer lowered the loud hailer and muttered something to the officer next to him who nodded and began speaking into a radio.

"Hello, Aubsie. You got the message then?"

Aubrey turned and looked into Vincent's gleaming green eyes.

"What's going on?"

Vincent always knew what was going on. He had a sort of knack for it. Probably helped, he thought, by living with a couple who worked for the local newspaper. Vincent always had all the news before anyone else.

"Attempted robbery," replied Vincent. "Down at the newsagents on the high street. They chased them back here. They've been up there for quite a while. They think the middle one has got a gun."

"Right."

Aubrey nodded thoughtfully. He knew about guns. One of

40

the old guys on the allotments had kept one in the corner of his shed, and Aubrey had seen him trying to shoot rabbits with it. It was probably all very interesting, but he still couldn't see what it had to do with him and Vincent. Why were they here? People with guns generally didn't bother cats; they preferred to bother other people. And even if it was a threat to them, what were they supposed to be doing about it? They could hardly swarm up the wall mob-handed and disarm him. If there was any real danger, they'd be much better off in their own homes.

He shivered. He didn't like being here. It reminded him too much of when he'd been picked up and taken to Sunny Banks. It had been not far from here that they'd got him, and he had avoided the area ever since. And he wasn't the only one who didn't like it round here, he knew. In the general way of things, all the cats tried to steer clear of The Meadows. Even those that lived there didn't usually stay any longer than they could help. They got away as soon as they could, preferring instead to take their chances on the street. In fact, Aubrey had learned pretty early on who was an ex-Meadows dweller and who wasn't. Cats that had lived in the flats were usually mean and stringy with a nasty light in their eyes, and they hung around together in packs. They weren't exactly aggressive, but they weren't over-friendly either. They were best avoided.

He looked around him. Unobserved by the police officers and the small crowd of passers-by who had started to filter in and gather round to watch the spectacle, there were at least twenty cats hiding in the shadows, their eyes gleaming, and all of them with a hungry expectant air. He looked back again at Vincent, puzzled.

As if reading his mind, Vincent said briefly, "Mice."

"Er…" Aubrey paused, confused. Mice? What was Vinnie on about? What mice? Where?

"When these flats were built," explained Vincent, "they screwed up. They put in all these pipes and under-floor heating and stuff. It was all supposed to be dead modern, but they didn't seal things off properly or something. Anyway, the result is that the whole place is alive with mice that live in the heating system. They get environmental health down here from time to time but it doesn't make any difference, they can't clear them out. They just come back again."

"Right."

Aubrey nodded and assumed a serious expression, trying to look intelligent. He still didn't have a clue what Vinnie was talking about.

"All this noise and banging about, it upsets them."

"It upsets the mice?"

"That's right." Vincent nodded and grinned. "And what does an upset mouse do?"

"Well, er…" Aubrey thought hard for a moment. What was the right answer? Frankly, he didn't have a clue what an upset mouse did. He'd never looked at one long enough to determine the state of its emotional wellbeing.

"An upset mouse, Aubsie old mate, runs." Vincent's grin grew wider. "You watch, any minute now and the whole place will be alive with them. And we'll be there to say hello."

Aubrey was about to speak, but then stopped and stiffened as the sound of a horribly familiar voice rose up and wailed out across the tarmac.

"He is a good boy. You are frightening him. My poor Carlos, he is scared." The woman strained her short, fat neck upwards towards the balcony, one hand shielding her eyes even though the afternoon was grey and overcast. "Carlos, it is your mother. What is it that you are doing up there with those boys?"

The boy on the left made a slight move forward, but was elbowed back by the middle boy who leaned over the balcony and carefully dropped a house brick down onto the upturned face of a young police officer.

Aubrey hesitated and then, as one with Vincent, he leapt lightly onto the roof of a car so that they could get a better view across the heads of the crowd. There, in the centre, was Maria, her podgy little arms upraised as she appealed to the gathering.

"You have got wrong boy. Yes, it is definite. Wrong boy. Police, they are making a big mess of the justice. Big mess.

Big fat mess. I am telling you this, all you people. This police mister plod, they are stupid. They have brain in bum. It is all mistake. Big fat mistake. My Carlos, he has done nothing wrong. He is with me all of the time. All of the whole damned time. He does not know these other boys. They are stranger. He has never seen them. It is definite. All is mistake."

"Don't look like much of a mistake from where I'm standing, Mrs."

The crowd rustled slightly and moved closer to the speaker. Another voice broke through.

"Yeah, mistake, right. Tell that to the poor bloke what they tried to rob in the high street. Anyway, if your lad don't know them other boys, what's he doing up there with them?"

The voices were angry. Maria wheeled round, her voice rising an octave as she thrust her face towards them.

"Huh! You are against us. Yes, this I know because it is the truth. It is fact. It is definite. You think we are here to steal your damned social services. Well, you can stick your damned social services. Yes, you can stick it all up the side of your bum. We are not needing your social service."

"Yeah." Another voice called out from the crowd, slightly shriller this time and more insistent. "Course you don't, Mrs. That's 'cos you send your kids out to rob our shops instead."

"That's right." A large red-faced man had pushed his way to the front and stood there, eyes narrowed and damp lower lip jutting forward. "What you doing here anyway, that's what I'd like to know? Why don't you get back to where you came from?"

"Yeah," shouted the woman standing next to him. "It used to be nice round here till your sort came. Why don't you fuck off back to your own country?"

"Oh shit," muttered the police officer who had been hit in the face with the brick and was now trying to stop his nose bleeding with a large white handkerchief, "That's all we need, a bloody race riot."

He leaned down and muttered urgently into the radio attached to his shoulder. Around him, the crowd seemed suddenly to swell and surge forward, so that for a moment

Aubrey lost sight of Maria. Time to go, he thought. Mice or no mice. The last thing he wanted right now was another confrontation with that mad cow. One sight of him and she'd be after him with a meat cleaver. Anyway, he'd achieved what he had set out to do. He'd done his bit, he'd been seen down here joining in, and now it was time to go. He turned to Vincent.

"I think I'll start heading back, Vin. Bit tired after last night."

Vincent turned and nodded back at him, his expression thoughtful.

"Yeah, maybe you're right." He gazed around him. "Looks like they're in for a long afternoon anyway. Could be hours before this lot clears."

Together, they jumped down from the car roof and picked their way carefully back towards the bins. Moses was gone, presumably woken at last by the noise. An unmistakeable shrieking floated across the damp afternoon air and followed them through the crowd.

"And I tell you another thing, all of you, your Mark and Spencer, your Tesco, your Mr Sainsbury, they are all rubbish. Big rubbish. Big fat rubbish. In my country—"

"If your country's so fucking good, why don't you go back there then?"

"Why the damned should I? My Carlos and me, we come here because it is what we choose. Not what you choose. What we damn please choose. And all the time you are pick, you are pick on us and you are trying to make us not welcome. My Carlos he want only to learn. He want to learn so that he can be doctor. Yes, good doctor. Best doctor. And I tell you something, ugly, fat, red person, when he is doctor he will not treat you! Yes, you are coming to his surgery and he will say fuck off and then off you must fuck and then you will die! Yes, all of you! You will die because world famous doctor my Carlos he will not treat you! And we will laugh." She stood tilting slightly backwards and folded her arms triumphantly across her large bosom. "Ha ha."

You had to give it to her, Aubrey thought, half appalled and half admiring, she wasn't short on bottle. Either that or she was even more bonkers than he'd thought. And then suddenly the crowd seemed to grow, and all Aubrey could see was legs running and people shouting. From somewhere in the sky came the crack of a gunshot followed almost immediately by another.

In the distance, the scream of sirens came closer.

Chapter Eight

"Where have you been?"

Yeah, thought Aubrey sourly, glaring at Jeremy. Where've you been? It was Friday evening and Molly was too busy cooking to have remembered that he was there. He should have been fed ages ago. Even worse, *The Archers* had started. His mood was distinctly grumpy. He hated being forced to listen to *The Archers*; even the chippy, little theme tune was enough to make him want to rip his own head off. He listened irritably for a moment to the dreary whine of some woman going on and on about a draggy pantomime which seemed to involve dwarves. Ambridge could do with a colony of dwarves invading the village, he thought. The script writers were missing an opportunity there; they hadn't tackled the vertically challenged yet.

He sighed quietly to himself. Whatever in God's name did they all see in it? Even Raj, who had never set foot in an Indian village never mind an English one, had been addicted to it. So much so that he had often listened to the repeat, as well as the omnibus on a Sunday morning. In the end, Aubrey had been forced to take evasive action until the end of the programme.

He got up and stalked over to the cupboard where his cat food was kept, and parked himself meaningfully in front of it.

Molly stopped stirring the sauce on the hob and peered across at the spattered cookery book that was lying on the work surface.

"Why isn't this thickening?" She frowned down again at the sauce. "Why are you so late, anyway? Did you have a meeting after school?"

Jeremy sat down at the kitchen table and ran his hand through his hair.

"I've been down at the police station."

"What?" Molly stopped what she was doing and turned to face him, spoon still in hand. Aubrey debated for a moment whether to tank over and catch the drips, but decided against it. He had to keep some dignity, even if he was in danger of wasting away.

"It's all right, don't panic. It wasn't for me. It was one of my tutor group."

"Which one? No, don't tell me, let me guess." She leaned back against the work surface and thought for a moment. "Jed Caparo."

"He's not in my tutor group," said Jeremy. "Thank God."

There was only one member of Jeremy's tutor group that was likely to have spent the afternoon at the police station, thought Aubrey.

"Anyway," said Jeremy. "Even if he was, I wouldn't have lifted a finger. I would have let the little shit rot in there. No," he paused. "It was Carlos."

Aubrey moved slightly closer, temporarily distracted from the sight of his empty food bowl. This was getting interesting.

Molly turned the heat off under the pan she'd been stirring and sat down opposite Jeremy. She folded her arms and frowned.

"Carlos? Is that the one that you were talking about the other day? The new boy? The one that was fighting in the cloakrooms?"

"That's the one. He started with us a couple of months ago. He lives over at The Meadows, just him and his mother. I checked his file before I went down to the police station. There's no father that I'm aware of, at least there was nothing on file. They came from Brazil originally, although they lived in London for a while before they came here. Camden, I think."

"So what's he done?" said Molly. "And why did you have to go? Why couldn't they get someone else?"

"Apparently there is nobody else. Like I said, there's no father, or not one that they're able to contact anyway. Carlos said that he lives in Spain but he doesn't seem to know where exactly. They don't seem to have an address for him, other than Madrid, which isn't particularly helpful. The mother doesn't speak very good English. And the bit that she does speak seems to be mostly abuse." He paused for a second, the recollection of Maria clearly still fresh in his mind, and then continued. "The police did get a solicitor for him – a young bloke off the duty list – which apparently they're obliged to do, but Carlos was refusing to say a word. In the end, the police asked him if he wanted someone else there, and for some reason the boy asked for me. The police rang the school and asked if I could come down. I've been down there all afternoon." He ran his hand through his hair again. "God knows why he wanted me there, the lad has barely said a word to me for the past eight weeks."

"So what's he done?" Molly repeated.

"Attempted armed robbery... threatening behaviour... resisting arrest... you name it."

Like mother, like son, thought Aubrey. Threatening people. Being a total arse. Must be hereditary.

Molly stared at him for a moment. "You're joking."

"Would that I were," Jeremy said heavily. "He wasn't on his own, though, if that makes it any better. There were three of them. Carlos, Jed Caparo – no surprise there – and a kid called Nathan. I don't know his last name, he's not in any of my groups."

"What's happened to the other two?"

"They had them all in separate interview rooms when I arrived, but Caparo had his social worker and foster mother there, and the other lad, Nathan, had his father. I saw him when I was leaving. I felt really sorry for him, he looked absolutely dreadful."

"I'm not surprised," said Molly.

Jeremy sighed. "It's pretty heavy stuff, even for kids from Sir Frank's. I mean, most of our lot aren't averse to a bit of petty thieving and helping themselves to the wheels from the odd car or two, but even they draw the line at armed robbery. According to the police, the three of them tried to hold up the newsagents in the high street with a gun, but when the shopkeeper pressed the panic button under the counter, they were the ones who panicked. They all ran out and legged it back to the flats."

"Where on earth did they get a gun?"

Jeremy shrugged. "Carlos says that he doesn't know anything about it. He swears that it wasn't his, anyway. He said that he didn't even know that Caparo had it with him, that he'd never seen it before. The first he knew of it was when Caparo pulled it out from under his jacket in the shop. Carlos said that when he saw it, he thought that it was an imitation."

"Do you believe him?" asked Molly.

Jeremy considered for a moment. "You know, I think that I probably do. He's in way over his head. He looked really frightened."

"Well, don't feel too sorry for him," said Molly. "They threatened the shopkeeper, don't forget. Poor old Mr Miller. He has enough trouble with the local children as it is."

"I know," said Jeremy, "but my guess is that in the event, they were far more frightened than Mr Miller was. Otherwise, why did they run away empty-handed? They had plenty of time to grab something before the police arrived. Anyway, they didn't get very far before they were chased."

Aubrey settled down on his paws. That was the trouble with humans, he thought, they just didn't think like cats. The newsagents was about halfway down the high street. The boys could have run one way or they could have run the other, but it was a fairly busy street even in the middle of the day. They couldn't have got very far before someone had picked up the chase and run after them.

"So what did Carlos say to the police?" asked Molly.

"Well, until I got there, almost nothing. Apparently, they'd hardly got more than half a dozen words out of him other than his name and address."

"But surely the police pressed him?"

"Well yes, of course, but saying nothing is child's play to most of the kids from Sir Frank's. They can keep it up all day, if necessary. It's the standard technique when asked a question in class. They know you'll get bored and either go away or ask someone else."

"So what did he say when you arrived?"

"The solicitor asked Carlos if wanted to be on his own with me for a moment and he said yes, so the police officers left the room."

"And what happened? Did he tell you how he came to be involved?"

"It was a bit of a garbled story, but from what I can make out, he just more or less got swept up in it. He was hanging around waiting to go into Science when Caparo sidled up and asked if he fancied a laugh. Carlos just said yes and followed him out of school, collecting Nathan on the way. You know, it's always hard for a kid to start halfway through the year in a new school, and even harder in a school like Sir Frank's. My instinct is that Carlos isn't a bad lad, but I suspect that he was so desperate to be accepted that when Caparo and his little gang offered him the chance to join in with something, he leapt at it, even if it meant getting into trouble."

Jeremy reached down and stroked Aubrey's head. They were both silent for a moment and then Molly said, "Where was his mother while you were talking to him?"

"One of the female officers had to take her to another room because she wouldn't stop shouting. Even then, you could still hear her halfway down the corridor."

"Did they let him go home with her?"

"Eventually. Anyway, I suppose that they had to. She is his mother."

"So what's going to happen to him now?"

"I don't know." Jeremy sighed. "I think that the police pretty much believe what he said and it helps that they haven't got anything against him on record, unlike Caparo who's already pretty well known to them. Also, Carlos wasn't the one waving a gun around. In his own words, he was just standing there. In any event, they haven't actually charged him with anything yet. He has to report back first thing tomorrow morning for further questioning."

"What about the other boys?"

"I don't know. I think that they were still there when I left."

50

"By the way," said Molly, "don't forget about tomorrow."

She nodded her head towards Aubrey as she spoke. Aubrey looked back at her. What was happening tomorrow?

Chapter Nine

Jeremy pulled up at the lights and turned his head to look at the passenger seat. Aubrey stared miserably back at him.

"Never mind, Aubrey. All done for another year. Soon be home and then you can have a nice big bowl of food."

Jeremy started to stretch out his hand to touch Aubrey's nose through the wicker grid of the cat basket, but pulled it back hurriedly as the lights changed. Aubrey rested his forehead against the side of the basket. Of all the things he hated, he hated cars the most. If you were inside them, you felt sick, and if you were outside them, they were trying to kill you. If he hadn't been so full up with food and sleepy after eating last night's leftovers, he would have been more on his guard when they didn't turf him out of their room last night. He would have taken evasive action and carried himself off to the airing cupboard which conveniently had a broken catch on the door, or gone somewhere else where they didn't usually think of looking for him, like the divan drawer under the bed in the spare room, which he'd learned how to hook out with a claw. Instead of which, he'd been caught. Done up like a kipper.

Lax though they were in most other matters, Molly and Jeremy were strict about him sleeping in their room with them. He could have kicked himself this morning when Molly brought his travelling basket into the bedroom. He should have known from experience that the only time they ever let him sleep on the end of their bed all night was when they wanted to make certain of his whereabouts in the morning. And they only ever wanted to make certain of his whereabouts in the morning when they wanted to put him in his basket. Which meant only one thing. The vet.

Aubrey brooded sullenly for a moment on the ruddy, broken-veined face, whisky-laden breath, and forcibly cheerful manner of the vet, Mr Jonathon Grimshaw. The vet at Sunny Banks had been bad enough but at least he had been business-like. He hadn't even bothered to pretend that he was interested in any of the inmates. It was a quick, jaws open, look round the teeth, needle in the scruff of the neck, and that was it. In out, job done, next please. But Grimshaw... Aubrey hunched his shoulders. It didn't fool him for one minute, all that pretend chuckling 'and how's this dear old chap today' stuff. The truth was that Grimshaw disliked most of his patients in general and he disliked Aubrey in particular, and that was fine because Aubrey didn't like him either.

From the moment that they had clapped eyes on one another when he had been to have his ear stitched that time, it had been hate at first sight and they had both known it. A little warm feeling rippled through Aubrey, in spite of his misery. At least he'd fought back this morning when Grimshaw had tried to come at him with the needle. A light scratch, just a quick scrape across the back of his wrist with the tip of a rapier-quick claw, and he had managed to leave a thin, red trail smiling in its wake. He had been rewarded with a look of pure venom. Aubrey had returned it with one of his own, narrowing his eyes until they were almost slits, fluffing up his tail and pulling back his top lip so that his broken tooth was particularly prominent.

If Jeremy hadn't been there, innocently unaware of the antagonism that was blistering the air, they would have gone straight for each other's throats, no question. When he thought about it now, though, he knew that having a go at Grimshaw had been a foolish thing to do. He had shown his paw too plainly, which had not been a good idea at all given that Grimshaw had all of the cards stacked very firmly on his side. Apart from the fact that in the great scheme of things Grimshaw was big and Aubrey was little, Grimshaw had at his disposal a cupboard full of needles and little bottles filled with lethal liquid.

He felt his stomach lurch as Jeremy suddenly braked sharply, throwing the cat basket forward with a dull thud against the dashboard.

"Sorry, Aubs," said Jeremy, changing gear and sliding forward more smoothly.

Aubrey closed his eyes. Being in a car was bad enough, but being in a car driven by Jeremy was sheer hell. Molly was a slow and sometimes hesitant driver, but Aubrey much preferred that, even if it made the journey a little longer. Jeremy's customary breakneck hurtle through the traffic was almost more than he could take.

"Nearly there. Not much longer now."

Aubrey opened one eye. Not much longer now? What was Jeremy talking about? Where were they going? They'd only been in the car for about five minutes; they weren't anywhere near home. He tensed as Jeremy suddenly turned a corner and parked, pulling up the handbrake in one quick screech that set Aubrey's teeth on edge. He opened the other eye and watched as Jeremy unbuckled his seatbelt and got out of the car.

"Shan't be a moment."

Aubrey sat up quickly and let out a small, low growl. Wherever Jeremy was going, he was going with him. He could, at a push, open the cat basket. He'd worked it out one night when he had been locked in the utility room by mistake and had been stuck for something to do, but he couldn't open a car door and he didn't fancy being trapped in there on his own. Anything could happen. Vincent had told him the story only the other week of some young cat called Bugsy who had been left in a basket on the back seat of a car when his owner went shopping. The car had been stolen and Bugsy had never been seen again. According to Vincent, he never would be either.

"The thing is, Aubsie old mate, and this is something that you may not know, but there's a lot out there that don't like cats. Difficult to believe, I know, but true, and that young Bugsy, he wasn't exactly what you'd call the co-operative type. Know what I mean?"

Aubrey hadn't been entirely sure that he did know what Vincent meant but he'd nodded anyway. He increased the volume of his growl and heaved himself against the side of the basket. While he thought it unlikely that any self-respecting car thief would look twice at Jeremy's beaten-up old Fiat, he wasn't taking any chances.

Jeremy walked round to the passenger side and opened the door. He peered down at Aubrey, a look of concern on his face.

"It's all right old mate, I'll only be gone for a couple of minutes."

Aubrey opened his mouth to growl again and then stopped. From over Jeremy's shoulder, he could see where they were and it was all starting to look horribly familiar.

Jeremy hesitated, frowning down at him, and then straightened up and looked around.

"Perhaps you're right. I'd better take you with me. It's not the sort of place to leave a cat on his own. Even a big old boy like you. Let's just let Molly know where we are."

Aubrey watched as Jeremy flipped open his mobile phone and tucked it into his shoulder while he reached inside the car to heave the cat basket out.

"No, Aubrey's fine... no, no problems. The vet said that he looks in good shape. I just wanted to let you know that we're going to be a bit late home... The Meadows... no, nothing's happened, I just wanted to check that Carlos is ok and find out what happened at the police station this morning. Ok, see you later."

Balancing the basket on one knee while he locked the car door, Jeremy slipped his mobile back in his pocket. Carrying the basket across his chest in both hands rather than by the handle, they set off together across the bleak tarmac towards the flats. They both knew why Jeremy was carrying the basket like this and Aubrey was not ungrateful. The last time Aubrey had been picked up in a basket by the handle, the handle had stayed in Jeremy's hand and the basket had plummeted straight to the floor. It had hit the ground with such a smack that Aubrey had thought for a moment that all his teeth would fall out.

He listened to Jeremy puffing and panting. Aubrey had put on weight since living with Molly and Jeremy, and he knew that Jeremy was already feeling under par, having witnessed him drinking the best part of a bottle of red wine last night and then shovelling down what looked like a whole handful of aspirin with his cup of tea this morning. He sat perfectly still, hoping that it would somehow distribute his weight across the floor of the basket more evenly and make it easier for Jeremy to carry.

The door to the entrance of the flats stood ajar, the combination lock that had once protected the entrance having long since been levered inexpertly out with a screwdriver, leaving a small dark hole in its wake. Jeremy shouldered the door open and walked towards the lifts. Aubrey watched as he punched ineffectually at the steel buttons.

"Why don't lifts in flats ever work?" Jeremy sighed and rested his head for a moment against the top of the basket and groaned. For the same reason, thought Aubrey, as the combination lock on the external door remained missing. Nobody who had any money or power could be arsed to do anything about it, and those that could be arsed to do something about it didn't have any money or power.

"Why did I drink so much last night?"

Jeremy sighed again, a great headache-laden sigh, and staggered towards the dank concrete stairwell, still carrying the basket. He paused for a moment to get his breath, leaning his back against the wall on which was scrawled the announcement that Darin is a nob in large white letters. Aubrey felt a small gagging rise in his throat and swallowed hard to push it back. It wasn't easy; the place stank, and it was a smell with which he was all too familiar. He had smelt it frequently before, most often round the back of the parade of shops where he'd hunted once or twice among the dustbins when he'd been desperate, just after Raj had died. It was a horrible stench, a combination of cooked cabbage and urine and vomit, all tangled together in a heap with unwashed human and wet mice. It was the kind of smell that hung on the air and wrapped itself around you, an evil little hobgoblin of a stink that poked its slimy, skinny fingers up your nose and down the back of your throat, and kissed your skin with soft, wet lips so that even if you washed a thousand times you would still catch its foul breath.

Raj had despised that little row of shops, Aubrey knew. It

was one of the few remnants of his tattered pride that he had been able to draw around himself. At least, as he had said frequently to Aubrey, his shop wasn't like one of those hell pits. At least his shop didn't stink of vermin and operate from behind steel grids. At least he didn't have the environmental health people permanently on his back. He did, however, have to deal with the same kind of customers. The kind of customers whose idea of a weekly shop consisted of jumbo packs of oven chips, cheap white bread, and six packs of strong lager, and the kind to whom in the end he was forced to give credit, because otherwise he would have had no customers at all.

"I am telling you, cat, it is a joke." Raj's voice had been hard and bitter. "These people, they say things about my shop, I have heard them behind my back. Yes, I have heard all the things that they say. And sometimes not behind my back but in front of it, as though I cannot hear, as though I am a deaf person. But my shop is clean. Every day I clean it. Wall. Shelf. Floor. All of it, it is clean. It is cleaner than the scum who come in and pretend that they are my friends so that I will let them pay another time."

He had sneered when he said it, but it had been a sad pulling back of the mouth that had lacked conviction and energy. Aubrey's heart had ached.

"Oh yes, it is always 'and how are you today, Raj?' and 'lovely weather we're having today, Raj' and behind my back they call me names. They call me paki. That is what they say. Paki, paki, paki."

And Aubrey had watched sorrowfully as Raj slugged down yet more whisky. He didn't know what a paki was, but whatever it was, Raj obviously didn't like it.

"And the thing is, cat, I should not be called a paki. It is not nice. No. Anyway, I am not a paki."

Aubrey couldn't have cared less whether he was a paki or not, but if Raj didn't like it then he didn't either.

"And what do they buy? I will tell you what they buy. They buy rubbish. They feed their children, their little, tiny children, their babies, on rubbish. And I must stock rubbish because that is what they buy. Except when they are stealing it. And when they are stealing it, I must let them, because what is the point of calling the police?"

None whatsoever, Aubrey knew. The last time Raj had apprehended a shoplifter and tried to involve the police, he had received a brick through his window for his trouble.

The thought of Raj sobered him and he sat quietly as Jeremy continued up the stairs, stopping on every landing to get his breath back and pausing finally outside a scruffy paint-blistered door.

"That's odd."

Jeremy placed the basket gently down on the floor and pushed on the door slightly with the flat of his hand. It swung open. He picked the basket up again and stepped cautiously into the gloomy, narrow hallway. Aubrey raised his head and tensed, suddenly alert. Something was wrong. The place felt eerily silent.

"Carlos?" Jeremy's voice came out on a slight squeak. He cleared his throat and tried again. "Carlos?" He stepped further down the hall and set the basket down on top of a small, battered, pine chest. Aubrey sat up straighter and watched through the wicker bars as Jeremy tiptoed across to a closed door and tapped on it gently with his knuckles.

"Carlos? Maria? It's me," he paused. "Mr Goodman." He listened for a moment and then raised his fist again. He hesitated for three seconds before tapping again, more firmly this time.

"Is anybody in there?"

Jeremy stiffened his shoulders slightly and grasped the door handle.

"It's me," he called again. "It's Mr Goodman." And turning the door handle, he stepped in.

To the right of Jeremy's shoulders, Aubrey had a clear view into the room. Lying on the bed and staring up at the ceiling, eyes wide open, lay Maria, one sparkly flip-flop dangling from the grubby little foot that stuck out over the edge of the bed. Across the side of her face and staining down into her neck flowered a large purple bruise.

Chapter Ten

"You should have seen her, Moll."

Jeremy took another swig of whisky and cradled the glass in both hands. He stared for a moment at the gently swaying amber liquid.

Aubrey sat curled up quietly at his feet, listening and sifting through the events of the morning. In his world, all life – even Maria's – was precious. God knew, it was cut short frequently enough, but if he was honest he had to admit to being more than slightly relieved that with Maria gone the threat to kill him had gone with her.

"I could see that she was dead straight away," Jeremy continued. "I mean, I could just tell. It's not like in those detective programmes on the telly. I didn't need to go up to her and hold a mirror to check if she was still breathing or anything. I just knew."

Aubrey had known, too. When he'd lived on the streets, he'd seen enough stiff and inanimate things, objects left where they fell, to know death when he saw it. He had guessed the worst before Jeremy had stumbled backwards into the hall, one hand over his mouth, and the other fumbling in his jacket pocket for his mobile phone.

"There wasn't any blood or, or… anything, was there?" Molly sat slightly forward, her face tense and her small hands clasped tightly together. She whispered the words and let them fall in a tiny hush, as though to speak out loud might somehow be disrespectful.

Jeremy shook his head. "No. Nothing like that. The police think that she was probably strangled."

Molly shuddered slightly. "God, how awful."

Depends on your point of view, thought Aubrey. What goes around, as one of the screws used to say in Sunny Banks, comes around. For the first time, he understood what it meant. Still, death threat notwithstanding, he wouldn't have wished this on her.

Jeremy nodded and took another gulp of whisky.

"Not nice," he agreed.

"Do the police think that it's the same person who killed Miss Jenkins and the others?"

"They're not saying. At least, not to me. But I suspect that they're probably hoping that it's not the same person."

Molly stared at him.

"Why ever not? Surely to goodness they don't want two killers on the loose?"

"Well, no, but Maria isn't like the other victims. Think about it. She's not elderly, for a start, and she didn't live alone. If it's the same man, or woman I suppose, who's going around doing these killings, it means that he or she is widening their field of interest. Which means that the population at large is at risk and not just the elderly." He took a deep breath and exhaled slowly. "The panic round here has been bad enough as it is, it'll go into meltdown when this gets out. It would be much better from the police point of view if they could put Maria's death down to some kind of domestic incident or something like that."

"But it was only her and Carlos living there," said Molly.

"Quite," said Jeremy.

For a moment neither of them spoke, and then Molly said, "What's going to happen about Carlos now?"

"Well," said Jeremy slowly, "I don't know, but clearly they're going to have to find him first. Apparently, they were going to send someone round anyway when he didn't show up this morning. It was just unlucky for me that I got there first. God knows where he's gone, but he's going to be in big trouble if he doesn't get back sharpish…"

He trailed off and they looked at one another.

Well, wherever he was, thought Aubrey, he clearly wasn't at home. The flat had been empty. The first thing that the police had done was to check all the rooms, including the cupboards, but there had been no trace of Carlos. He turned the thought over in his mind. The boy must have known what had happened, surely. It would have been impossible not to know. He would have heard if someone had broken in during the night. And even if he hadn't, even if he had slept right through it, he must have noticed that his mother wasn't around in the morning. Aubrey chewed it over for a moment.

If Carlos had nothing to do with his mother's death, if he had gone into her room in the morning and found her lying like that on the bed, then the natural thing to do, the obvious thing, would be to go for help. Run to a neighbour, for instance. He checked this thought. No, the people that lived in The Meadows weren't the kind of neighbours that you'd run to. Run from, maybe, but not to. But he could have gone somewhere else for help – one of the shops on the parade, perhaps, or he could have just rung for an ambulance or the police. If he was afraid of being in the flat on his own, he wouldn't have had to stay indoors, he could have waited outside until they arrived. So maybe, he thought slowly, Carlos really didn't know that his mother was dead. Perhaps, terrified by everything that had happened, he had done a bunk the night before. But in either case, whether Carlos had anything to do with it or not, where was he now? He seemed to have vanished into thin air.

As if reading his thoughts, Molly said, "Where do you think he's gone?"

Jeremy shrugged. "Who knows? He could be anywhere. When Carlos was questioned at the police station yesterday, it was quite clear that they haven't got any relatives or friends in this country. From what I could gather, they came to England because his mother thought that she could make a better life for them, but they didn't know anybody when they arrived. They spent their first few weeks here living in a bed and breakfast near the airport."

"It's possible, I suppose," said Molly, "that he might have gone back to where they used to live in London. There might be somebody there that he could have run to."

"It's my guess," said Jeremy, "that the police will look there first."

"You don't think that the police seriously suspect him of having anything to do with it, do you?" Molly sounded shocked.

"Well, it has to be a possibility. And, for reasons already stated, it could well be their preferred option." Jeremy fell silent for a moment.

"Yes, but his own mother..." Molly looked at him, appalled.

He wouldn't be the first son to kill his mother, Aubrey thought. He'd known it happen even in the cat world. And, to be brutally honest, Carlos had more reason than most. He shuddered slightly. Imagine living with Maria every day; it didn't bear thinking about. She'd be enough to try the patience of a saint. He would defy even Molly to find anything good to say about her.

"But what reason would he have?" continued Molly. "I mean, I know you said that she was irritating, but so are lots of people. They don't die for it."

Jeremy sighed. "I don't know, Moll. I honestly haven't got a clue. If you'd asked me if he was the sort of kid that was capable of something like that, I would have said no. But who knows what goes on inside people's heads? Anyway, he's only been with us for half a term or so. I don't really know much about him, and we didn't get an awful lot from his previous school, just a few lines which didn't do much more than confirm his date of birth and the fact that he'd been enrolled there. All I know for sure is that his mother is dead and that he's done a bunk."

Whatever way you looked at it, Aubrey thought, it wasn't looking good for the boy. At the very least, the police would want to question him. The chances were that even if he wasn't directly involved, he might have seen something. Or perhaps he knew something. Even if he didn't know that he did.

Molly swallowed hard. "What do you think will happen next?"

Jeremy shrugged his shoulders. "I'm not sure. They were starting to question the neighbours and so on when I left. I've given my statement, so I guess they'll just get on with things now. I suppose that I might have to go back again if they want to check anything. One thing to be grateful for is that at least they knew who I was. I mean, I didn't have to explain what I was doing there or anything."

You might have had a bit of trouble, thought Aubrey. It wasn't every day that a local teacher pitched up at a murder scene with a cat in a basket.

Molly stared at him horrified, as the thought occurred to her.

"You don't mean that they might suspect you? Why on earth would you have any reason to kill her? She was practically a stranger to us. You just happen to teach her son, that's all." Her voice sounded suddenly small and slightly shaky. "You only got involved in the first place because Carlos asked for you."

"Well, you know what they say," Jeremy took another mouthful of whisky and drained the glass.

No, thought Aubrey, and looked at him with interest. What do they say?

"First person to find a dead body," continued Jeremy, "is usually the last person to see it alive. First rule of crime fiction."

"Oh, that's nonsense. They can't possibly suspect you." Molly spoke quickly, her words tumbling out in a rush. "What possible reason could you have? It's ridiculous. It was probably someone who broke in, someone who went there to steal things and she disturbed them or something like that."

You must be joking, thought Aubrey. Even he had seen that there was nothing in there worth stealing.

As if echoing his thoughts, Jeremy said, "I shouldn't think that there was a lot in there to steal. If you were going to go burgling, you wouldn't pick The Meadows. Even a very dim burglar wouldn't pick The Meadows. Anyway, the police said that there was no sign of a break-in."

Molly frowned. "But I thought you said that the door to the flat was open?"

It was, thought Aubrey, but it hadn't been forced. There was no sign of any breakage anywhere. He ran the scene back through his mind. Jeremy had placed his basket on the floor and had just pushed the front door with the flat of his other hand, and it had swung back. He had closed it behind him, but there hadn't been an answering click. Now he thought about it, there hadn't been any noise at all.

Doors, as Aubrey knew, came in different shapes and sizes, and generally he classified them as those that he could open and those that he couldn't. But external doors were slightly different. At Raj's shop there had been two types of external door – the one at the front that clicked shut and locked automatically when you pulled it to, and the one at the back that had huge bolts at the top and bottom and needed a big key to secure it. He'd watched Raj lock up many a time, and had seen him turn the key and put it back on its hook on the wall.

He mulled it over. If Maria's door was one of those that needed a key to secure it, it was unlikely that she would have left it unlocked. So, did that mean that she had let in whoever it was? She must have done, he thought. Nobody would leave a front door unlocked in a place like The Meadows. Anybody could walk in and, in this case, he thought soberly, anybody had.

Chapter Eleven

Jeremy sighed and slapped the last of the exercise books that he'd been marking down onto the pile by his feet. He threw his pen on top of them.

"I wonder why I bother sometimes."

Molly looked up from the magazine she was reading.

"Why? What's up?"

"Well, I've just finished marking what I thought was a fairly simple exercise that I set for Year Nine." He nodded down at the pile of books. "Just a straightforward task, nothing difficult. All they had to do was take two or three words at a time and put them into a sentence, and then tomorrow we were going to swap the sentences around the room and try to build them up into a story. There was nothing complicated, nothing too much to think about, no hard words like adolescent, hormone, and intellectually challenged. Just simple ones like water and bucket."

"And?"

"Three of the words were 'horse', 'hay', and 'man'. Jake Carlyle has written, 'hay man, borrow us your horse'.

"Perhaps he doesn't know what hay is?" suggested Molly.

"Perhaps you're right," Jeremy acknowledged gloomily. "In fact, you probably are. He's probably not entirely certain what a horse is. I should have thought of that. God, what sort of world is this where kids don't even know what a horse is?"

Aubrey was with Jeremy on that one. Even he knew about horses. In fact, he'd been quite friendly with one at one point. It was a large bay and lived in the field at the back of the railway station. Aubrey had dropped in to see him now and again. They hadn't exactly communicated, but it had been nice to have some company from time to time, especially after Raj had died. Now he thought about it, he'd lost touch with quite a few of his friends from the old days. Since he'd got sprung from Sunny Banks, he'd got out of the old routine. There was Tony, too. He had been friends with Tony for a long time. One of the inmates of the psychiatric wing of the local hospital, Tony was a gentle, dazed-looking young man with kind eyes and a soft mouth. He had come across Aubrey in one of the little enclosed gardens one day and had started talking to him. According to Tony, he was the secret heir to the throne and was due to be the King one day, which was why they kept him locked up. Aubrey had been quite interested and had been more than willing to listen, especially as the young man had fed him bits of crumbled digestive biscuits which he had fished out of his pockets from time to time. He made a mental note to look Tony up again. He was probably wondering where he'd been.

Molly closed her magazine and laid it on the arm of the chair. "You seem very down this evening. Has something happened at school?"

Jeremy reached across the sofa and tickled the back of Aubrey's neck. "No, not really. Just another crap day at the madhouse known as Sir Frank Wainwright's. We've had the date of the Ofsted inspection, but we all knew it was coming so it's no surprise."

"When is it?"

"Three weeks. Nicely balanced. Just enough time to get everyone stressed off their heads without there being enough time to put anything right. Mind you," he added, "I don't suppose they give ten years' notice."

He got up and walked across to the window. Molly and Aubrey watched the set of his shoulders as he stared out at the rain, the drips falling in big sorry sobs against the glass. Jeremy continued talking, his back still to the room.

"All the kids were full of what's happened about Carlos today. It's all they've talked about all day. It's all everyone's talked about all day: the staff, the dinner ladies, everyone. Even the contractors that are supposed to be fixing the roof were talking about it. The whole place is buzzing with it." He sighed.

It was hardly surprising, thought Aubrey. It wasn't every day that a boy got his mother murdered and then made himself the chief suspect by disappearing, even at Sir Frank's.

"How did they know about it?" asked Molly. "It's not even been in the local paper yet."

"Some of the kids live over at The Meadows. The place has been swarming with police all weekend. They could hardly have missed it. Anyway, these things always get around."

Molly nodded.

"What are they saying?"

"Well, there are a number of different versions of events doing the rounds, depending on who you talk to, but most of the kids are suddenly his new best friend on the basis that he's a murder suspect and he's done a runner. On the other hand, the dinner ladies always knew that he was a bad lot and think that hanging is too good for him." He smiled suddenly. "Most of the staff are trying to remember who he is without quite admitting that they haven't got a clue. And of course, the Head is doing her pretending to be all concerned act. Like she gives a shit," he added bitterly.

"What do you mean, pretending?" asked Molly.

"The fact is," said Jeremy flatly, "the only person that the Head is even remotely interested in is herself. Therefore, the fate of Carlos is only of concern to her insofar as it might have a direct effect on her personal wellbeing. She makes all the right noises, of course, but there's nothing behind it; nothing other than sheer naked self-interest, anyway. She does this special look."

Jeremy turned to face Molly and contorted one side of his face, pulling back the corners of his mouth and scrunching his eyebrows up into an expression of mock sympathy. It looked uncannily like her, thought Aubrey. He'd seen the Head once when she'd called round to give Jeremy some reports to write and a load of other work to do after he had been ill with 'flu and was at home recovering. All it needed, he thought, was a smudge of sticky pink lipstick across the front teeth to complete the picture. Molly laughed.

"She called me into her office this morning," Jeremy said.

"She was obviously desperate to get hold of the inside info. I was barely over the school step before she'd collared me. She must have been watching at her window, waiting for me to arrive." He paused and reflected for a moment. "I guess she must have heard all about it the same way that she hears about everything else, through one of her bum-licking coven."

"What did she say?"

"Oh, she didn't mess around, she was straight in there. Rats and drainpipes weren't in it. She wanted to know what I thought Carlos had done, where I thought he might be, and what the police had said to me. But above all, she wanted to make sure that I hadn't spoken to the press. Her actual words were, 'It wouldn't do to let the media pre-judge matters.' Of course, what she really meant was, for God's sake don't let the school be dragged into it. She must think I'm stupid."

Aubrey watched as Jeremy pushed his hands down hard into his pockets, his knuckles straining tight against the fabric of his trousers. He was obviously upset.

"Do you know," Jeremy continued more slowly, "she didn't once ask about Carlos? About Carlos himself, I mean. I don't think she even knew who he was. In fact, I'm sure that she didn't, because she had a set of the school mugshots out on top of the filing cabinet. And then when she'd finished grilling me, she called a staff meeting before school started. A special briefing she called it." He paused and then added, "She makes me sick."

"What did she say at the briefing?"

"It was pathetic. Everybody already knew all about it by then, of course, although they all pretended that they didn't." Jeremy paused and smiled grimly. "She'd obviously got it all well-prepared. She was probably up half the night writing it. It was all wrapped up in sad smiles and that caring little whispery sort of voice that she uses."

Aubrey knew that voice, it was the one that she had used when she had marched up the front path with an armful of work for Jeremy to do. It sounded like nothing so much as a mouse scuttling across a wooden floor on little, scrabbly feet.

Jeremy crossed the room and sank down in an armchair.

Leaning back, he stared at the ceiling and let his arms flop over the sides. He continued.

"It was all about how we must protect the kids, and not let speculation and gossip run rife, and how it could be very damaging for their tender young minds and how it was all very tragic and all that. Oh yeah, and of course Carlos hadn't been with us for very long, so he's not really one of ours, and whatever you do, don't talk to the papers."

"I suppose there's no news of Carlos?"

"No. Not a whisper. God knows where he's gone. I just hope that wherever he is, he's indoors somewhere. I'd hate to think of him being out on a night like this."

All three of them jumped suddenly at the sound of a sharp rat-tatting on the front door. Molly and Jeremy looked at each other.

"I'll go," said Jeremy, and heaved himself out of the chair.

Aubrey stiffened at the sound of voices in the hall and then felt his heart drop. He knew that great booming tone. He watched with dread as the sitting room door slowly opened and Rachel and Clive walked in.

"Rachel," said Molly brightly, rising from her chair to greet them. "And Clive. What a nice surprise. How lovely to see you. We heard that you were coming back."

"Drink?" said Jeremy.

"Just a small one," said Rachel, dropping herself into the warm chair that Molly had just vacated. "We were on our way to pick Caleb and Corrina up from the Young Christians Ethical Craft Group, and we thought that we'd just drop by to say hello. We wanted to let you know that we're back and to give you our new temporary address. And also," she looked across at Clive, her expression arch, "we wanted to share our good news with you."

Molly looked enquiringly towards Clive, who was standing with his back to the fire, arms behind his back and legs astride.

"Just been offered a new post," said Clive.

Why, thought Aubrey wearily, did he always speak in those stupid, clipped tones? Did he think that it made him sound important or something?

"Not just a new post," said Rachel. "Rather more than that, darling."

She leaned confidentially towards Molly, her head tilted slightly to one side. She looked, Aubrey thought, like a mentally retarded turkey.

"A headship," said Rachel triumphantly.

Jeremy handed a glass to Clive.

"Where?" His tone was suspicious.

"Bishop's."

"Bishop Caulfields? But that's…"

"Yes," said Rachel, her voice rushing swiftly between them like a determined dodgem car. "But privileged children need spiritual guidance as well, you know. Even more so, in many respects. And Bishop's were so keen to have him, they practically begged."

"Prayed long and hard about it," said Clive gravely. "As you can imagine."

"Oh yes," said Jeremy shortly. "I can imagine all right. After Africa and everything, it must have been a real struggle for you." He paused and poured himself a glass of wine. "Well, you'll be interested to know Clive, that after the last Ofsted inspection – you remember that one, the one that you were off sick for – Sir Frank's is going to be put into special measures unless things have improved. Which, astonishingly, they haven't."

"Oh dear," murmured Rachel, and then turned brightly to Molly. "Do you know, Molly, it does sometimes seem as though things are almost meant to happen. Clive had already applied for Bishop's while we were still in Africa, but we had no idea then that we would be coming back anyway."

"Well, God certainly does move in mysterious ways," said Jeremy.

"Well, obviously, Jeremy, we're all dreadfully upset about Clive's aunt, such a dreadful thing to happen, but what with inheriting the house and the new job and everything, it does all seem to have fallen into place somehow."

"Hasn't it just," said Jeremy, rather sourly, Aubrey thought.

"Of course," continued Rachel, "there's an awful lot of

work to do on the house, especially the garden. It's an absolute jungle." She sighed.

"You're going to live there, are you?" asked Molly.

"Oh yes. It's a lovely house, in spite of what has happened."

Great, thought Aubrey. It was bad enough when old Jenkins lived there. He'd have to warn Vincent and the others.

Rachel continued. "Dear old Aunt Louisa. She was over ninety, you know. And of course, there's still the funeral and everything to arrange."

"Will it take a lot of arranging?" asked Molly.

"Well, no, not really," admitted Rachel. "The police have said that we can go ahead now, but she didn't have many friends left. Most of the people she knew are dead. The only friends she had were those that she knew at The Laurels. And Clive is her sole beneficiary, so really everything should all be quite straightforward. And of course, the children think it's terribly thrilling," she added. She smiled mischievously at Molly.

"What is?" said Molly. She looked, Aubrey thought, puzzled.

"Well, you know, a real live murder! Caleb's planning to charge some of his friends to look at the actual place where, you know, it happened!"

"He's got some, has he?" said Jeremy.

"Some what?" Rachel looked confused.

"Friends," said Jeremy flatly.

"What Jeremy means," said Molly hurriedly, "is what with you just having come back and everything, the children haven't really had a chance to settle in yet. Anyway, poor Miss Jenkins. It was a terrible way to go."

"Awful," agreed Rachel. "We could hardly believe it. It was a dreadful shock to us."

"Must have come as a bit of a surprise to her, too," said Jeremy. "She had her head caved in, didn't she?"

"No point dwelling on it," said Clive.

For a moment, they all fell silent, and then Rachel turned to Molly and said eagerly, "Did you hear about the woman that got herself murdered over at The Meadows?"

71

Aubrey stirred slightly and crept closer to where Molly was sitting. He tucked himself tightly around her feet. If Rachel noticed him she'd start making a fuss about all her allergies and then he'd have to go out.

"Apparently it was the son," Rachel continued. "It seems that she wouldn't give him money for drugs and so he shot her and then he strangled her."

"Oh really?" said Jeremy. "Bit pointless, wasn't it?"

"What?" Rachel looked puzzled.

"Bit pointless," repeated Jeremy. "Bit of a waste of energy. I mean, if he shot her, why bother to strangle her? Unless," he added thoughtfully, "he just liked it."

Rachel shuddered and drained her glass.

"How awful."

"Doesn't surprise me," said Clive. "Only surprise is that it hasn't happened before. All the same over at The Meadows. Heard all about it first hand from Bill, the Chief Super. Belongs to our church. Course, he was drugged up to the eyeballs, like they all are."

"The Chief Superintendent?" asked Molly, startled.

"The boy," said Clive impatiently. "Said to old Bill, best thing to do with kids like that is give 'em a bit of harsh punishment. Give 'em some of their own medicine. Short, sharp shock. Not so short either, if I had my way."

"How jolly Christian of you," said Jeremy.

From beneath the kitchen table where he was watching a spider, Aubrey listened contentedly as Molly and Jeremy loaded the dishwasher.

"Thank God for that. I thought they'd never leave."

"They're not so bad," said Molly.

"Yes," said Jeremy flatly, "they are."

He reached over to the table and picked up the two small pieces of paper that were lying there. He peered down at them.

"Honestly. I don't know how they've got the nerve leaving these tickets. Fund-raising for Bishop Caulfield's? Since when did Bishop's need funds? All they have to do is pull a long face and say that they're down to their last three laptops per pupil and the parents are stampeding the gates with open cheque books."

"Well, they've gone now," said Molly. She paused for a moment and then she said slowly, " Why didn't you tell them about Carlos?"

"What do you mean?"

"Well, when they were talking about what happened over at The Meadows, you didn't mention that he was a pupil at Sir Frank's. You never said that you even knew him, let alone that you'd been down at the police station with him."

"Because," said Jeremy, "I couldn't stand any more of that hang 'em high stuff. Or, even worse, they might have suddenly decided to get all concerned about him. Imagine that." He walked over to the window and looked out at the rain which was continuing to sheet down.

"You didn't see the boy, Moll. When he was down at the police station, he was absolutely terrified. He was all big eyes and badly-cut hair. At one point he was shaking. I think that Carlos will have enough problems when they find him, without Rachel and Clive trunking in and praying all over him."

Aubrey emerged from under the table and padded over to Jeremy. He looked up and nudged Jeremy's calf with his chin.

"See?" said Jeremy. "Even Aubrey agrees with me."

Chapter Twelve

From under the kitchen table, Aubrey yawned. He stretched out a paw and pushed the radiator control slightly higher. It was one of a number of things he could do that Molly and Jeremy didn't know about. He rolled onto his side and pushed his stomach towards the heat. From the other room he could hear the faint clacking of the television. He needed to go to the toilet; he'd needed to go for ages, but he'd been waiting for the rain to stop. He heaved himself up and padded over to the window. It was still chucking it down. He shifted position slightly but it was no good, he was bursting. He'd have to go out there, he couldn't hold it in much longer. In the past, he'd always sneered at those cats whose owners kept a litter tray indoors for them, but there were times, he had to admit, when they had a certain benefit. Now being one of them.

He jumped down and slipped out through the cat flap, hurrying down the garden to his special place. No fun being out on the streets tonight, he thought. On nights like this the romance of the road was thin, to say the least. He shivered as he felt the rain hang in fat droplets on his fur and seep right into him. He felt chilled to the bone. After Raj had died, it had been on nights like this that he had been most at risk. He had needed to be on constant alert against the danger of being kicked in the ribs by a passing stranger, or terrified into heart-stopping immobility by the sudden rough barking and hot breath of a dog in his face. It had been on nights like this that his life had hung in the balance more than once.

He quickened his pace as the cold wind gusted down the garden and shook the leaves in the trees, flattening the tops of the plants and tinkling the wind chimes that hung in the branches of next door's tree. He contemplated for a moment calling on Vincent, and then changed his mind. No point, probably. If Vincent had any sense he'd be tucked up in front of the fire on a night like tonight. Just like he was going to be any minute now. No cat that had any viable alternative would be outside on a night like this.

He scrabbled the earth back over the hole that he had dug and began to shake the last of it free from his paws, but then stopped and looked upwards as something caught his eye. If he wasn't very much mistaken, there was a light showing in the garden shed. He sat perfectly still for a moment and watched it. There it was again. It was definitely a light. A small, yellow light that leaped for a moment against the glass of the little square window and then went dark. He frowned. Somebody was in Molly and Jeremy's shed. Somebody was in their shed and using what looked like a torch, or maybe it was a candle.

Aubrey thought for a second and then crept silently across the grass, lifting each paw in slow motion, a lithe grey shadow moving ghost-like against the silver light. He paused and listened. There was definitely somebody in there, he was close enough to hear them now. A tiny but distinct rustling noise, and then something that sounded like sniffing filtered out into the night air. He sat back and thought about it. Whoever was in there had no right to be in there. That shed was his territory. The broken panel at the back made it easy to slip in and out, and he liked the dim, cobwebby light and the lovely peaty smell of damp earth and half-used bags of compost that lay stacked in the corner. The clump of old sacking piled up on the bottom shelf was also perfect for curling up on when he felt like being on his own.

The other thing was, Jeremy kept his tools in that shed, and some of them had cost quite a lot of money. All right, Jeremy didn't use them very often, and in fact only the other day he had said something to Molly about selling some of them to raise a bit of cash to help pay for the renovation work on the house that Dave was supposed to be doing. But that wasn't the point. The point was that they were Jeremy's, and if someone was in there nicking them then he, Aubrey, ought to do something about it. But, what?

He flicked his paw across his left ear and had a quick wash

while he thought about it. Of course, it might be an animal in there, in which case he could ignore it. He didn't feel much like a fight tonight. It probably wasn't doing any harm, and most animals didn't have much use for power tools. On the other hand, it might not be an animal. He moved slightly closer and listened harder. It would have to be a bloody big animal to be making that much noise, he thought. And an animal wouldn't be able to flick a torch on and off like that, far less light a candle. Not even the twins could do things like that, although they could probably make somebody do it for them. It must be a person. He stepped back and measured the leaping distance to the sloping roof. The window was set just underneath it. If he flattened himself across the slope and peered downwards, he'd be able to see into it.

He sprang upwards and landed four-square in one movement on the battered roofing felt. Crouching down, he held his breath for a moment. Clearly, whatever was in the shed was doing the same thing. For a moment there was absolute silence, and then the rustling noise began again. He peered down.

***

"What is it, what's the matter Aubrey?"

Molly bent down and scooped him up. Aubrey wriggled impatiently out of her arms and jumped down again.

"What is it? What's the matter with him?" Jeremy looked up from the television.

"I don't know. Shut up, Aubrey. Stop being so noisy."

Aubrey continued to yowl, raising the pitch to the next level and twisting himself upwards in a half-hoop. Molly turned to Jeremy.

"I think that he wants something."

Aubrey was momentarily stunned into silence. He'd spent the last two minutes jumping up and down on the arms of their chairs, and it had finally dawned on them that he was trying to attract their attention. Give him strength.

"Perhaps he wants something to eat?" said Jeremy.

"He can't be hungry," said Molly. "I fed him only an hour ago."

"I'll give him some of his biscuits to shut him up," said Jeremy.

Jeremy got up and strolled through to the kitchen. Aubrey followed. Jeremy reached down and tickled Aubrey's ear.

"What's up, old boy? Are you still hungry? Do you want something else to eat?"

Jeremy reached towards the cupboard where Aubrey's biscuits were kept, glancing towards the window as he did so. He reached up to pull down the blind and then stopped. Walking closer to the window, he leaned over, hands on the sink, and peered out into the night.

"Moll," he turned his head and called through to the other room, "I think there's someone in our shed."

He spoke slowly and turned back to the window, peering out more intently and shading his eyes with one hand against the glare of the kitchen light. He twisted around as Molly came in. "I could swear I just saw a light down there. Look, there it is again."

Hooray, thought Aubrey. At last.

Molly and Jeremy looked at each other.

"Call the police," said Molly.

Jeremy looked doubtful.

"It's probably nothing," he said. "I expect it's just one of next door's security lights reflecting on the window or something. The bloody things are always going on and off for no reason. I'll go down and check."

"No." Molly caught him by the sleeve of his jersey and held it. She turned and grabbed the phone from the shelf with her other hand. She held it out to Jeremy. Her hand shook. "Call the police."

Her face, Aubrey noticed, had gone suddenly white and had a sort of pinched look.

"It's gone now," said Jeremy, "I told you, it's probably just a reflection from next door's lights."

"Jeremy," Molly spoke slowly, and took a deep breath. "There's a killer on the loose out there. What if it's him? He's

77

already killed four people. Five, if you count Carlos's mother. What if he knows that it was you who found her? He might think that you witnessed something and he's come to find you." Aubrey gasped as she reached down and snatched him up, clutching him tightly to her. "For goodness sake, we can't take any chances…"

Her voice trailed off and her eyes widened in horror as all three of them turned to the window and watched as the shed door opened. A dark shape hesitated on the threshold and then began to creep slowly down the path towards the back door.

Chapter Thirteen

"Can I stay here?"

Aubrey stretched out along the arm of the sofa and ran his eye over the boy. Shivering and wet, the fake fur on the hood of his parka hung in sodden clumps around his sharp-featured face. He looked exactly like a drowned rat. Stick a tail on him and you wouldn't be able to tell the difference. The poor kid looked like he hadn't eaten in days. Thin to start with, he looked practically emaciated now.

"I don't know, Carlos," said Jeremy, running his fingers through his hair, the worry line between his brows suddenly deepening. "There are a lot of things to think about. It's not that simple."

It might not be up to you anyway, thought Aubrey. It might not be your decision. In fact, it almost certainly wouldn't be. As Aubrey had quickly discovered at Sunny Banks, once authority got involved, all concept of free will went straight out of the cat flap. But whatever Jeremy decided for now, whether he let the boy stay for tonight or whether he didn't, surely he would have to let the police know that Carlos was with them? It would only make matters worse if he didn't tell them.

Aubrey felt suddenly anxious. He didn't want Molly and Jeremy to go getting themselves into trouble, and certainly not for the sake of a kid of Maria's. Apart from anything else, what would happen if the police took Molly and Jeremy away? There'd be nobody to feed him.

"How did you know where we lived, anyway?" asked Jeremy.

"All the kids know where the teachers live."

Aubrey watched as Jeremy stared blankly for a moment, his mind clearly absorbing the implications of what Carlos had just said. Don't worry, he thought. It was a compliment in a way. Jeremy had been at Sir Frank's for over ten years, so all the kids presumably knew where he had lived previously, too. But in spite of that, nothing had ever happened. He and Molly hadn't been firebombed, or stoned to death or anything, when they were putting out the milk bottles.

He looked up as Molly came in with a bacon sandwich and a mug of hot chocolate. They all fell silent as the boy wolfed the sandwich down, and then Jeremy spoke.

"How long have you been in our shed?"

Carlos shrugged his shoulders evasively.

Jeremy continued. "Well, if you haven't been in our shed, where have you been? You know everybody's looking for you, don't you?"

Carlos nodded and wrapped his thin fingers around the steaming mug of chocolate. Aubrey looked at him more closely. When exactly had Carlos run away? It might have been almost as soon as the police had let him return home, in which case he probably didn't know that his mother was dead. The same thought had clearly just occurred to Jeremy. Aubrey watched as he glanced across at Molly, who raised her eyebrows back at him. He listened as Jeremy cleared his throat, trying to feel his way forward.

"Er…" Jeremy paused.

Aubrey inched up closer to him in a show of solidarity. Poor Jeremy. It was bad enough trying to tell a kid that his mother was dead, without the added strain of adding that she'd been murdered and that he was currently occupying the number one spot of chief suspect. Jeremy cleared his throat and tried again.

"Er, Carlos… about your mother…"

Carlos wiped his mouth with the back of his hand and took another gulp of hot chocolate as he waited. Aubrey felt his heart suddenly constrict. Poor little sod. He had exactly nothing going for him. From a chaotic insecure background with an absent father and a dead mother, Carlos was just like some of the kittens that he had seen in Sunny Banks. Tiny, little, starving creatures, they had been found abandoned in bins and boxes, and they had sat patiently where they had been left, waiting for their fate. Fear, hunger, and cold had been the only things that they had ever known. One of them, he recalled, had been brought in with burnt feet. One of the screws had called it Sizzle. He had thought it was funny. Aubrey hadn't. He felt a sudden spurt of anger. He turned his head and stared desperately at Molly.

"The thing is," said Molly gently, leaning forward and reaching across to stroke the back of the boy's hand, "your mother is dead, Carlos."

Carlos nodded. "I know."

"You know?" Jeremy sat back, the relief stamped across his face. Oh well, thought Aubrey, that was one hurdle over. Only another nine hundred and ninety-nine thousand to go.

Carlos nodded again and looked at the floor, the words dropping from his mouth like small, hard pebbles. "I saw her."

They all fell silent for a moment, and then Carlos spoke again.

"Mr Goodman, do the police think I done it?"

Aubrey tensed and narrowed his eyes, watching as Jeremy opened his mouth to tell what would clearly be a comforting lie. But there was no point in pretending, it would only make matters worse in the long run. The boy was going to find out soon enough, and whatever else he was, he didn't appear to be stupid. In Aubrey's opinion, the sooner Carlos faced up to his predicament the better.

Jeremy swallowed hard and then said, "To be honest, Carlos, it doesn't look very good for you at the moment."

Carlos stared miserably around the room, his gaze coming to rest finally on Aubrey. Slowly, almost unconsciously, he stretched out a thin, grubby hand and began to stroke Aubrey's back. Jeremy continued.

"Look, Carlos, I know it's probably not what you want, but we're going to have to tell the police that you're here. They'll find out anyway, and it will look better if we tell them first."

Carlos's hand paused mid-stroke.

"And what will happen then, Mr Goodman?"

"I don't know," Jeremy admitted.

81

God, Aubrey thought, these kids are so street-wise, so smart, but they still automatically assume that the grown-ups will always know what to do. In his opinion, Jeremy should have called the police as soon as he'd pulled open the back door and seen Carlos shivering on the threshold. That was what he should have done, that was what a responsible person in his position would have done. But, he reflected, it was exactly the same instinct that had made Jeremy pick him at Sunny Banks that had prevented him from immediately turning Carlos over to the law, and who was he to criticise that? He also knew that if Jeremy had rung the police, there was every possibility that pandemonium would have broken loose very shortly afterwards. Once the police knew that Carlos was with Molly and Jeremy, everything would depend on who they sent to pick him up.

Some of the local police weren't exactly known for their hands-off approach. He and Vincent had seen two of them arrest a shoplifter in town only last week. You'd have thought that the poor bloke had gunned down at least half a dozen shoppers and danced in their blood, instead of merely trousering a couple of packets of cheap socks and a polyester shirt from the department store. The police had come roaring down the high street in a squad car, screeched to a stop, and pinned him up against the wall before the guy had a chance to blink. They had his hands twisted up behind his back and a full and public confession in a matter of seconds.

In Aubrey's opinion, it had only been the fear of so many witnesses that had stopped them from giving the guy a good kicking. They had clearly been itching for it. Ironically, the school's liaison bobby was the worst of the lot – a fat, ruddy-faced character who looked like he'd just cycled in from Toy Town, Aubrey had often seen him as he swaggered through the primary school gates as though he was entering Dodge City.

If the two officers that Aubrey and Vincent had seen in town the other day were sent to collect Carlos, they would come tearing up, lights and sirens blazing, and Carlos would be carted off and questioned, and that would almost certainly be the last they saw of him. For all he knew, Jeremy and Molly would be taken down to the police station and questioned, too.

He looked at Jeremy anxiously. If Molly and Jeremy got slung into the big house for any length of time, who knew what would happen? He felt his heart beat suddenly faster. When would they be let out? They could be in there for hours, days even. There would be nobody to give him his dinner. Or worst of all, what if he got shoved in a cardboard box and carted off to Sunny Banks again by some do-gooder? No, he forced himself to calm down and breathe more easily. Molly and Jeremy would never let that happen. They just wouldn't. Nevertheless, a slight unease had crept in and started to wriggle about at the back of his mind. He tensed slightly and listened harder.

"Do you want to tell me what happened?" said Jeremy.

Good thinking, thought Aubrey. Once Carlos was back with the police, he might just simply clam up again and they'd never get the story out of him. It was better that he told everything to Jeremy and Molly now, and then at least there would be one version to refer to.

Carlos looked at him for a moment and then nodded.

He began to speak slowly at first, hesitating over the words and spacing them out as though they were rationed. Anybody else might think that he was making it up, thought Aubrey, feeling his way for each lie. But Aubrey knew differently. Aubrey knew about liars. Raj's shop had been full of them; customers with their ready excuses about why they couldn't pay this week, next week, sometime, never. Liars spoke far more quickly than Carlos was doing. Liars had more words than they knew what to do with. What Carlos was doing, Aubrey knew, was telling the truth. Telling the truth and concentrating on getting it right. He waited.

"When the police finished questioning me and that," said Carlos, "when they let me go, me and Mum just went back to the flats. That copper, the one with the grey hair, he said that I just had to promise to stay in and not go out no more that night." He stopped and then burst out, "I didn't know that Caparo had a gun, Mr Goodman. Honest. I didn't. I swear. I never knew nothing about it. I wouldn't have gone with them if I'd known. Caparo said it would just be a laugh. He said we were just going to bunk off school for the afternoon and go and put a scare up old Miller. He never said it was going to be serious or nothing. I never knew about the gun," he repeated. "Honest. I swear on my life."

Jeremy nodded. "It's ok, Carlos. I believe you. Carry on."

Carlos sniffed and grazed the end of his nose with the cuff of his parka.

"When we got home, first off I was going to do like what they said. You know, like just stay in and watch the telly and listen to music and stuff, but, like, straight off, as soon as we got in, she starts going on. Like screaming and that." He paused for a moment. "Honest, Mr Goodman, she does my head in when she starts all that." He raised his voice suddenly and screeched, "You are a no-good. You are a bum like your father. Yes, no-good bum. Bad bum. What for is it that I work so hard? Work so hard that my fingers are only bones? Why is it that you do this to your poor mother? Why is that I am keeping you when you do all this and turn my poor fingers into bones? You will never be best doctor. You will be only big fat bum like your father."

Aubrey looked at him admiringly. Pretty good, he had to admit it. He sounded just like her. You would have thought that Maria was in the room with them. The kid had a future as a mimic, if nothing else. Carlos continued.

"I tried to ignore her, Mr Goodman, honest. That's what I always do when she starts, but this time she wouldn't shut up. I mean, I knew I was in big trouble and all that, I didn't need her to keep telling me. She just kept going on and on, and everywhere I went she kept following me round and shouting, like even into my bedroom and that, so I went out again. I had to. I couldn't stand the sound of her voice no more. I didn't even take my parka off."

"Did you lock the door after you?" said Jeremy.

Carlos nodded. "We always lock the door. Mum was strict about that."

Aubrey thought for a moment about the implication of what Carlos had just said. So, he was right. The door had been locked, and Maria had unlocked it to let in whoever had killed her. Unless, of course, it was Carlos, who didn't need to be let in because he had his own key.

"Ok," continued Jeremy, "and then what happened? You left the flat, so where did you go next?"

"Well, I just walked around for a bit, just over the waste ground round the back of the flats and that, and then I thought, what if the police see me? Cos, like I was in enough trouble as it was, and I'd promised them I wouldn't go out no more that night. If they saw me outside, they might take me back to the police station. And anyway, I was hungry and I didn't have no money to get no chips or nothing, so I thought I'd better just go back home."

"Did anybody see you in that time?" asked Molly. "Was there anybody else around?"

Carlos shook his head. "I don't think so. There weren't nobody else out. It was raining."

"How long were you walking about for?" asked Jeremy.

Carlos shrugged. "I don't know."

"Well, try and think," Jeremy persisted. "An hour? Half an hour? Ten minutes? Think about it, Carlos. Try to remember, because the police will ask you and it might be important."

There was no 'might' about it, thought Aubrey. The fact was, that unless it was Carlos himself who had done it, whoever had killed Maria had almost certainly done it in the space of time that Carlos was out of the flat.

Carlos frowned. "Honestly, Mr Goodman, I don't know. I'd tell you if I did."

"Well, what time did you go out?"

Carlos shrugged again and looked helplessly back at Jeremy.

"Haven't you got a watch?"

Carlos looked at him blankly. "What for?"

Aubrey sighed inwardly. Quite. What for? It was a stupid question. In his experience, the world was divided into those that told other people when to move, those that moved when they were told, and cats. Carlos didn't need a watch for the same reason that Aubrey didn't. Aubrey didn't need a watch because, apart from the fact that he couldn't tell the time, he didn't need to tell the time. And neither did Carlos. At school, he had teachers and bells to tell him when to move, and at home he had Maria.

Jeremy took a deep breath and exchanged glances with Molly. He continued.

"Ok, forget about the time for now. So, what happened next? Don't rush, take your time and try to tell us exactly as it happened."

Carlos thought for a moment and then spoke slowly, again feeling for each word in an effort to get it right.

"I went back up to the flat and the door was open. Like, it was shut but it wasn't locked. I thought Mum might have taken some stuff down to the bins and forgot to lock the door behind her. I thought it was a bit strange, because she don't never forget, not even if she just steps outside or something." He paused for a moment and then continued. "Anyway, I went in and I noticed straight off that the telly was turned off."

"Was that unusual?" asked Molly. "Was the television usually on?"

Carlos nodded.

"It was always on. It was only turned off when we went out or if we had a visitor. Mum was strict about that, too, but we never really had no visitors. Anyway, I knew she couldn't be out because of the door, and, anyway, her handbag was in the kitchen and she never goes nowhere without her handbag."

He paused and swallowed hard. It had, Aubrey realised, finally dawned on Carlos that his mother was dead and she wasn't coming back. She had gone somewhere where she wouldn't need her handbag ever again.

Chapter Fourteen

For a moment, the three of them sat in silence. Aubrey could see that Carlos was struggling not to cry. Outside, the rain continued to patter against the windows.

"Go on," said Jeremy gently.

Carlos swallowed and pressed his lips tightly together. He took a deep breath through his nose and then exhaled slowly.

"After a while, she still hadn't come back up from the bins so I thought she might be lying down in her bedroom or something. She didn't normally but I thought, like, what with all the upset and everything, she might have a headache. I thought it was, like, odd that she hadn't locked the door when she come back in, but I thought she might just have forgot." Carlos paused and his voice cracked slightly. "And I felt a bit guilty and that, like, for everything that happened and then just running off and making her more worried, so I thought I'd take her a cup of tea and some biscuits. You know, to like, say sorry and that."

Now Aubrey thought about it, he remembered. There had been a mug of what had looked like cold tea on the table next to the bed. It had obviously been there for some time, because it had what looked like a faint film floating across the top of it.

"I looked in the cupboard for some biscuits but I couldn't find none, so I made a mug of tea and I took it into her room." Carlos stopped and swallowed. "The door was closed so I opened it and she was lying on the bed, and at first I thought she was asleep. I mean, like she looked like she was asleep. And then I took the tea over."

He speeded up now, the words suddenly rushing and tumbling from his mouth as though he couldn't get them out quickly enough.

"And I put it down on the bedside table, and I saw the

bruise on her face, and I touched her arm, and I said, 'Mum.' And then I said it again. 'Mum.' And I leaned right over and I couldn't hear nothing. I couldn't hear her breathing, so I shook her by the shoulder and her arm just sort of flopped over and was just sort of hanging over the side of the bed, and her mouth was open and her eyes were staring, and I knew she was dead. And then I didn't know what to do so I run out."

Aubrey looked at him closely. He could see that Carlos was still struggling not to cry. Did he blame him for running away? Probably not. In his position, he might very well have done the same. The poor little sod had been terrified.

"Carlos, why did you run away? Why didn't you call an ambulance or try to fetch help or something?" asked Jeremy.

"There weren't no point. There weren't nothing anyone could do for her."

"But in that case, you should have called the police," said Jeremy.

"I couldn't do that, Mr Goodman."

"Why not?" Jeremy's expression was puzzled.

"Mum always said that we mustn't have nothing to do with the authorities. She said it again and again. That's partly why she was so upset about having to go to the police station and everything. I didn't know what to do," he repeated. "I could see that she was dead. But when people die, you have to tell someone. You have to fill in forms and stuff like that."

"Well, yes," said Jeremy, his tone slightly puzzled. "Of course you do."

"We're not legal, Mr Goodman."

"What?" said Jeremy. "What do you mean, you're not legal?"

"We're not legal," repeated Carlos. "We ain't got no visas or permits or nothing."

"You mean you're illegal immigrants?" Jeremy sounded confused.

Carlos nodded. "We been in this country for six years. Before that, we lived in Brazil. That's where I was born. When we first come to England, we lived in a bed and breakfast and then we lived in a house in Camden, but we only had two rooms and we had to share a bathroom and kitchen with all the other families. Someone Mum knows said they could get us a flat so we come here."

"But how did you get a council flat if you're illegal immigrants? People round here wait years for council housing."

Aubrey knew Jeremy was resisting adding, even for The Meadows.

Carlos looked confused. "We didn't get it off the council. This bloke that Mum knew, he got some other bloke to get it for us. Mum used to pay him the rent. A little, fat bloke. He used to come round Friday afternoons in a blue van."

And how much did she pay this 'bloke', Aubrey wondered grimly. Considerably more than she would have had to pay the council, he suspected. But surely, Maria had worked for the council? She had said so to that man who had turned up at Mr Telling's place. It was Social Services who had sent Maria to Mr Telling in the first place. He listened carefully.

"I thought your mother worked for the council?" said Jeremy. "Didn't she need a work permit or something?"

Carlos shook his head. "No. She works for an agency. The council don't check agency workers."

Jeremy thought for a moment.

"What about your father, Carlos? Can we contact him?"

Carlos shook his head. "I ain't seen him since I was three."

"There's been no contact at all? No address to write to? When was the last time that you heard from him?" asked Jeremy.

"He sent me a birthday card when I was five," said Carlos. "But it didn't have no address in it. It just said 'to Carlos from your daddy'. I've still got it," he added.

Molly stood up suddenly.

"I'll go and make up the bed in the spare room. We can talk about what to do next in the morning."

Chapter Fifteen

Aubrey padded quietly across the landing on his way to the airing cupboard. Downstairs, Molly and Jeremy were still talking, the rise and fall of their voices filtering softly up the stairs. From the spare room, a thin shaft of light fell through the slightly open door. Aubrey paused. From inside came the faint sound of sniffing, and then something that sounded like a crow gulping. He pushed his nose round the edge of the door and stared. Sitting up in bed and lost in a sea of Jeremy's pyjamas, his long, thin limbs sticking out like the spokes of a broken umbrella and the blue and yellow striped scarf that he had been wearing under his parka still tucked around his neck, Carlos was crying as though his heart would break. Aubrey watched for a second, and in that moment Carlos looked up and saw him.

For a moment, they stared at each other and then Carlos spoke, his words squeezing out from behind his tears on a hoarse whisper.

"Cat… cat…"

He patted the bed clothes as he spoke, palm downwards in a gesture of encouragement. Aubrey hesitated and then trod gingerly across the carpet. He sniffed at the hand that the boy dropped down to him, ready to pull back at any moment. Was this a trick? Was the boy a cat-hater like his mother? He didn't think so. He hadn't shown any sign of it, but you couldn't be too careful.

"Hello, cat." Carlos gulped and smiled at him through his tears.

Aubrey jumped lightly up onto the bed, willing to be friends but poised to spring down again at the slightest hint of anything untoward. Carlos leaned over and wrapped his thin arms around him, burying his wet nose in the warm fur of

90

Aubrey's neck. For a moment, Aubrey stayed perfectly still and then, gently, quietly, he disentangled himself and sat back. Carlos sat up straighter and pushed his back up against the wall behind the bed. He reached across and stroked the top of Aubrey's head with a cold, thin hand.

"Hello, cat," he whispered again. "I'm Carlos."

There didn't seem to be anything to say to this. Aubrey tucked his tail neatly round his paws and waited. Carlos smiled at him again and sniffed, his long eyelashes sparkling with the ends of tears.

"I like cats. I like dogs, too, but I like cats better. I always wanted a cat, ever since I was little, but Mum wouldn't ever let me have one." He paused as though thinking, and then continued on a confidential note, leaning forwards slightly and lowering his voice. "There used to be street cats in Brazil, you used to see them everywhere, but I wasn't allowed to touch them. Mum said that they all had diseases. When we came here, I found some wild cats round the back of the flats. They were living in this old car that someone had just left there. I used to feed them. I never told no-one. I used to take them tins of meat and stuff that I nicked from our cupboard, and milk sometimes, too, if I thought Mum wouldn't notice. I gave them all names and I used to go and see them every day after school. My favourite was called Pele. He was a famous footballer. The real one, not the cat," he added. "He played for Brazil." His hand drifted to his scarf and patted it as he spoke. "My granddad gave me this."

Aubrey tucked his paws underneath him and settled down on the duvet. Carlos wasn't such a bad lad. He couldn't help it that Maria had been his mother. He hadn't chosen her any more than Aubrey had chosen his. It wasn't his fault that Maria had been a crazy, cat-hating lunatic. Carlos continued.

"One of the cats had kittens once, five of them, and I looked after them till they got bigger. I made them a bed in a cardboard box, a proper bed, and I put a cushion in it and an old blanket that I got out of our airing cupboard. One day, I came home from school and someone had moved the car. I don't know where they went after that. I looked for them but I couldn't find them. I never saw them again."

He fell silent for a moment, the memories of the cat family clearly still fresh in his mind.

"I used to go on and on about having a cat, but Mum wouldn't ever give in," Carlos's voice was reflective now, calmer. "She said it was because they weren't allowed in the flats but really it was because she didn't like them. Other people had cats, I told her, but she said that if they got found out they'd have to leave, they'd get thrown out. She said they'd get ejected." He paused for a second and then added, "She meant evicted."

He wiped his nose on the sleeve of Jeremy's pyjamas, one hand still resting on Aubrey's warm back.

"I wish we had got ejected, and then we could have left there and gone back to Camden." His voice cracked suddenly. "I hate that flat. I hated it right from the first time I saw it. I never wanted to go there in the first place, not right from the beginning. It's horrible living there. It stinks. It don't matter what you do, it don't matter how much you clean it, it always stinks. And there's always people fighting and kids crying. You can hear them in the flats around us. Screaming and shouting and chucking stuff about. Someone in the flat above us chucked a table out once. I saw it go past the window."

He paused and his voice calmed down again. He sniffed and wiped his nose for a second time on the sleeve of Jeremy's pyjamas. His eyes were still wet but at least, thought Aubrey, the tears had stopped rolling down the end of his nose. Perhaps he was starting to feel a little bit better.

"I never wanted to go there in the first place," he repeated. "I told Mum, I said that we should have stayed in Camden, it was better in Camden, at least in Camden we had some friends. I know we only had two rooms, but we would have got something else in the end. At least in Camden I didn't get called no names." He continued stroking Aubrey, his gaze fixed on the far wall. "At school all the kids call me Pedro. It's crap."

Tell me about it, thought Aubrey. Try being called Aubrey. Although it could have been worse, he supposed. Jeremy had been reading John Aubrey's *Brief Lives* at the time. He could have ended up being called Brief.

Carlos continued.

"It's all crap, everything. All of it. We only came here in the first place because Mum said we would have a better life, but I didn't want no better life. I liked the one we had. When we was in Brazil, that's all Mum used to go on about, all the time, this better life. She used to do cleaning for this English couple and that's what started it, that's where she got the idea from in the first place. She started learning English, and she used to come home with these English magazines what they gave her. She used to spend hours looking at them, especially the ones with pictures of houses and gardens in them. She used to cut them out and stick them in a book, and then when she'd had a few drinks she used to practise talking, saying words and that in English."

He turned his head for a moment and stared at the wall.

"Oh Carlos, when we go England all will be better. Yes, it is definite." Aubrey watched the bitter twist of his mouth as he mimicked his mother's distinctive voice. "In England, Carlos, we have house, we have garden. In England, you will go to good school. You will take examinations and you will be doctor. Good doctor. Famous doctor." He turned back to face Aubrey, his eyes blank with misery. "And so we come here, and we never had no house and we never had no garden, and look what's happened. She's dead."

He spoke on a dull, flat tone, the pain behind his words pushing for release. "And the thing is, cat, there weren't never going to be any better life. When we come here, it weren't never any better. Not from the start, and it weren't never going to be. I could have told her that right from the beginning. We didn't have nothing there and we ain't got nothing here. When we was in Brazil, you know what she was? You know what she done for a living? She was a cleaner. That's what she done. She cleaned people's houses. And when we come here, you know what? She's still a cleaner. At least in Brazil we was meant to be there; at least we was in our own country. At least people didn't look at us like we was dirt."

His voice cracked suddenly on a harsh sob, and the words came spitting out like firecrackers. "She used to say it was all for me, she used to say it was to give me a better chance and that, but I didn't want no better chance. I was all right where we were. But then Grandad died and Dad left us and went back to Spain, and we didn't have no money so we had to move to the city so Mum could get a job. But the thing is, cat, Mum was brought up in the country and she hated the city. So she used to daydream all the time about starting again somewhere else. She never stopped going on about it, especially after she started working for the English couple. 'Yes, Carlos, we will go to England and we will be rich. All will be well. You will be doctor. Brain doctor. It is definite. You will mend brains. You will be famous and we will be rich. We will go to England and forget about your no-good bumface of a father and we will be very rich."

Aubrey stared at him. All this talk about mothers had stirred up an unsettling thought. For the first time, it occurred to him that maybe his own mother hadn't abandoned him after all. He had always assumed that she had just upped and left, that the bundle of kittens that she had presented the world with had been too much for her. He didn't blame her, he never had. But maybe, just maybe, it hadn't been like that at all. Maybe she had gone to do something, get them some food perhaps, and something had prevented her from coming back to them. Perhaps she had met with an accident, perhaps she had been hit by a car when trying to cross a busy road. Nobody would have bothered about her, she would have just been left where she fell. Another dead cat on the road, another mess of blood and fur for the crows to pick at. He pushed the thought quickly away before it could get too tight a grip. There were enough things to worry about in the here and now, without tormenting himself about the past.

He inched closer to Carlos as the boy tipped his head back, and Aubrey saw the quick gulping movements of his throat as he tried to choke back the sobs that were now threatening to erupt in a torrent of tears .

"And now, cat, stupid cow's gone and got herself dead."

Chapter Sixteen

Aubrey nodded cautiously and then glanced sideways at Vincent, who was managing to look both grave and sensibly non-committal at the same time. He focused his gaze on Rupert again and tried to compose himself, but it wasn't easy. Rupert had a rolling eye and it was giving him the heebie-jeebies. It was difficult not to keep staring at it. Rupert was clearly working himself up, a fact which didn't bode well for any cat present.

Aubrey huddled further into himself and felt his spirits sink a little lower. The sooner he got out of here the better. He should be at home with Molly and Jeremy, where he was needed, not sitting here being forced to listen to this lunatic. Molly had been very near to tears this morning when the police had come for Carlos and, truth to tell, Aubrey had felt a little bit wobbly himself. The police had arrived and taken Carlos first thing, and to Aubrey's dismay, it had been the same two officers that had arrested the shoplifter in town. They had come screeching up in a squad car minutes after Jeremy had phoned the police station, and had kicked open the gate and stormed up the garden path as if they were raiding a crack den instead of simply removing an underweight boy of fourteen in a borrowed sweatshirt that was several sizes too large. Poor Carlos. He had barely had time to get himself dressed before the police officers had barged up the stairs and dragged him out. He hadn't even had time to wash. He had looked pathetically small against their huge bulk.

Aubrey had watched from the landing windowsill as they had bundled him into the back of the waiting squad car, the largest officer pushing the top of his head down with the flat of his hand as though Carlos might resist at any moment. Jeremy had come running up the path behind them, shirt hanging out, and breathless and panting. He had only just managed to pull open the door and climb in the back of the car next to Carlos as the engine was starting. At the last minute, Carlos had turned and waved at him. He pushed the thought away and tried to concentrate on Rupert instead.

He assumed an expression of intense interest and let his mind wander off again. He was a fool to have got himself caught up in all this business with the twins. Although, to be fair, he didn't see how he could have avoided it. Moses had been waiting for him just outside the back door this morning, and there had been no opportunity to slide away and pretend that he hadn't seen him. Anyway, even if he had been able to give them the slip this time, they would only have caught up with him later. Moses might be a dim little twit but he was a persistent dim little twit. Moses had been given a job to do and Moses would do it, come hell or high water. Rupert and Roger had sent Moses specifically to give him a message, and give him a message was what Moses would do, even if it took him to the middle of next week. And, as Aubrey knew from experience, it would have been no good trying to frame any sort of excuse for Moses to take back. Moses would have forgotten it before he'd jumped the garden fence. Anyway, it was difficult to construct a sentence composed solely of words of one syllable. No, the fact was that he'd had no choice but to follow Moses down to the allotments and join the meeting with the rest of them. Even the loathsome Carstairs from next door was here, which was a first. Whatever was going off, it was clearly something serious.

He forced himself to pay attention as Rupert continued talking.

"And the way I see it, we gotta do something about this and we gotta do it now. Know what I mean? We know, we all know, if we let them get away with it this time, they'll be walking all over us. They'll be taking over. We gotta show them that we mean business. We gotta show them the paw."

Aubrey nodded along with the rest of the cats. He didn't like the sound of this; he didn't like the sound of it at all. Of the twins, Rupert was well known to be the least stable, and looking at him now it wasn't difficult to see why. He was crouched over, his piercing blue eyes barely focused, the left one rolling skywards and the right one beaming in on each cat in turn like a search light. His long, thin tail lashed rapidly from side to side with nervous tension. Aubrey wouldn't have been surprised if he'd started foaming at the mouth. He was clearly working himself up to something big.

"We all know, everybody knows, that this side of the railway bridge is ours. It's always been ours. Them cats got no business down the high street. Stand on me, if we don't sort it now they'll be all over the allotments next, and then where will we be?"

Aubrey resisted the suicidal urge to yawn.

"Nowhere, that's where we'll be," said Rupert. "Nowhere."

A number of the cats murmured agreement, and Aubrey's heart sank still further. Nowhere was about right. He felt his shoulders slump slightly. He really could do without all this. For a start, he doubted that Rupert actually knew what he was asking. Start a turf war with those cats over the railway bridge and who knew where it would end? There was nothing to gain from any of it. He'd seen it all before when he was out on the streets. In the end nobody won, except the vets who cashed in on stitching all the cats up afterwards. This, he reflected gloomily, was definitely the down-side of having a permanent address.

Aubrey's brow furrowed as he thought about Molly and Jeremy. They had enough to worry about at the moment, what with Carlos and Dave and everything, as well as that Ofsted thing that Jeremy seemed to be getting so anxious about. He didn't want to add to their troubles by coming home with one ear and half his fur missing. Besides which, if he got hurt in a cat war, they'd have him straight down to that bastard Grimshaw who would almost certainly lose no time at all in finishing him off.

Roger, the other twin, suddenly looked across at him with eyes narrowed down to slits of blazing blue.

"Something up, Aubrey? Look like you got something on your mind."

97

Aubrey shook his head and sat up straighter. He hadn't been aware of Roger eyeing him up. Compared to most of the others, he was a relatively new cat on this particular block, and Roger was undoubtedly taking his measure. He needed to pay more attention. What he said and did now would set the pattern for the future. If he played it right on this occasion, it could pay considerable dividends later. Roger continued to stare at him.

"Hear you had a bit of trouble over at your place last night," he said.

Aubrey stared back at him. How the hell did Roger know about that?

As if in answer to the unspoken question, Roger said, "Saw the police car this morning. The lad gone now, has he?"

Aubrey nodded, frowning slightly. The thought that Roger knew anything about Molly and Jeremy and his life with them made him feel suddenly uneasy, although he couldn't put his paw on why exactly.

The sound of Rupert's voice, suddenly demanding, interrupted his thoughts.

"So, we got to do something, we got to act now and we got to have a plan. We won't get nowhere without a proper plan. Any of you got any ideas or suggestions, let's have them."

Yeah, thought Aubrey, right, let's have them. That was a laugh for a start. The last time anyone had suggested anything to Rupert, they'd found themselves at the head of the queue in the taxidermist's waiting room. Without waiting for an answer, Rupert continued, "Now, what I'm thinking is this…"

Chapter Seventeen

Aubrey trailed slowly and reluctantly down the left side of the high street, his gaze fixed firmly on the pavement. His mind was quietly seething. He should be at home now, tucked up in a nice pile of clean washing, and sleeping the sleep of the innocent. Instead of which, he was out here freezing the tips of his ears off, checking out the high street for escape routes and high-rise attack points. Rupert had it all planned out for tomorrow night, and every cat at the meeting had been given a job to do, even Vincent. Although being Vincent, he'd got himself a nice cushy little number making sure that there was water and food available in the abandoned shed that the twins used as their headquarters when there was a skirmish on. It wasn't exactly a difficult task, especially as he'd make Moses do most of it for him.

Aubrey was also feeling vaguely disturbed about Winston, the milkman. He liked old Winston, they all did. Even when he caught them on his float, he just laughed and chucked them off. When he'd set off this morning, he had seen Winston standing next to a squad car, talking to a police officer who had been scribbling things in a little notebook. The fact that Winston was just standing there was peculiar enough in itself. Winston was always moving. Up and down the garden paths with his crates of milk, jumping on and off the float, Aubrey didn't think that he had ever seen him still. But there he had been, just standing and talking to a police officer.

Police officers, in Aubrey's experience, were more or less welded to their cars. They rarely got out of them, and only stopped to talk to people when they'd done something wrong. But what could Winston have done wrong? He could hardly have been speeding in his milk float. As he had watched, Winston had pulled down and locked the shutters on his float, and then got into the squad car with the policeman.

Aubrey looked up and spotted a small, black and white, short-haired cat jogging smartly towards him. He quickened his step and tried to assume a bright, interested expression.

"All right, Lupin?"

Lupin nodded curtly back, his nasty, foxy little snout twitching and sniffing the air as he trotted briskly past. It was no coincidence that he'd run into Lupin, Aubrey knew. Lupin had been sent out to do the rounds and check up on everybody, and he would be straight back to Rupert and Roger if there was the merest hint that they weren't doing what they were supposed to be doing. Aubrey didn't like Lupin; he didn't like him one little bit. Along with the rest of the cats, he wouldn't trust Lupin as far as he could throw him, but also along with the rest of the cats, he always made sure that he kept on the right side of him. Lupin was Rupert and Roger's trusty lieutenant. One wrong word from Lupin, and the single mother cat problem would be solved at a stroke.

Outside the newsagents, the one that Carlos and the other two lads had tried and failed to hold up, the news placard was being buffeted about by the wind, the metal of the stand clattering to and fro on the pavement. The pictures of Maria and the other murder victims were clamped within it. The headline, 'Town Gripped By Terror – Police Clueless', was spattered by small drops of sporadic rain. Aubrey paused and stared at it for a moment. Perhaps it was the photograph that the press had used, but from where he was standing Carlos looked nothing at all like his mother. He didn't have those mad black eyes, for a start.

Next to the newsagents were the offices of Donaghue and Stevenson where Molly worked. He'd never been in the building, but he'd been in the car outside when Jeremy had picked her up after work once. He looked up at the windows longingly for a moment and wondered about calling in on her, but changed his mind. Much as he could have done with a bit of comfort, she'd probably only panic and think that he was lost or something, and she had enough to worry about this morning. He probably wouldn't even get as far as her office anyway, even if he could work out which one it was. There was bound to be some jobsworth in there whose sole purpose in life was to eject cats from buildings. There usually was.

A pity, he thought. He could do with a nice warm lap to sit on for half an hour. Down the high street the small icy wind started to blow harder, lifting small pieces of litter and twirling them up in the air before sending them dancing on their way. Aubrey shivered and moved slightly faster. Ah well, it was no good moaning about it. The sooner he got this job over and done with the sooner he could get back home and curl up in the warmth.

He reached the end of the street and surveyed back along its length. As far as he could tell, there were four-and-a-half possible escape routes – the four being side streets which ran off the main street, and the half being a narrow, covered alleyway which led down the side of the chemist's. He'd investigated the alleyway when he'd been out on the streets. The problem, if he recalled correctly, was that it didn't lead anywhere other than a yard with recycling bins in it. Somewhere to run at a push, but no good if you were being pursued as it effectively led to a dead end. Aubrey turned back and looked up ahead. Up on the right was the twenty-four hour garage, and beyond that lay the industrial estate and The Laurels. Rupert hadn't actually said to go that far, but it might be worth a look. There was nothing obvious on the high street anyway.

Aubrey knew The Laurels quite well. Most of the neighbourhood cats did. It was great for ratting, and more than one homeless cat had set up shop in the crumbling old barn and greenhouse which stood in its grounds. Aubrey had slept in it a few times himself when he was between addresses, and he still visited from time to time, just to keep it on his list, so to speak. He remembered now that the last time he'd been there he had been almost trodden on by two people carrying something. It had been just before the break of dawn and still not quite light when their dark shapes had come staggering out across the car park. They had been holding something that looked like a roll of old carpet, carrying it between them, and huffing and puffing under the weight of it. Aubrey had only just had time to skip back into the shadows before they tripped over him. He had meant to go back and investigate but he'd forgotten all about it until now.

He ran rapidly across the road and moved quickly forward, keeping close to the dusty hedges that banked the mostly boarded-up terraced houses lining the route on this side of town and linking it to the industrial estate. He flicked his eyes to right and left, ready to duck under a hedge at any hint of trouble. While a busy street was always a dangerous place, deserted streets were even worse. A cat out walking was very easily spotted, and there was less cover. He quickened his pace. He had forgotten how quiet it always seemed after the busy high street, and he found the silence slightly unnerving. He reached the end of the road and skirted quickly past the twenty-four hour garage.

Ahead of him lay a maze of short intersecting roads, all lined with low-rise, flat-roofed units bearing names like Colin's Electrics and Jack's Autos. He glanced up to the right and sniffed the air. Dino's Diner. Good old Dino's. It had been a very reliable source of pickings when he'd been on the road. He hesitated for a moment but then pushed on. He wanted to get this job over and done with. He could always call in on his way back and see if there was anything going, and it wasn't as if he was hungry. There had been a slight confusion over feeding duties this morning, with the result that he'd been fed twice – once by Jeremy before he went to have his shower, and then again by Molly before she left for work. It was as good a way as any to start the day, even if it did leave him feeling a bit stuffed.

Up on his left, the chimneys and upper storeys of The Laurels loomed over the squat, functional premises that lay scattered around its feet. It looked as out of place as a maiden aunt at a drugs bust. Never beautiful at the best of times, it stood dank and foreboding; a great, gothic pterodactyl of a building, the bare branches of the surrounding trees reaching blackly up into the sky like witches' fingers.

Aubrey stopped and considered for a moment, half-closing

one eye as he scanned the height of the building. Was it a possibility? He couldn't see why not. It wasn't exactly what Rupert had in mind, but then who knew what crazy ideas went on in Rupert's head? The advantage of The Laurels was that most of the cats already knew it, and if they could all get there safely and planned the route properly, and there was no reason why they shouldn't, The Laurels had the potential to provide just about everything that they required. It was more or less deserted at night, apart from a caretaker who had a small flat in there. It had unlit car parks at the back and front, and plenty of roof space and chimney pots set at various different levels, all of which were excellent for cover. Just as importantly, there were no near neighbours to come running out to see what all the commotion was about. The more he thought about it, the better it seemed.

At the big, wrought iron gate, Aubrey paused and looked about him and then squeezed through the gap underneath. He stopped on the threshold and hesitated for a moment, then slipped round the side of the building towards the back of the house. The former walled kitchen garden was one of the few remaining spaces around the house that hadn't been sold off for development, and was now laid out for cars with hard tarmac underfoot. Beyond it was a small patch of overgrown land on which sat the old barn and a crumbling greenhouse whose broken panes made it easy for cats to slip in and out of. Around the edges of the car park, the big trees stood clumped together and made it seem dark compared to the daylight at the front. Aubrey waited for his eyes to adjust before starting to move slowly forward. Only a very foolish cat would step into half-darkness without being very sure of what lay beyond.

The car park was empty, other than a small minibus with the legend The Laurels painted along the sides. Several overflowing dustbins and a pile of empty, flattened cardboard boxes leaned against the far wall. Aubrey stared at the wall and shuddered. Running along the top of it was a turret of broken glass set into a layer of thick, grey concrete. One of the other cats that he had met there in his homeless days had told him that it had been put there by the previous owner, a strange old man who had lived alone. Clearly, nobody had ever got around to removing it. The long, thin shards glittered like jagged diamond teeth in the watery sunlight that was struggling to break through. Aubrey ran his eye over it. Whoever had put it there had meant business. It was just as well that he'd come to take a proper look. He had forgotten all about the glass. It would be pitch black out here at night, and an unwary cat could easily shred itself to pieces by trying to leap the wall.

He glanced over towards the narrow iron steps that were fixed to the back of the building. He'd never really looked at the steps before. He had always been more interested in the grounds than the house. He let his eye travel upwards. The steps appeared to lead to some sort of small platform with a door let into the wall. Presumably, it gave access to the interior of the building. He stared at it thoughtfully for a moment. The platform was too small to be of much use – it wouldn't hold more than about a dozen cats, and that would be a tight squeeze – but there was a narrow ledge that ran off it along the side of the building that looked as if it might be wide enough for a cat to walk along. More to the point, it might also serve as a take-off and landing point.

He walked over to the bottom of the steps and looked up. It was difficult to tell from here. He'd have to go up and see for himself. And then he'd definitely go home. He scrambled quickly up the steps and stepped out onto the platform. From here, he could see the layout of the different roof levels and chimneys. It was even better up here than he'd thought. There were ambush points all over the place. He ran his eye along the ledge and began to tread his way along the length of the building. He felt pleased. Coming out to The Laurels had been inspired. Apart from anything else, it would tell Rupert that he'd done a thorough job, which, he reflected, might be necessary. He hadn't been altogether comfortable with the sideways look that Lupin had given him earlier. It had been just a touch too appraising for his liking. Well, sod Lupin.

He braced himself and jumped lightly across to the next roof level. Easy. No problem. Even a little cat like Moses could manage that. He walked round the edges and stared down. It was perfect. It couldn't be better. He let out a small sigh of satisfaction. He'd done his bit and now, at last, he could go home. Raising his eyes, he glanced to his left along the row of attic windows. It might be an idea to take a quick look in through some of them before he set off. There might be a way into the building which could be handy if they needed to beat a hasty retreat.

Unlike the windows in the rest of the house, the attic windows were small and grimy, the paint on the frames cracked and peeling. They didn't seem to have been cleaned in years. Aubrey trod carefully along the ridge and peered briefly through each one in turn. There was nothing of any interest to see. The rooms were dark and gloomy, and every window was shut. Each room was more or less empty, other than a stained mattress or two and a few broken chairs. The contents, if there had been any, had obviously been cleared out after the death of the last owner. He half-turned and then stopped as something caught his eye. In the last room, something had moved among the shadows. Something quite big. He crept closer and then jumped back, almost losing his footing as three figures suddenly leapt up and began to shout and point at him.

His heart banged against his ribs as he moved swiftly backwards and out of their line of vision. Pausing for a moment to catch his breath, he turned carefully and placed his paws evenly in front of him. He steadied himself, his breathing coming more easily now, and turned the corner back towards the small platform. Whatever the people in the room had been doing, they clearly hadn't been expecting a large tabby cat to be peering in at them.

He moved cautiously forward. There wasn't a lot of space to spare on the ledge and it would be easy to miss his footing and fall. That in itself wasn't a problem for most felines, but it could be catastrophic if there was a pack of enemy cats waiting to catch you below. He hesitated and looked down as the sound of an engine filtered upwards. A battered blue van was pulling up in the car park. He watched as Dave climbed out, Rascal snapping and jumping around his heels.

Aubrey sighed and huddled closer against the side of the building while he waited, the chill wind ruffling his fur. If he tried to descend the steps now, he would be seen. Rascal would be bound to detect him, and then Dave would recognise him. Without Jeremy's protection, there would be nothing to stop Dave setting Rascal on him. He would just have to sit it out. Ah well, whatever Dave was doing here, presumably he would have to leave at some point. Either that, or he would go inside the building, and then Aubrey could be down the steps and leg it out across the car park before he came out again.

From somewhere below, he heard a door open. He watched as a pair of trainer-clad feet came into view. Dave slumped back against the van and folded his arms, the bulging canvas tool bag that he habitually carried around with him slung down at his feet. Aubrey eyed it for a second, momentarily distracted. He didn't think that he'd ever seen Dave open it.

"We can't leave it there indefinitely." Dave's voice floated up on the cold air.

"I don't see why not. It's not like it's going anywhere, and anyway, nobody ever goes in there."

Aubrey stiffened. He knew that voice, he was sure of it; he just couldn't place it for the moment. Was it one of those guys that Dave occasionally sent to Molly and Jeremy's to do some work when they complained that the renovations were taking too long? Most of those guys spoke in strange foreign accents, but there had been one or two that spoke English. He listened harder.

"In case it's escaped your notice, the whole town is crawling with police. They've already been over here asking questions. The old barn is just the sort of place that the Odd Lot are likely to go poking around in."

"They've been asking questions everywhere, not just here. Anyway, they've already been all over the place, including the old barn. Why would they need to look again?"

"Why do they ever do anything? Use your brain, in so far as you've got one. The point is, there's a full-scale murder investigation going on out there. The Laurels is one of the things that most of the victims had in common. We can't afford to take the risk."

Aubrey frowned to himself. What was in the old barn that was so interesting? The last time he'd been in there it had contained nothing but an abandoned lawn mower, a broken deck chair, and a few old oil drums and paint cans. The next time he got a moment, he'd go over there and take a look.

"Well, if you're so keen, you move it. Anyway, where are we going to put it?"

"I don't know. I just know that we can't leave it where it is, it's too risky. And the longer we leave it, the worse it's going to get."

Aubrey watched as Dave lit one of his roll-ups, one hand cupped around the lighter against the wind.

"We could always put it in the back of your van and cart it off somewhere."

That voice. It was driving him mad. If only he could think where he'd heard it before.

It was somewhere quite recently, too.

"You must be joking." Dave drew heavily on his roll-up and coughed. "What if I got pulled over for something and they wanted to look in the back of the van? Anyway," he continued, "I don't want it in the back of my van. And even if I did, which I don't, then what?"

"I dunno. The woods maybe?"

"Don't be ludicrous. Half the town go walking their dogs in those woods. How long do you think it would be before it was found?"

"Look, just leave it, mate. Even if the police do go looking in there, which I doubt,

why should they think it's anything to do with us? More importantly, when's the next drop?"

"Next Friday. Which means that we need to get this lot moved on toot-sweet, if not

sooner. Anyway, where's this cracked window pane you want me to have a look at?"

Aubrey held his breath as the two men walked around the side of the house, Rascal trailing along behind them and snuffling the ground. Aubrey slipped quickly down the steps.

He wanted to get home now and tell Roger and Rupert about his plan. He looked back just as he got to the gate. The man that had been talking to Dave had stopped and was standing with his back to him, pointing up at one of the windows. Along the side of one his trainers was a splash of green paint.

Chapter Eighteen

Aubrey jumped the back wall and strolled down the garden path, feeling quietly contented. He'd done himself a bit of good checking out The Laurels, and no mistake. Rupert had been well pleased with his report and even Roger had given him an approving nod. Lupin had merely thrown him a sour look, which he had ignored.

He slipped through the cat flap and made straight for his food bowl. He hadn't realised what an appetite he'd worked up. From upstairs, he could hear the faint murmur of voices. He twitched his ears slightly, one of them sounded like Carlos. Jeremy must have brought him back.

Aubrey munched rapidly through his food. He was glad now that he had resisted the temptation to come home first before reporting back to Rupert and Roger. Now, he could relax and enjoy the rest of the day. From overhead, the drumming sound of the shower filtered down. He turned his head slightly as Jeremy entered the room.

"Hello, Aubrey, I didn't hear you come in."

Jeremy reached over him and lifted the telephone from the shelf.

"Moll? It's me."

Aubrey continued eating, one ear on Jeremy's conversation.

"No, they haven't charged him with anything. He's adamant that he doesn't know anything about it and the police obviously haven't got any evidence to suggest otherwise. Anyway, I've brought him back here."

The low, rapid buzz of Molly's voice in reply sounded troubled, a bit like a fly in a bottle.

"Moll, I know what you're saying but what else could I have done? I couldn't have left him in there with all the drunks and the mad people, and there was, literally, nowhere else for him to go. They couldn't get hold of anyone from Social Services for ages, and they could hardly have sent him back to the flat."

Aubrey watched as Jeremy rubbed his forehead and sighed.

"I know, but that's the problem. He doesn't seem to be anybody's responsibility. Even Social Services were trying to shove him off onto someone else. As soon as they realised that I was DBS checked, the pressure was on."

Aubrey finished eating and started a leisurely clean of his paws. He couldn't hear what Molly was saying but she didn't seem too keen on having Carlos as a house guest. He could see her point. Having the boy there as an emergency measure was one thing, but this was something else. He listened as Jeremy continued.

"According to the social worker, some woman called Zanna, they're already stretched to breaking point. The chances of getting a foster home for him are roughly nil. The only alternative is Alderman Wenlock House."

There was silence for a moment, as though Molly was absorbing what Jeremy had just said. Aubrey didn't know what this Alderman Wenlock House was, but the mere mention of it seemed to have brought a chill into the room.

"Ok, that's fine." Jeremy sounded relieved. " Yes, I'll take him this afternoon. You're quite right, he can't keep wearing my old sweatshirts. I didn't think of that. I guess he'll need socks and underwear and so on as well. See you later." He paused and smiled into the receiver. "Love you, too."

He replaced the receiver and looked down at Aubrey who was still washing.

"Well, Aubrey, that's one thing sorted. And now for the next."

He picked up the receiver again and pressed the keypad. Aubrey watched as he took a deep breath.

"It's Jeremy Goodman here. Is the Head available?"

He covered the mouthpiece and whispered down at Aubrey, "Thank God, she's in a meeting."

He turned back hurriedly to the receiver.

"No, don't disturb her. Can you just let her know that I

won't be back in school this afternoon? I'll explain tomorrow."

He put the receiver down quickly and turned to Aubrey.

"If it rings, don't answer it."

Aubrey grinned. That was one of the things he loved about living with Molly and Jeremy. They just made him laugh. They both turned round as the door opened and a newly-showered Carlos came in. He looked anxious.

"Is it all right, Mr Goodman? Did she say that I could stay?"

"It's fine, Carlos. You can stay here until things get sorted out, but you're going to need some fresh clothes and so on. The police said earlier that it was ok now to go back to the flat."

Carlos nodded, his face blank. Aubrey looked at him. It was difficult to tell what the boy was thinking. Perhaps he didn't want to go back to the flat. Really, all things considered, it would be perfectly natural if he didn't. After all, the last time he'd been there he'd seen his mother lying murdered across her bed. Not the best of memories to carry away with him. On the other hand, it might well be the only place that he really did want to go. With everything else in his life suddenly ripped out from under him, it was the one place that he didn't need permission to be.

"Or, if you prefer," said Jeremy, "I can go and get anything that you need. If you give me a list and tell me where things are, I'll get what you want and bring them back. Only the thing is, you mustn't go out if I leave you here on your own. You do understand that, don't you? You know that you were only allowed to come home with me on certain conditions?"

Carlos nodded again. Aubrey looked across at Jeremy thoughtfully.

"On second thoughts, maybe it's better if we go together. You can wait in the car if you prefer."

Smart thinking, thought Aubrey. Jeremy wasn't quite as naïve as he sometimes seemed. None of them really knew the boy and, in spite of appearances, there was every possibility that he might do a bunk if he was left alone. There was no point in putting temptation in his way. Hell, he would be tempted himself if he was in Carlos's shoes.

Aubrey felt a faint slither of anxiety struggle up and wriggle its way through him. Had Jeremy really done the right thing in bringing Carlos back home with him? A lot of people wouldn't have done it, he knew. Rachel and Clive wouldn't have dreamed of it, for a start. To attract the charitable attention of those two you would have to be a lot more interesting than a snot-faced, council flat kid from the wrong side of town. Carlos would have to have survived a war-zone and been both orphaned and horribly maimed in the process, at the very least. So really, he reflected, what else could Jeremy have done in the circumstances? Especially given that Carlos appeared to have nowhere else to go.

"We ought to get something to eat before we go back to the flat. You must be starving. Come on, let's go and see what we've got."

Chapter Nineteen

Aubrey stretched and then followed them across the kitchen, tail erect. Apart from the possibility of a food opportunity, he was interested to see what Jeremy would come up with. Molly did most of the cooking. Apart from the fact that she was usually home earlier than Jeremy, his culinary skills stretched about as far as an oven chip sandwich, and he only did that when Molly was out and he couldn't find anything else that he fancied in the freezer. Jeremy's signature dish, reserved for the rare occasion when Molly was ill in bed with a cold or flu, was beans on toast with a slice of cheese on the top. Sometimes, if he was feeling a bit cheffy, he piped a bit of tomato sauce around the edges. Aubrey liked it when he did that because for some reason it always put him a good mood, with the result that Aubrey got a bit of cheese as well. In common with most cats, there was almost nothing that Aubrey liked better than a lump of cheddar.

Jeremy opened the fridge door and peered in. He turned hopefully to Carlos.

"Er, what sort of food do you like? I'm afraid cooking's not really my strong point." He glanced across at the clock on the kitchen wall. "I think we've missed the chip shop, but we've probably got some oven chips in the freezer."

"I'll cook if you like Mr Goodman. Got any dried pasta, some garlic? Tinned tomatoes?"

Without waiting for an answer, Carlos reached across and opened the nearest cupboard.

"That was delicious, Carlos. Absolutely lovely."

Jeremy looked up appreciatively from his dish and scraped round the last drop of sauce with the edge of his fork. From underneath the table, where he was having a quick wash, Aubrey nodded in agreement. He didn't know what it was, but

113

the stuff that Carlos had put on a saucer for him was the absolute business. Did they do it in cat food packets? he wondered. He came out from under the table and flopped down next to Jeremy's chair.

"Where did you learn to cook like that?" asked Jeremy. "Did your mother teach you?"

Carlos smiled back at Jeremy and shook his head. With a sudden shock, Aubrey realised that it was the first time that he had actually seen Carlos smile – smile properly, that is. It lit his eyes and completely transformed his face. The lad was actually, he thought, rather good-looking. Carlos reached down to stroke him, and he responded by giving him a quick affectionate lick across the back of his hand.

"No, I taught myself. Mum used to do a lot of cleaning jobs in the early mornings but she worked in the evenings and at night as well, offices and factories and that. I got fed up with toast and chips and stuff, so I got a book out of the library."

"You got a... book... out of... the library?"

Jeremy stared at him open-mouthed, his fork suspended in mid-air. It was unheard of. The kids at Sir Frank's, having worked out how to bypass the alarm system, thought that a library was somewhere you went to nick CDs. Most of them had been banned years ago. If they wanted a book, they stole a new one from WH Smith.

Carlos nodded. "Yeah, I went to the library in town. At first, they wasn't going to let me join because I didn't have no ID or nothing, but then I remembered my timetable, like from school, so I got that out and they let me use that." He thought for a moment. " I s'pose they thought they could always get contact with me through school, like if I didn't take the books back and that."

Aubrey thought it was more likely that someone at the library had felt sorry for him. Carlos continued.

"Anyway, I thought, well, like, it couldn't be that difficult. Loads of people do it every day so I reckoned I could teach myself. When we lived in Brazil, Mum always used to do the cooking. She used to cook a lot, especially when granddad lived with us. She used to make proper meals and puddings and cakes and stuff, but since we come here she's always working or too tired. I mean," his tone was suddenly anxious lest Jeremy should think ill of his mother, "she never used to just go off and leave me without anything. She always used to give me money and that to buy stuff with."

"So you taught yourself?" The amazement was still evident in Jeremy's tone.

Carlos nodded.

"Have you chosen cookery as one of your options at school?"

Carlos looked back at him, a pained expression etched across his face.

Aubrey sighed inwardly. It was a stupid question. A boy choosing cookery at Sir Frank's was tantamount to asking for your head to be kicked in and your arms and legs torn off and thrown to the neighbourhood dogs. Unfair, but there it was. In Aubrey's experience, cooking was usually done by girls, like Molly, unless you were big, hairy, sweaty, and frightening, like the bloke who cooked at the local steakhouse and who had fed Aubrey on the odd occasion that he'd passed by in his homeless days. He would have passed by more often, but there was something slightly unnerving about a bloke who habitually had a meat cleaver in his hand.

It was an odd thing, thought Aubrey. All this stuff about girls and boys. As far as Aubrey was concerned, it made no difference. Live and let live was his motto. Well, unless you were a rat, obviously. Or a mouse. But there were others that thought differently, he knew, both in the cat and the human world. He sighed and flopped over to his other side.

Aubrey watched sleepily as Jeremy started clearing the plates. He smiled slightly to himself. He might be a cat, but he and Carlos had far more in common than Jeremy could ever begin to imagine. Parentless and left to their own devices at far too young an age, neither Carlos or Aubrey had exactly got off to a good start in life.

He gazed fondly at Jeremy's kindly face. Considering that they were both human and that they both had two arms, two legs, and a head, Jeremy and Carlos were about as far apart as it was possible to be. The idea of Jeremy coming home to find his own safe, comfortable mother lying strangled on her bed was about as likely as Carlos suddenly discovering that he had been picked to accompany the next manned space shuttle. It was Aubrey's guess that the only thing that Jeremy had ever come home to was a cooked meal, a warm, clean study bedroom, and parents who were interested in what he'd been doing that day. It had almost certainly been a loving, safe, and uncluttered existence, and as a result Jeremy was a generous, affectionate, big-hearted person. He could afford to be. He had never known anything different.

How different from Carlos, he thought. Carlos appeared to have only a very dim memory of his father, and from the time he had come to England he had lived a precarious and lonely existence in a home that he wasn't legally entitled to occupy, with only the company of a volatile, half-crazy mother. And now he didn't even have her. Whatever way you looked at it, Carlos was well and truly on his own. Just like Aubrey had been until Jeremy had picked him. So what else could Jeremy have done in the circumstances, other than bring him back home with him? It was a question hardly worth asking.

He looked across at Jeremy as he slammed the dishwater door shut, and a sudden doubt assailed him. Was it possible that Jeremy was being played for a fool? Were they all being played for fools, come to that? Had the boy killed his mother? Could he have had anything to do with the deaths of Mr Telling and the other elderly people? Surely not. What possible reason could he have? Looking at Carlos now, it was unimaginable. Surely if he had anything to do with any of the murders, he would be back at the police station, banged up in a cell right now, not sitting in Molly and Jeremy's kitchen drinking a can of Coke. Anyway, whatever the truth of the matter, whether Jeremy had been right or whether he'd been wrong to bring Carlos back with him, he was here now and that was all there was to it. It was too late to take him back and say that he'd changed his mind. Carlos was a person, not some inconvenient baggage. Unlike a cat who had stopped being cute, he couldn't just be tipped out with the family rubbish and forgotten.

Jeremy turned back to face them.

"Carlos, about your mother…"

His tone was low and gentle, and Aubrey could hear that he was searching for the right words. He listened with interest. If Jeremy was going to say what he thought he was going to say, it was going to be very difficult. It wasn't the kind of question that was easily asked.

Jeremy plunged back in.

"What I'm trying to say is, well, the thing is, have you got any idea, any idea at all, who might have hurt your mother? Do you know who might have wanted to do this thing to her?" He stopped, and was obviously trying to gauge Carlos's expression. The boy's face remained blank. Jeremy continued. "It's important that, if you do know anything, you tell me because… because…"

He trailed off again. Now it had come to it, Aubrey knew that he didn't want to say it, but the truth was that it was important because if Carlos did know anything then he might be in danger, too. In fact, he suddenly thought, if it came to it, they might all be in danger. He shivered suddenly and tucked his tail tightly around himself, glancing instinctively across at the bolt on the bottom of the back door.

Carlos shook his head.

"No. Honestly, Mr Goodman. If I knew anything, I'd tell you. Honest, I would."

Interestingly, thought Aubrey, he believed him for the most part. But did he detect some slight flicker? Was there something that Carlos wasn't telling? His instinct told him that there was. He watched as Jeremy stood quietly and waited for Carlos to continue.

"We didn't really know anybody, not even the people who lived in the other flats. Well, like, Mum knew the people that she cleaned for and that, she knew their names and stuff but she didn't know anything else about them." Carlos thought for a moment. "And she didn't know anybody else," he repeated.

"Did she ever go out apart from work? Did she ever meet anybody?"

117

"No. She only went to work, that's all she did, she never went out nowhere else. And when she came home, she just used to watch the telly. It was one of her favourite things. She used to like all those programmes about dancing and that. The telly that we had when we lived in Brazil was black and white, and it was always breaking down. One of the first things we got when we come here was a colour telly. She saved up for it."

"So she didn't have a boyfriend or anything?"

Carlos looked scornful. But that didn't mean anything, thought Aubrey. To Carlos, his mother had probably seemed about one hundred. The thought of her having a boyfriend would be beyond his imagination. But, he thought, on the other hand, if she'd never gone out and nobody had ever come to the flat then he was probably right. Also, and possibly more to the point, what kind of lunatic would choose Maria for a girlfriend?

"Did anybody ever ring or call round at the flat?" asked Jeremy.

"No. I told you, we didn't know anybody. The only person who ever came to the flat was the rent man. The fat bloke in the blue van."

Oh yes, thought Aubrey, the fat bloke in the blue van. Aubrey had his own ideas about this so-called rent man, and they were the kind of ideas that had Dave Blubberman Builder stamped all over them. Except that it didn't really add up. Dave couldn't have had anything to do with Maria's death. It didn't make sense. Given that it would take a thermo-nuclear device to part Dave and his wallet, why would he want to kill somebody who was not only poor but who was paying him rent money from the little that she did have? He couldn't for the moment work it out.

"Well," Jeremy persisted, "was there anything different about her lately? Anything unusual or out of the way? Was there any little thing that you noticed, anything at all?"

"Like what?" Carlos looked puzzled. As well he might, thought Aubrey. It would be better asking if there had been anything normal about Maria. It would have been more

118

noticeable for a start.

"I don't know… something. Anything."

Life on the street had taught Aubrey to read faces as easily as twitching a whisker. Get it wrong and you could find yourself on the business end of a large boot. He sat and watched as a new thought flitted across Carlos's mind like a bat in twilight.

"Yes?" Jeremy asked, hopefully.

"Well, she did seem a bit different, this last week."

"Yes?" Jeremy repeated, trying to keep the eagerness out of his voice. "Different in what way?"

"Well, she seemed, like, pleased about something." Carlos looked thoughtful, considering. "Like something good had happened, like she'd won on her lottery ticket or something."

Probably nicked something, thought Aubrey. Probably managed to strangle a few cats.

"Did she say what it was that she was pleased about?" Jeremy leaned forward, looking hopeful. "Did she tell you what it was?"

Carlos shook his head.

"No, but she said about us getting a computer." He paused. "She was always going on about us getting a computer, but this time she said it was definite. She got some leaflets from that big electric shop in town, and she said that I could pick which one I wanted. And she said that we could have some other things, too. A new telly and that, a proper big one to go on the wall, with DVD and everything." Carlos looked blankly across at Jeremy. "But she was always saying things like that. It didn't mean nothing. I just thought maybe she'd got another cleaning job or something."

Aubrey looked at Carlos thoughtfully. So, Maria had been pleased about something, and from the sound of it, that something had quite a lot to do with money.

Jeremy stood up suddenly and fished in his pocket for his keys.

"Come on, let's go and get some of your stuff."

"Can Aubrey come?"

"I don't really think so, Carlos. He doesn't like going in the car. Come on, we won't be long and he'll still be here when we get back."

Aubrey watched from the sitting room window sill as they walked down the front path. Five days after Raj had died, some of the local low-life had broken into the shop and trashed the place. Not content with stripping the shop shelves and emptying the deep freezers, they had made their way through to the back rooms. They had jumped on and broken Raj's precious photographs in their frames, and smashed the little china elephants that had adorned the mantelpiece. They had broken some of the windows as well, hurling bricks and stones and then running off. Aubrey had seen it for himself. He hoped to goodness that nothing similar had happened at Maria's place.

Chapter Twenty

"I think that he might know something, Molly. I think that there might be something that he's not telling me."

Jeremy leaned over her shoulder and looked down into the saucepan that she was stirring. Molly nudged him away. Aubrey slipped through the cat flap and joined them.

"It won't be long, just be patient. It's nearly ready," said Molly. "What sort of thing?"

"I don't know. I could be wrong, but it's just a feeling I've got that he's holding something back. It's niggling away at me but I can't put my finger on exactly what it is."

"Where is he now?"

"Upstairs in the study. I left him playing games on the computer."

"How did he react when he was back in the flat?"

Jeremy thought for a moment.

"He looked a bit sort of dazed, I suppose, as if he wasn't quite with it. I guess it's not surprising really, given everything that's happened. I told him that he could stay in the car if he preferred while I went in and got his clothes, although I would have had to lock him in, just to be on the safe side. But he wanted to come in with me, he insisted. I half thought of trying to stop him, I wasn't sure that him going back inside the flat was the right thing to do. I didn't want him to be traumatised any more than he already is, but in the end it seemed better to let him have his way. Anyway, I don't suppose that I could have physically stopped him."

"How was it? Had the police left it tidy?"

Jeremy nodded.

"Oh, yes. I went in first, just in case, but you wouldn't have known that they'd been there. Everything was put back exactly as they found it. Even Maria's handbag was still lying on the work surface in the kitchen where she'd left it." He paused. "Carlos asked me if he could bring it back with him."

Aubrey's heart gave a sudden tug. Like Carlos had needed to ask. In the absence of any other next of kin, the handbag and its contents was, just like everything else in the flat, now his.

Jeremy sighed and reached up over Molly's head to pull a bottle of beer from the cupboard.

"I suppose at some point the flat is going to have to be cleared out," he said. "It can't just sit there empty. And he can't live there on his own, he's only just fourteen. Even if he could live there, once the Council get wind of the sub-letting, they'll want the flat back. Given his age, they're not even under a duty to re-house him. If they can't find a foster carer, they'll just have to stick him in the children's home." He wrapped his fingers around the beer bottle and held it for a moment. "I guess someone will have to do something about his mother's things as well, and then there's the furniture and so on to think about, too."

Molly looked up from the saucepan that she was still stirring.

"I can't imagine that Carlos will want any of it," she said. "He won't have anywhere to put it, for a start. Once the police have finished with everything, someone will have to start making some arrangements."

No prizes for guessing who that might be, thought Aubrey.

"Is there anything worth keeping?" continued Molly.

Jeremy shook his head and leaned back against the work surface.

"Not from what I could see. There may be one or two bits, but it mostly looked like cheap self-assembly stuff and even that looked second-hand. The only thing that looked half-way decent was the television. It looked to me like they were living on pretty much the bare minimum."

Molly nodded. "Well, if it comes to it and it's what Carlos wants, I suppose we could arrange to have it cleared. We'll have to talk to him about it. There's a man in town who does house clearance, he does it for some of our clients sometimes when they've inherited a property. He's pretty honest and he'll give a fair price, so at least Carlos will have a bit of money in his pocket. I suppose we could open an account for him if he hasn't already got one. In the meantime, though, what's going to happen about paying the rent and the other bills?"

"I've been thinking about that." Jeremy frowned. "My guess is that whoever was collecting rent from them will lay low for a while. I mean, he can hardly turn up at the police station and ask for arrears because he's almost certainly sub-letting illegally, and he won't approach Carlos because he doesn't know where he is. I think that the best thing for the time being is to just say nothing and see what happens. And as for the utilities, electric and gas and so on, that can wait for a few weeks until things get sorted. I mean, nobody's using anything there, and even if the flat got cut off it would hardly matter, would it?"

Molly nodded.

"I guess not. Did he manage to get everything that he wanted?"

"I think so. I took a couple of those big bin liners so that he could just shove everything in." Jeremy reached into a drawer and pulled out a bottle opener. For a moment, he simply stared at it and then he slowly prised the top from the beer bottle.

"I think I must be losing it."

"What do you mean?"

He looked up at her. "Do you think that I'm being stupid about all this? I mean, he's not the only kid at Sir Frank's with a hard luck story. Far from it. Do you think that I'm getting too involved?"

Molly sighed.

"No, not really. What else could you have done? I don't suppose that if it came to it I could have left him at the police station, either. In a way, we took responsibility by letting him stay when he turned up in our shed. If we were going to hand him over to the authorities, we should have done it there and then."

Aubrey nodded silently in agreement. Molly was right. It was all a bit late in the day now.

Molly continued.

"My only concern is what's going to happen to him next. I mean, he can't stay with us indefinitely."

"I know," said Jeremy. "But where else can he go, apart from Alderman Wenlock's?"

Aubrey felt the same slight chill that had descended the last time that Alderman Wenlock House was mentioned.

"I mean," Jeremy continued, "everything seems to be left in limbo. The police have made loads of noise but nothing's actually happened, which must mean that they haven't got enough evidence to go any further, at least in relation to Carlos. And Social Services seem to have vanished into thin air. For the time being, at any rate."

He leaned back against the work surface and thought for a moment. "We know that Maria was almost certainly strangled. My guess is that the police have got some sort of forensic evidence that says that Carlos couldn't have done it."

"Like what?" Molly sounded puzzled.

Jeremy shrugged. "I don't know. The marks on her neck maybe, or the size of his hands? Something like that, I guess. Otherwise, why would they let him go? If they really thought that he had anything to do with Maria's death, they wouldn't dare run the risk. Carlos would be locked up right now. With all these other murders going on, there's no way they'd let him walk free."

"What about all that business with the gun at the newsagents?"

"That seems to have dropped off the agenda for the time being, at least as far as Carlos is concerned. He's told them repeatedly that he didn't know anything about the gun. He swears that he thought they were just going to go and try and get a rise out of old Miller. He said that Caparo told him that they were just going to have a laugh. I'm sure that he's telling the truth about that. Anyway, the police have got more important things to think about right now."

Molly nodded.

"There's something else that will need to be arranged, something that nobody seems to have thought of yet."

"What?"

"Maria's funeral."

Aubrey nudged round the door and made for the stairs. He didn't like talk of funerals. From what he could gather, they were something to do with putting people in holes or burning them or something. The whole idea gave him the shivers. Far better to be a cat and just creep under a friendly bush and let nature take its course.

Upstairs, next to the computer, the contents of Maria's handbag were spread out across the desk. Carlos was staring at the pathetic rubble, his face pinched and white against the bright blue and yellow stripes of his woollen scarf. In amongst the crumpled tissues and unmatched earrings with the backs missing, sat old bus tickets and several biros bearing the logo of a national bank. A scuffed, brown leather purse had revealed the princely sum of one pound and twenty-seven pence. In the pocket compartment had sat a tiny cracked mirror, a pink plastic comb, and a broken rosary. Carlos picked up the purse and ran the tips of his fingers across the worn leather.

Aubrey jumped up and settled himself against the side of the computer. Carlos looked at him sadly.

"You know, the thing is, Aubrey, she never really had anything. Even her clothes she used to get from them charity shops in town. She used to talk big but that's all it was, just talk." He swallowed and gripped harder on the leather purse. "She worked all the time, all the hours she could get. She was always working. But it didn't make no difference in the end. We didn't have nothing in Brazil and we didn't have nothing here neither. She used to try, though, she used to buy me jeans and trainers and that. She used to come home well-pleased but the stuff she got, it was always the wrong sort. I never told her, though. I used to say it was great, just what I wanted. She got me a mobile phone, too. She knew all the other kids had them so she got me one. It's a right crap pay-as-you-go. I think she got it off the market."

He put his hand in his pocket and withdrew a small, shiny, mobile phone. He stared at it ruefully for a moment.

"I pretended to Caparo and some of the others that it was a punishment. That she took my smartphone away because I'd been giving her lip and she made me have a cheap one instead to teach me a lesson." He sighed. "It don't make no difference. She might as well not have bothered. No-one ever phones me anyway."

Aubrey cocked an ear slightly to show that he was listening. He had discovered that he liked sitting next to the computer when it was switched on. It was warm and it made a nice comforting humming noise. Carlos continued.

"She used to think that she was going to win the lottery. That was the big plan. Every week, she was sure of it. Everything was going to be all right. She used to go down town and buy a ticket, and then she used to come back and say, this week, Carlos, this week we will be lucky. It is definite. This will be our lucky week."

He smiled. "She never even won a tenner."

Aubrey stretched out a paw. Not quite touching, but in reaching distance if needed.

Carlos stared down at his hands for a moment.

"When we come here, when we first come to England, she used to pretend that my dad would be coming, too. I knew, really, that he wouldn't but I never said nothing." Carlos smiled again, the same sweet smile that Aubrey and Jeremy had seen earlier in the day. "She used to say, 'Very soon now, Carlos. Very soon. Any day now, Daddy will be joining us. Daddy will be coming to live with us again.' That was all she wanted really. All she ever wanted. She didn't ask for much else. She just wanted to be a family. She wanted to be like everybody else. But I couldn't tell her." His voice cracked suddenly and he dipped his head. "I couldn't say it to her. I couldn't say we wouldn't never be like everybody else."

He turned his head towards the window and stared into the distance for a moment before continuing.

"You know what I used to do, Aubrey? It sounds really stupid, but I used to pretend things for her. I used to make stuff up to tell her so that she would feel good. Like I used to say that we'd had a test in school and I come second in the whole class. I never used to say first because she might not have believed it, but I used to say second and she used to be really happy. And sometimes I used to say I'd been picked for the football team, and then I'd stay late after school and just hang around town on my own. And then when I come home, I'd tell her about all the goals I scored." He paused again. "Truth is, Aubrey, I never got picked for nothing."

His voice cracked again and he took a great gulp of air before continuing. Aubrey inched closer.

"She was a right pain in lots of ways as well, she used to drive me mad, but she was good at lots of things, too." He thought for a moment. "She could sing, she was a good singer when she tried, she was often singing, and she could dance, too. That's why she liked all those dancing programmes on the telly. She was good at sums as well. Especially good at sums. Funny that. I'm crap at maths, probably take after my dad, but she was good. She could do adding up straight in her head, she didn't even need to write it down or use a calculator or nothing." He dropped his head into his hands. When he spoke again, his voice was muffled.

"I don't know what's going to happen now."

From downstairs, a babble of voices suddenly soared upwards and crashed through the ceiling. Aubrey sat up straighter, suddenly alert. He knew that voice, and whatever she had called round for, it was almost certainly nothing good.

Chapter Twenty-One

From downstairs, the sound of Rachel's voice rose and fell, her strident tones spiralling above the more moderate notes of Molly and Jeremy. Aubrey slipped down the stairs and sidled silently round the door. Carlos, with a face full of tears, had stumbled back to his room and was lying on his bed and, much as Aubrey loathed Rachel, he was curious to know what she wanted. Also, he was starting to get hungry.

"For goodness sake, Molly. Do see sense." Rachel peered over Molly's shoulder. "I think you need to turn the heat up a bit on that."

Aubrey watched with interest as Molly's shoulders tensed. She was normally such a placid person, but he could see that it was taking her all her willpower not to turn round and twat Rachel right between the eyes with the hot spoon.

"And really, Jeremy," continued Rachel, turning to face him, "I do think that you might have considered Molly in all of this. What on earth were you thinking of? For goodness sake, the boy is a murderer. He's killed at least four other people as well as his own mother, and several more for all we know. How could you have him here, under your own roof?" She paused and gulped for breath. "He's a cold-blooded killer."

"Oh, don't be ridiculous, Rachel," Jeremy said irritably. "The police clearly don't think he poses any danger or he wouldn't be here, would he?"

Rachel pursed her lips.

"Be that as it may. Speaking personally, it's not a risk that I would care to take. Nor, I believe, would any other sensible person. I just couldn't believe it when Clive told me what you'd done."

Aubrey looked across at Jeremy, puzzled. How had Rachel and Clive got onto it so quickly? Surely Molly couldn't have told them?

"How does Clive know about it?" demanded Jeremy.

"Your head teacher phoned him," said Rachel. "She wanted to know if, in the unlikely event of Carlos being innocent, there was any possibility of him transferring to Bishop Caulfield's on a bursary. Of course, there isn't," she added hurriedly. "It's full to bursting as it is. We've got a waiting list as long as your arm. And of course," she added, "Bishop's is a Christian school."

Aubrey turned round and looked at her. Oh terrific. Sir Frank's wasn't much, God knew, but at present it was about the only small area of stability in Carlos's life. And the Head couldn't wait to get rid of him. What a charmless cow she was.

"Sorry, what's Bishop's being a Christian school got to do with it?" asked Jeremy.

Rachel stared at him, a slight frown crinkling her broad brow.

"Bishop Caulfield's is a faith school, Jeremy. I thought you knew that." She paused and added gently, "We only take Christian children"

As if, thought Aubrey, Jeremy was some sort of half-wit.

Jeremy nodded thoughtfully, his expression blank.

"I'm sorry, I may be missing the point here, but how do you know that Carlos is not a Christian? Has anybody asked him?"

"Well…" Rachel started to bluster, her face colouring.

Aubrey suppressed a grin. He was beginning to enjoy this. Jeremy continued, his tone smooth and his face still blank.

"Or did you mean, Rachel, that Bishop's only take special Christian children, the special Christian sort that come from nice, little, special Christian homes where there's lots of nice big money? The kind of special Christian homes where they employ special cleaners like Maria to do their dirty work? For less than the minimum wage, usually," he added flatly.

Rachel stared at him, her mouth working to find the right words. Jeremy rushed in before she could find them.

"Anyway, when you think about it, it would actually be better in a way if Carlos wasn't a Christian, wouldn't it? If he was, in fact, a godless little heathen. Then Clive could have all the pleasure of bringing him into the flock. An ideal candidate, I would have thought. A lad in trouble and all that, just the sort that Bishop's should be welcoming in with open arms." Jeremy paused and looked thoughtful for a moment. "You know, it's a pity really that he's not disabled as well. You'd get double martyr points for that. Remember the Good Samaritan, Rachel. And I'm sure that our dear Lord would approve."

"There's no need for sarcasm, Jeremy. Anyway, that's not really the point," said Rachel, her tone still flustered .

No? thought Aubrey. What was the point then? Was he missing something here? Didn't this Christian stuff mean that they had to go round being good? He was sure that was what Rachel and Clive had said before. Or something like that, anyway. Ah well, maybe he was wrong. Maybe it meant something else entirely.

Aubrey could see that Jeremy's chin was starting to jut out and that he was making a conscious effort to pull it back in. He felt suddenly angry. Jeremy had enough on his plate right now. He had enough to worry about, without engaging in a shouting match in his own kitchen with horrible, old, bucket-faced Rachel. He didn't quite know what it was about Rachel, but somehow she seemed to manage to take Jeremy from nought to sixty in terms of rage within seconds, and with apparently no effort at all. It was quite a feat really, considering that when Jeremy had told Molly about the sight of a gang of Year Nines gaily scattering chilli powder across the keyboards in the school's one and only computer room, he had hardly seemed bothered at all. Aubrey had been amazed about that. He had made the mistake of licking some chilli powder once when one of Raj's customers had knocked a bottle from a shelf. It had taken him a week to get over it.

Rachel sighed and gave Jeremy a pitying look.

"The point is, Jeremy, that you know as well as I do that there are proper agencies to deal with these things. They have people who are trained in this kind of thing. People who are experienced and who know what they're doing." She turned to Molly. "I know that you mean well, but you must see that you're letting your heart rule your head here. You can't just rush in and take a boy like that off the street and bring him into your own home. You must see that. You and Jeremy, of all people, should know that it's irresponsible. Apart from anything else, you don't even know anything about him. And have you given any thought to what's going to happen afterwards? Even if he hasn't done any of these horrible things, even if he's completely innocent, which I very much doubt, have you any idea about what's going to happen to him when it's all over? Who's going to have him then? He can't stay with you forever." She paused and stared at Molly's back. "I'm only thinking of you."

Molly turned the heat off under the pan and turned to face her. She gave a small but weary sigh. Aubrey knew just how she felt.

"What do you suggest, Rachel? Clearly you have some sort of plan."

"That's why I'm here."

Rachel spoke quickly, her tone eager. A bit too eager, for Aubrey's liking. People like Rachel always had a plan, and he had the distinct feeling that whatever she was about to suggest, it would bode no good at all for Carlos. Her voice had exactly the same note to it, sort of pleased and excited, as the little, fat woman had who had declared Aubrey to be what she called a rescue cat, and then shoved him head first into a cardboard box so that she could bundle him off to Sunny Banks in the back of her car.

"I've been looking into it," continued Rachel. "There are quite a number of agencies that operate through the Church. Organisations that have properly trained people to deal with situations like this. I could get in touch with someone and you could place him…"

"No." The word exploded from Molly like a gunshot.

Aubrey jumped, and both Jeremy and Rachel looked startled.

"I'm sorry, Rachel." Molly took a deep breath and lowered her voice. This time, she spoke more gently. Aubrey could see that she was making a tremendous effort. "I know that you mean well and that you're only trying to help, and I appreciate it. Really, I do, and so does Jeremy, but Carlos is staying here. With us. He's been through a terrible trauma, he has just lost his mother in the most appalling circumstances, and if we can give him a home for only a week or two then it will at least be something. And anyway, it isn't our decision. The police and Social Services have released him into our care, and it will be up to them to move him somewhere else. It's out of our hands now."

"Well," said Rachel grimly, "be it on your own heads, but don't say that I didn't warn you." She looked from one to the other and back again, and then shrugged her shoulders. "Oh well, I can't say that I didn't try." She glanced down at her watch. "I must fly. I'm chairing the Parish Women For Equality and Diversity Prayer Group Meeting tonight."

She reached across and pecked Molly on the cheek.

"Do think about what I've said, Molly. Please. Anyway," she added, "you know where to find me if you need me."

Molly, Jeremy, and Aubrey listened in silence as the front door banged shut behind her.

"She can't help it. She thinks that she's doing the right thing," said Molly.

"So did Hitler," replied Jeremy.

Molly turned the heat back on under the saucepan. "How do you 'chair' a prayer meeting anyway?" she asked. "Aren't you supposed to just go and pray? I thought it was supposed to be pretty much an individual thing."

Jeremy laughed.

"Oh, it's easy if you're Rachel. She just takes over and tells them what to do. She needs to make sure that they're all praying for the right things, that is, the things that she's decided that they should pray for, all the right Rachel-type things as decided by St. Rachel. It wouldn't do to have any of them praying off-message; who knows where that type of thing could end?"

Jeremy was right, Aubrey thought. Let them have their own way, and before you knew where you were they'd be putting in sneaky little prayers of their own and spoiling everything. Anyway, who cared? It was dinner time, and at least Rachel hadn't parked herself there for a whole evening's lecture. And at least she hadn't brought Clive with her. Or their hideous children.

Molly shuddered slightly. "God, she's wearing."

"I know." Jeremy took a long, slow draught of his beer. "And you know what's really annoying? She's probably right."

Chapter Twenty-Two

Aubrey jumped lightly from the end of the bed. As a special concession, he was still being allowed to sleep with Carlos, to keep him company Jeremy had said. But he didn't want to wake him now. He sat on the floor for a moment listening to the light rustle of Carlos's breath, and then made for the door. The battle was on for tonight and he wanted to get there early. Lupin was doing the roll call and, besides, he wanted to have a look in the old barn before the scrap got started. He was intrigued to know what was in there that Dave and the other man had been so concerned about.

He turned and hesitated as Carlos stirred and opened his eyes.

"Aubrey," Carlos whispered quietly. "Where are you going?"

Aubrey's heart sank, although he wasn't surprised that Carlos had woken. After Rachel had gone, she had left behind her an edgy, jagged feeling. Like a cold east wind, it had rattled round corners and spiked itself right through the house, and it had stayed there all evening. They had all gone to bed early. Even Jeremy, who usually stayed up to watch the late news, but in spite of that they hadn't slept. Both Molly and Jeremy had been wide awake way past their usual time. The strip of light under their door had been extinguished eventually but the sound of their voices had continued to drift through the wall, a low anxious rumbling that had lasted until long past midnight.

Carlos had finally fallen asleep, the events of the day taking their toll, but he had been restless and fitful, muttering to himself and dragging the quilt this way and that until Aubrey had felt almost sea-sick with the effort of hanging on.

He watched as Carlos swung his thin limbs out of the bed

and walked towards the window, his legs leaden. He stared out into the blackness and pressed his forehead against the cold glass.

"I heard what that woman said." Carlos's voice was hard and strained. "I heard all them things that she was saying about me."

Aubrey would have been surprised if he hadn't heard. Rachel had the kind of voice that would carry in a force ten gale. Carlos turned back to face him, his voice bitter and his expression suddenly old beyond his years.

"And that social worker down at the police station, as well. That Zanna woman. She was just the same. Gobbing off right in front of me. Like I couldn't hear her, like I was deaf or something. You know what she kept on calling me, Aubrey? The problem. That's what she called me. The problem. Like I was some kind of virus or... or..." he paused, searching for the right expression through which to vent his feelings, "Something what gets left on a bus, something what nobody wants to touch. She never even spoke to me, not once. She didn't even look at me."

Aubrey watched as he clenched his fists.

"It was like I haven't got no name or something. It was like I was invisible, like I didn't exist. I felt like shouting. I felt like going, 'I am Carlos. I am here. My name is Carlos." He paused and the momentary defiance fluttered away. He sounded suddenly defeated. "It was horrible at the police station, Aubrey. The room was really small and it smelled funny and it was dark, even though the light was on. I had to sit on this hard chair and Mr Goodman sat next to me."

Aubrey listened intently. It sounded a bit like his cell at Sunny Banks – a nasty, smelly, little cage with a dank concrete floor and a dark, depressing interior. At Sunny Banks the sour, fetid stench of the previous detainees had hung acrid on the air, and at times he had felt like he couldn't breathe. It had been even worse when they had sluiced out the cells with cheap disinfectant. The horrible, choking, chemical sweetness had fought with the smell of the bodies of twenty incarcerated cats, and the result had usually been a draw. It hadn't seemed to bother the screws – presumably they were used to it – but it had bothered him. There had been times when he would have given eight of his mythical nine lives for just one gulp of fresh, sweet air.

He pulled his thoughts back to the present as Carlos continued.

"The thing is, Aubrey, if Mr Goodman don't want me here, if he don't let me stay, if he lets that woman tell him what to do, where am I going to go? What am I going to do? Now Mum's gone, I ain't got nobody else, only Mr Goodman. And Mrs Goodman, I s'pose." Carlos paused again and gulped. "I like it here. It's a proper house. It's clean and nice, and people don't go chucking furniture out of the windows. And," he repeated, "I ain't got nowhere else to go."

Aubrey sat perfectly still. He still had a bit of time before he needed to leave. Let the boy get it out of his system and then, with a bit of luck, he'd get back into bed.

Carlos crossed back to the bed and sat on the edge.

"I'm not going to that Alderman Wenlock place." He lowered his voice. "Jed Caparo got put in there when he was between foster families. He told me about it. They used to lock them in their rooms at night, and there was a warden there who used to put boys heads down the bogs." His voice lowered to a frightened whisper. "And some of the boys killed themselves. Jed Caparo said it was before he went there, but some of the rooms are still haunted. He said if you were bad or if they just didn't like you, the wardens took the light bulbs out and made you sleep in one of them." His mouth tightened suddenly. "They can't make me go there. If they do, I'll run away again. And I ain't going back to The Meadows neither, even if they let me. I ain't never going back there."

Aubrey wasn't surprised. He had only seen the inside of it once, when Jeremy had discovered Maria's body, but the flat in which Carlos had lived with his mother had been pretty cold and cheerless, an impression not improved by Maria's lifeless body lying on the bed. His guess was that the prospect of living there now was about as joyless as moving into an open grave, especially when you compared it with Molly and

136

Jeremy's house.

"And if I got sent somewhere else, I wouldn't be able to see you no more, neither. It's not like you could get on a bus and visit me or anything." Carlos dropped his head in his hands and caught his breath on a sob. "If Mum was here, she'd know what to do."

If Maria was here, thought Aubrey, they wouldn't need to know what to do. He watched as Carlos breathed in deeply and then exhaled, his thin ribcage expanding and contracting with the effort.

"When we was there at the flat, I went into her bedroom." He turned his head sideways and looked at Aubrey. "I wasn't going to, I already decided, I made my mind up before we went, but in the end her bedroom door was open and I couldn't help it. I couldn't stop myself." He gulped hard and moistened his bottom lip with the tip of his tongue before collecting himself and continuing. "They stripped her bed, Aubrey. They took all the bed clothes and sheets and everything right off. You could see the mattress. Why do you think they done that?"

Evidence probably, thought Aubrey. It must have been the place where she died. After all, it was next to impossible that Maria had managed to get through to the bedroom after she had been strangled, so the murderer must have chased her in there. He ran the scene through his mind. Maria would have almost certainly fought back but, he suspected, she had instinctively run through to her bedroom as a place of safety. The man must have run after her, knocking her across the face and causing the large bruise, before pushing her down on to the mattress and fastening his strong hands around her neck and squeezing the very life out of her.

He listened as Carlos continued talking.

"She got that mattress off the tip. She bought me a new one on instalments from the shop in town, but she got hers off the tip. She got one of the council workers to help her bring it home in his council van, and she scrubbed and scrubbed until I thought her fingers was going to start bleeding. And I never helped her."

He gazed mournfully at Aubrey.

"Aubrey, who do you think could have done this to her? Why would anybody want to hurt her? I know she was, like, a bit annoying but…"

A bit? Only totally, thought Aubrey.

Carlos continued.

"I mean, like, she did argue with the neighbours and that, but she weren't the only one. She weren't no worse than anyone else. Sometimes they was all at it, especially in the summer when it was hot. Those flats didn't have no air-conditioning or nothing, so all the windows would be open. One of them would start and then they'd all be popping their heads out and having a go. Like a load of mad jack-in-the-boxes. I had a jack-in-the-box once," he added sadly. "My dad sat on it when he was drunk and broke it."

For a moment, Carlos was silent and then he said slowly, "I never told Mr Goodman, but somebody did come to the flat once."

Aubrey stiffened. He'd known there was something.

Carlos continued. "I only saw the back of him. I never saw his face, and I never said nothing because I was supposed to be in school. Mum had gone to work and I went off to get the bus like usual, but then I changed my mind. We had games and I ain't got the proper kit, so I just went back home again."

He paused for a second as though remembering.

"This bloke, I saw him knocking on our door so I skipped back down the stairs and hid round the back of the bins. He was there for ages, knocking and looking in the windows. I thought he'd never go. I didn't know whether to tell Mum when she come home, but in the end I never told her. She would only have thought that we was in trouble about something. And he wasn't wearing a suit or nothing like that, just jeans and trainers. So he weren't no-one important. He was probably just trying to sell something."

The improbability of anybody being dull-witted enough to try door-to-door selling in a neighbourhood where the majority of new goods to pass the thresholds had usually been stolen from somebody else, seemed to strike both of them at the same time.

"Or, well, something like that anyway."

Carlos raised his head slightly and stared out across the room. He gave a deep sigh.

"Tell you what, Aubrey, I couldn't half do with a smoke."

Don't even think about it, thought Aubrey. A wisp of smoke in a house of non-smokers could be detected at five hundred paces. Molly and Jeremy would be in here quicker than you could say fire extinguisher. As if reading his thoughts, Carlos looked directly at him and said, "Mr Goodman never said I couldn't smoke."

Only, thought Aubrey, because he didn't know that you wanted to. He watched as Carlos sped quickly across the room and pulled on his jeans, trainers, and parka. Wrapping his long, woollen scarf round him with one arm, and wriggling down with the other into one of the black bin liners that he'd brought back with him from the flat, he pulled out a battered cigarette packet and a small plastic lighter. Pausing only to stuff his pillows down under the duvet, Carlos crept slowly down the stairs.

Out in the garden, Carlos pinned his shoulder blades back against the side of the shed and took a long, slow drag on his cigarette. Aubrey watched as he tipped his head back and blew out a long, thin column of smoke towards the sky.

"One thing school's good for, Aubrey," Carlos whispered down to him, although there was nobody out there to hear him. "At least you can always borrow a few fags off one of the fag barons. I've only got one left."

He straightened up and huddled into himself as he shook his last cigarette from the packet and lit it from the stub of the first.

"And I ain't got no money either." He inhaled deeply. "I s'pose I could ask Mr Goodman for some but it don't seem right somehow."

No, it didn't. Aubrey agreed. Molly and Jeremy would, he was fairly sure, have given Carlos some money if he'd asked them for it, but he could hardly go and shake them awake in the small hours of the morning and ask them for some fag money. Anyway, time was passing and he needed to get a move on. He moved sideways and slipped quickly away into the shadows. Carlos seemed less upset now; he'd be all right.

Chapter Twenty-Three

Aubrey hurried down the high street. It was funny how different it all looked at night. During the day, it was a jolly, bustling little thoroughfare. People and cars and buses were coming and going all the time. It had a general sense of purpose, a busy atmosphere that was hardly ever dulled, even when it was raining. But at night, it was a different prospect altogether. When the shops were closed up and the workers from the offices had gone home, the pavements were still and shrouded in ghostly layers of moonlight. The doors were locked and barred, and the only sound was that of the distant drone of traffic as it moved along the bypass to the west. In the window of Bateman's, the old-fashioned men's clothing shop, the plastic dummies in their chunky-knit cardigans and flannel trousers seemed horribly life-like. Aubrey could almost imagine that they were leaning down to have a look at him. Their whole aspect appeared sinister, like a gang of malevolent pensioners. One of them was wearing a pair of thick, dark-rimmed glasses that had slipped sideways.

Aubrey averted his eyes and moved more quickly, breaking into a run as he gathered momentum. At least at this time of night he didn't have to keep an eye out for the traffic. He reached the top of the high street and glanced right before crossing the road towards the all-night garage and the industrial estate, but then stopped. For a moment, he stood perfectly still. He could sense somebody behind him. He turned and looked. From halfway back down the road, a hooded figure was panting towards him, the ends of its blue and yellow woollen scarf fluttering in the night air. He sat down on the kerb and waited for Carlos to catch him up. It would have been no problem to simply outrun him, but it seemed heartless somehow. Anyway, they were friends.

"Aubrey." Carlos chugged up to him and stopped, breathing

heavily. He leaned over and clutched his side with one hand. "Hold on, mate. I'll come with you. I can't sleep anyway."

Aubrey sighed inwardly and moved forward, slowing down his pace so that Carlos could keep up with him. He began to thread his way through the industrial estate. He didn't really want the boy with him, not tonight. Although he didn't mind in a general sense, and in fact would usually welcome his company, Carlos was in enough trouble as it was. He didn't have Molly and Jeremy's permission to be out, and if they went into his room and found the bed empty except for the pillow that he had stuffed down it to make it look as if he was in there asleep, all hell would be let loose. However, there was very little that Aubrey could do about it now. On any other night he would have simply turned round and gone back home in the hope that Carlos would follow, but tonight was different. Tonight he had no choice but to carry on. He had to be there with the others or they would all think that he'd bottled it.

At the thought of what lay ahead, his pace slowed even further. It wasn't that he minded having a scrap. In almost any other circumstances, he rather enjoyed it. It was just this particular scrap that he objected to. Rupert's instruction had been to wait up on the section of flat roof overlooking the car park at The Laurels. The enemy had been told that the bundle was going to take place in the car park, and the task of Aubrey and the other cats was simply to leap down and surprise them. When he'd heard the great master plan, Aubrey had been sorely tempted to just take off and hit the road again. Of all the things that he didn't want to do, about top of the list was leaping off a roof into the darkness and straight down into a mass of hostile cats. The only thing that had kept him from leaving the neighbourhood then and there was the thought of Molly and Jeremy. That and the fact that Rupert would hunt him down and tear him limb from limb. But there was no denying it. All in all, whichever way you looked at it, it didn't exactly have the hallmark of being a good night out. And on every step of the way, he had no doubt that from somewhere in the shadows Lupin would be watching him, watching and just waiting for him to put a paw wrong.

Aubrey quickened his pace as the great gothic pile of The Laurels loomed up in front of them. He thought about the glittering shards of glass set into the top of the far wall and shuddered. God help any cat that got stuck up there. Or any person, come to that. Thank goodness he'd remembered to tell the others about it. He reached the gate and glanced quickly around. He couldn't see any sign of the other cats yet. Good. That meant that he still had the time to have a look around the old barn and see what Dave and the other man had been so interested in. He slunk under the gate and winced at the clunk of the latch and the following groan as it creaked forward across the tarmac against the weight of Carlos's hand. He waited for a second. A small light went on in the house. He glanced across at Carlos. Even if the caretaker had heard the gate opening, it was dark. They'd be over at the barn by the time he came out to see what was going on.

Together, Aubrey and Carlos made their way across the car park and slipped through the bushes and weeds on the other side towards where the old barn and greenhouse stood. Aubrey stopped and looked at it for a moment. Something was different. For a moment, he couldn't work out what it was, and then he realised. The barn door was shut, and glinting in the moonlight was the shape of what looked like a new padlock. In the past, the door had always been slightly ajar and dropping slightly on one side where one of the hinges was broken. Now it looked as though it had been mended and made secure. He advanced cautiously towards it. It didn't matter that the door was shut. Doors generally were shut and there would be another way in. There was always another way in. What he was more interested in was the fact that someone had bothered to shut it. He walked slowly round the side of the building looking for an entrance, eyes scanning up, down, and sideways. And then he saw it. Up on the slope of the roof there was a hole in the corrugated metal, the jagged rusted edges just visible against the sky.

He scrambled rapidly up the side of the building, his paws and feet instinctively catching at claw holds and propelling him upwards. From below, Carlos watched him as he reached the jagged edges of the hole and lowered himself down, holding on with his front paws for a moment before dropping to the floor.

The smell hit him before his paws touched the ground. It was a sickly sweet, cloying smell that permeated the whole atmosphere and hung on the air. He knew that smell. It was the same smell that had clung to the room in which Raj had died, a smell which had gathered momentum over the period of days in which Raj had lain undiscovered, until it had filled every crack and crevice and finally seeped into the very fabric of the furniture.

He ventured slowly forwards. The barn still contained the broken lawnmower, its spiky shape clearly outlined in the dim light. The deckchair and old paint cans and oil drums were still there, too. He frowned. That shiny new padlock had been put on the door for a reason, and it wasn't to protect some broken kit and a few old cans of paint. Something else was in here, and it was that something that was causing the smell.

The only thing he could see that was different was what looked like a roll of old carpet pushed against the far wall. Moving to one end of it, he flattened himself against the floor and peered along its length. The smell here was strong. At first he could see nothing, but then, between the folds, a strange shape became visible. He screwed his eyes up and peered harder. It was a small dark object, but it had what looked like little spokes sticking out of it. He looked at it thoughtfully. If he had to bet a pack of cat food on it, he'd say that it was a hand. Did he have time to wriggle down the carpet and find out what it was for sure?

He jumped backwards suddenly, startled as sounds broke through the still night air. He turned his head towards the noise. A scuffling and grunting noise, and a half-choked muffled cry was followed by silence. Badgers probably, he thought, or a fox. But time was getting on, he needed to get back over to the car park. He could always come back here after the scrap, if he wasn't too tired. Whatever was rolled up in the carpet was almost certainly not going anywhere.

He scrambled quickly back up the wall and climbed out

through the hole. Standing on the barn roof, silhouetted in the moonlight, he peered down. Carlos was nowhere to be seen. He thought for a moment. Carlos had probably got bored and wandered off. Or maybe he had realised what trouble he would be in if Jeremy and Molly woke up and found him gone, and had started to head for home. Aubrey hoped so. His ears flicked suddenly and he turned his head towards the house. From the car park came the almost imperceptible tread of an army of cats on the move.

Chapter Twenty-Four

Aubrey dropped noiselessly to the ground and ran quickly towards the car park. Where was everybody? He could have sworn that he'd heard them a couple of seconds ago, but the car park appeared to be completely empty. Suddenly he caught sight of a small white flash at the top of the fire escape and looked upwards. They were already up there, he could see them now. They were streaming up the fire escape and marching along the ledge round the side of the building and then disappearing into the darkness.

He watched for a moment and then sped silently across the tarmac and began to climb the fire escape. He reached the top and paused on the small ironwork platform, staring out into the darkness before slipping quickly along the ledge towards the flat roof. Reaching the corner of the ledge, he leaned slightly backwards and gathered himself up. In one graceful bound, he leapt to the flat roof opposite and landed among a carpet of cats, each one poised ready to spring as soon as the word was given.

"Got here all right then, Aubs?"

Vincent's green eyes gleamed out from the darkness. Next to him, Aubrey could see Moses, his little face looking worried but resolute.

"To tell the truth, Vin, I'm not sure that this is such a great idea…"

Before he could continue, the sibilant hiss of Lupin reverberated across the roof top. The battle was on.

Aubrey barely had time to think before the huge push from behind propelled him forward and then caught him in a great rushing of air, and he found himself sailing through space along with thirty other cats, each of them twirling their tails in graceful helicopter fashion like feline sycamore leaves, paws spread straight before them Superman-style. The cats below had slunk commando-fashion into the car park, one at a time, bodies low to the ground and eyes narrowed, clearly suspecting a set-up. They had been watched from above by thirty pairs of eyes as they had prowled warily around. For several moments, there had been complete silence, and then the cats on the ground had looked up in horror as the opposition started to drop from the sky with great blood-curdling yowls.

Aubrey landed four-square on all paws and immediately lashed out at the nearest cat. It was a lesson that he'd learnt early in life and one which had rarely failed him; strike first and ask questions later. He drew breath and gathered himself up in readiness to lunge again, and felt Vincent streak past him, eyes narrowed and ears back.

"Be first, my son," he muttered to Aubrey as he leapt on what looked like a big fur hat. Aubrey nodded back in agreement. As usual, Vincent was right. When it was one-to-one fighting, there was no point in being second. The cat that he had attacked had limped away to regroup, but was followed almost immediately by a big, soft, grey animal that started towards him but then skittered back again in fright at the expression on Aubrey's face. Aubrey grinned to himself. This was too easy. He might have put on a bit of weight since he'd come to live with Molly and Jeremy, but he was still a big, powerful cat. Not bad for one who had lived on his wits and hadn't so much as smelled the inside of a tin of cat food for the first few months of his life.

To one side, he could see Moses hanging on for dear life to the back of a large white cat, claws dug firmly in while the cat swung from side to side in a desperate attempt to dislodge him. Good old Moses. He might not be very bright but he was bloody brave. The white cat was almost three times his size.

Aubrey tensed his shoulders ready to launch himself again, trying to decide where to plunge in among the great teeming mass of fur and claws that had seemed to gather itself up into a great ball and was now rolling round and round the yard in a huge feline bundle. Hovering slightly above it, small thistle-like tufts of detached fur floated on the breeze, and over his head a yellow fluorescent collar suddenly flew upward, its little bell tinkling merrily across the cold night sky. In the far corner, he spotted Lupin trotting purposefully around, snout twitching and not a whisker out of place. He was bristling with importance. He had clearly designated himself Director of Operations, but was managing, as usual, to be the only cat present that was not actually doing anything.

For a moment Aubrey distracted himself by toying with the idea of creeping around the edges of the yard and ambushing him. It was incredibly tempting; it would be so easy, almost too easy. If he kept to the shadows, he could leap on him from behind and give him a bloody good battering, and he'd never know who had done it. Just the thought of it made him feel good all over, but he dismissed the idea as quickly as it came. Lupin might not see who'd had a go at him but someone else would, and all the good he'd done himself with Rupert and Roger in finding the flat roof and suggesting it as an attack point would be undone in an instant. Somebody would be bound to spot him and tell the twins, it was how they operated.

To his left, he could see Rupert now, nose-to-nose with a huge black and white beast, one eye rolling skyward and his fur crackling with all the gusto of a true lunatic. His back was arched so highly that he was almost standing on his claws. Aubrey shuddered slightly. He wouldn't like to be in the black and white cat's place. He might be bigger than Rupert, but Rupert was definitely more insane. Rupert also had the added protection of Roger, who Aubrey could see now was covering him while at the same time despatching a sleek-looking tortoiseshell. There was something chillingly and menacingly detached about Roger, he thought. While Rupert clearly enjoyed his work, with Roger it was always business, never personal.

Spotting a gap, Aubrey threw himself back into the melee and found himself next to Vincent.

"All right, Aubsie?"

Aubrey paused for a moment to get his breath and then nodded. For several minutes, neither cat spoke as they dealt swiftly and silently with the cats in front of them, and then Vincent spoke again.

"I reckon we'll be finished here in a few minutes. Half of them have done a runner already."

Aubrey looked around him. It was true, the yard was much emptier than it had been ten minutes earlier, and the great fighting bundle had been reduced to a few isolated scraps between individual cats. On the ground lay pieces of torn collar, and in one place what looked like the tip of a tail. Aubrey looked away. It looked distinctly like the tip of the tail of the cat that Rupert had been eyeballing. But all in all, the whole thing had gone pretty well, considering. Much better, in fact, than he might have expected, given that Rupert had master-minded it. After the initial chaos when every cat had seemed to be fighting every other cat regardless of which side they were on, it had all settled down into a good old-fashioned bundle. The best bit had been finally seeing Lupin get what he deserved by way of a good kicking. He grinned. If he ever met that big fluffy cat with the strong-looking legs and the white patch over one eye, he would shake it by the paw, even if it was one of the enemy.

Vincent arched his back slightly and stretched his sleek paws in front of him.

"Let's hope this keeps them quiet, for a while anyway. I mean," he continued, as he sat upright again and straightened his collar, "I like a good scrap as well as the next one, but there's got to be something a bit more in it, something a bit more personal, know what I mean?"

Aubrey nodded again and yawned. The left side of his head felt slightly sore and he could feel a warm trickle of blood behind his ear. He'd have to keep that hidden from Molly or she'd have him straight down to Grimshaw's. He felt suddenly tired. He'd acquitted himself well, he had nothing to worry about, and right now he could do with a little something by way of food, followed by a good long kip on a nice big pile of clean washing. But first, he'd take another quick look in the barn. It would save him from coming back tomorrow.

Across the yard, he could see the few remaining cats from

the other side slinking away now, flattening themselves against the walls in an effort to make themselves invisible, the air of defeat hanging heavily over them. From the look of it, it would be some time before they started demanding a re-match.

"Might as well make a move then," said Vincent, stepping lightly forward. "I'll just have a word with Roger and make sure that there's nothing else to do."

"I'll catch you up, Vin. I just want to make a quick check on something." And with that, he sped off back across the car park and towards the old barn.

Reaching the barn door, he stopped and stared down at the ground. There had been some kind of disturbance here. He looked more closely at the flattened grass. It was recent. The marks of something or someone being dragged were clear. Had it been here before? He couldn't be sure. He had been so focused on getting to the scrap that he hadn't stopped to look around, but had simply jumped from the roof and hit the ground running. He turned his head to the right. Lying to one side and caught among the lower leaves of a bush, the blue and yellow colours of the Brazilian national football team were damp and smeared with mud.

Chapter Twenty-Five

Aubrey turned and ran quickly back towards the house, his heart in his mouth. Ignoring the few remaining cats that were washing and smartening themselves up before heading for home, he skirted the edges of the car park and climbed the fire escape. He would have a clear view of the surrounding area from the rooftop. If Carlos was injured and lying in the grounds somewhere, he'd have a better chance of spotting him from up there. He climbed to the highest ridge and stared out across the urban skyscape surrounding him. The industrial estate was dark and silent, the small fleets of white vans parked in front of the various units ready for the morning. In the grounds of The Laurels, the last of the cats began to tramp wearily through the gate which Carlos had left open earlier. Of Carlos himself, there was not a sign. He slid quickly down from the ridge and made his way towards the small attic windows, peering in each one in turn. Short of getting into the house somehow, it was the only thing left that he could think to do. As he reached the third window, something white passed in front of the grimy glass and seemed to float there. Aubrey paused. There was something vaguely familiar about the white shape, which had now stopped moving and seemed to be staring back at him. He moved closer. Thin fingers curled around the window catch and began to unfasten it. Aubrey inched closer still.

"Aubrey, Aubrey." The familiar voice croaked through the gap.

There was no mistaking it now. Aubrey moved up to the hand and sniffed at it. Trembling, Carlos knelt down on the window sill and reached through the narrow gap of the open window. Tenderly, he stroked the top of Aubrey's warm furry head with the tips of his fingers.

"Aubrey, Aubrey," he whispered. "You have no idea how glad I am to see you, mate."

Aubrey wriggled through the gap and jumped into the room. He didn't have a clue what Carlos was doing in there, but whatever it was, it clearly wasn't a matter of choice.

He looked curiously around him. By the moonlight that filtered into the room, he could see that it contained a single chair and some small cardboard boxes stacked on an old wooden table in the corner. The air in the room was stale and unpleasant. It held the same depressing lack of hope as Sunny Banks. All it needed was a pack of desperate cats and a smelly food bowl chucked down on the floor and they could have been banged up in a rescue centre. Funny old life, thought Aubrey. This time, I'm the one who can get out. Carlos knelt down and buried his face in the thick, warm fur of Aubrey's neck. Aubrey could feel the heat of his breath.

"Aubrey, I never done nothing."

Aubrey felt the narrow shoulders start to shake, and the hands that were clutching him begin to tremble slightly.

"Honest. I never done nothing. I was just standing there. I was waiting for you to come back out and this bloke just come up behind me and grabbed me round the neck. He dragged me round the front of the house and made me walk up all the stairs, and then he shoved me in here and locked me in."

He stopped abruptly as the sound of footsteps outside the door came to a halt and a key scraped against the lock. They both watched as the door handle twisted round. In the split second that it took for the door to open, Aubrey dashed across the room and threw himself under the table in the corner. His instinct told him that whoever was on the other side would not be pleased to see him in there with Carlos. He watched from the shadows as Carlos stared at the man, his eyes wide with fright.

"Right, let's have some answers. And don't start giving me none of your lies. I've seen you before, you little bastard."

The man strode over to Carlos and grasped the front of his parka in both hands. He pulled him up towards him so that they were almost nose-to-nose.

From his hiding place Aubrey stared, totally transfixed. The man was practically foaming at the mouth. His small grey eyes were sparking with anger. This was the man that had been in Mr Telling's house with Maria that day, and it was the same man that he had seen talking to Dave in The Laurels car park. He was sure of it. He hadn't seen his face properly on either occasion but he recognised the voice for sure now. He dropped his gaze to the man's feet. Sure enough, there was the splash of green paint caught along the side of one his trainers. But now that he could see the face as well, there was something oddly familiar about that, too. A soft soot fall of memory shifted at the back of his mind and then swirled and settled. He had seen this face somewhere before, or someone very like him. It was just that for the moment he couldn't remember where. One thing was for sure, though, the man had obviously seen Carlos heading towards the old barn but he hadn't seen Aubrey.

The man released his grasp on Carlos and stood back.

"Who are you? Why are you following me around? What do you want?"

"I wasn't following you... honest." The words sounded hoarse and cracked as though Carlos was shaking them free from a dry mouth.

"I've told you once already. Don't give me none of your lies. You think I didn't see you that day over at The Meadows, don't you? I saw you all right, cringing round the dustbins and spying on me. What were you doing over there? Why were you watching me? Why weren't you in school where you were supposed to be, with all the other kids?"

Carlos stared mutely back at him. The man continued.

"When I heard the gate open tonight and looked out of the window, I knew it was you straight away. I recognised your stupid scarf." The man paused for a moment and stared at him. "What team is that, anyway?"

"Brazil," muttered Carlos miserably, his hand instinctively reaching for his throat where the scarf should have been.

The man's eyes narrowed. He was, thought Aubrey, putting the proverbial two and two together.

"Do you live over at The Meadows?"

Aubrey held his breath.

"No. I just go over there sometimes."

"Why? What's so interesting over there?"

Carlos shrugged. Aubrey let his breath out again. Clever lad. He was adopting the classic adolescent defence. When in doubt, plead indifference. Only Aubrey saw the almost imperceptible quick nervous swallowing and the very slight flutter of Carlos's left hand.

"What's your name?"

"Dan."

"So, why are you following me around, Dan?"

"I'm not. I don't even know... who you are. I've never seen you before. Honest. I was just waiting... for my cat."

"I hate cats."

There didn't seem to be anything much to say to this. For a moment Carlos and the man stared at each other, the man's chest still bulging with barely suppressed rage. Suddenly his expression changed. Aubrey watched as his chest slowly subsided, collapsing down like the air going out of a balloon. The man tilted his head slightly to one side and ran his eye over the length of Carlos's body. Aubrey swallowed hard. He didn't like the look of that expression. He'd seen something very like it on the faces of the crack dealers when they had hung around outside the little parade of shops where Raj's News and Groceries had been.

"Do you like money?"

The man tilted his head to the other side while his hand jangled in his pocket, turning over the loose coins. Aubrey looked at him, confused. What sort of question was that? Show him a human who didn't like money. More to the point, what was the right answer? He watched as Carlos cleared his throat and flicked his tongue over dry lips. Carlos was clearly equally at a loss.

"Er, yes. No. Sort of."

The man smiled suddenly, a thin split of a smile that threw his cheekbones into sharp relief and seemed to Aubrey more terrifying than his rage.

"I thought you would." He stared pointedly at Carlos's shabby parka. "I can see that a few quid wouldn't go amiss."

He moved closer to Carlos and placed a hand on his shoulder. With the other hand he tilted Carlos's chin up towards him and looked deep into his eyes.

"You and me, we could be mates. You can call me Rick." The hand holding Carlos's shoulder squeezed down on it. Aubrey watched as the fingers tightened their grip. "I do you a favour, you do me a favour. Because," the hand squeezed down still harder, "that's what mates are for. Mates stick together. Mates never grass on one another, do they?"

He let go of Carlos and reached down into the inside of his jacket. He pulled out a half bottle of whisky and took a long hard swallow. With the other hand, he patted Carlos gently on the head.

"You be a good boy and stay here quietly until I come and get you."

And with that, he turned and left the room, banging the door shut behind him. From the other side came the unmistakeable sound of a key turning in the lock.

Aubrey crept out from under the table and ran towards Carlos. For a moment Carlos stood perfectly still and then, slowly, he sank to his knees.

"I've heard about blokes like him." Carlos's voice sounded small and frightened. "They get everywhere. They get you on your own and they do pervy acts on you, and then they give you money to shut you up." He paused and swallowed. "Like a rent boy. William at school said about it. It happened to him when he was in Year Seven and some bloke was supposed to be looking after him when his mum was at work, only the bloke what done it to him was a right tight wad. He didn't even get the rent."

Carlos shifted his legs from under him and sat cross-legged on the hard floor. Aubrey moved closer and settled down next to him. For a moment, they both sat in silence.

A new and even more scary thought seemed suddenly to strike Carlos, hitting him so hard in the chest that he almost stopped breathing. He turned and stared at Aubrey, his eyes

155

wide.

"Aubrey, what if he's gone off to get all his pervy mates?"

Aubrey stared back at him. He wasn't sure what a perv was but he knew what mates were. He had just been formulating a plan for when the man returned; Aubrey would jump on his back and stick his claws hard into his neck, which would give Carlos the opportunity to jump up and escape through the door. By the time Rick realised what was happening, Aubrey could be out of the door, too, or better still, the little window which was still open. Rick wouldn't be able to follow him out there, the gap wasn't big enough.

But his plan wouldn't work if the bloke had his mates with him. He couldn't jump on all their necks.

"They'll probably take it in turns to do loads of pervy stuff to me and then they'll kill me afterwards." Carlos's voice was low and hoarse, his eyes practically bulging now. "That's what they do. They have to kill you afterwards in case you tell anyone, even if you promise cross your heart and hope to die that you won't. That's where he's gone now. He's gone to ring up all his mates, and then they're going to jump in their cars and come up here and do things to me, and then they're going to kill me and bury me. Probably in a forest," he added.

For a moment Carlos was silent. Aubrey watched him as the thoughts whipped up and whirled around his head in a frenzy of fright. He could almost hear them exploding in great cluster bombs of fear.

"And they'll film it." Carlos's eyes began to fill, and his bottom lip started to wobble slightly. "They always do that. They'll have one of those digital camera things, and they'll film the whole thing so that they can pass it round to all the other pervs." Carlos could barely breathe now. "And then it'll be on the internet and everybody in the whole world will see it. And all the pervs will know who I am. Except that they won't. I'll just be the kid without a name, the kid in the film, the one that got killed."

Carlos stood up and walked stiffly over to the window. Aubrey joined him and jumped up onto the window sill. Together, they stared out into the night. The first streak of morning light was just starting to poke its fingers across the sky. In the distance, they could hear the slow creep of a milk float, the whine of its electric engine quietly audible beneath the clinking clash and clatter of milk bottles.

"He thinks I know something, Aubrey," Carlos whispered. "But if I did, I'd tell him, no problem. My dad, he always used to say brave men die young and then he used to laugh. When I was little, I didn't get what he meant. I thought being brave was good. I s'pose I still do, really." He stood silently, lost in thought. "But if I knew something, Aubrey, I'd say. Straight off, I'd tell him whatever it is that he wants to know, but I don't know what it is." He thought for a moment. "It must be something to do with that time he came knocking at our flat, that was the only time I ever saw him. But I never saw him do nothing. There weren't nothing to see. All he done was knock at our front door and look in the windows. The only thing I saw was his back. I wouldn't even have known it was him if he hadn't said nothing."

He gazed down at Aubrey, his expression still frightened but his breathing more regular now.

"And he's been drinking," he said flatly. "See this, Aubrey?" Carlos raised his chin slightly and pointed to a small, fork-shaped scar. "My dad did that. He went to wallop me once when I was getting on his nerves because I kept asking him questions. He'd had a few and he missed, but he caught me on the chin with his ring. There was blood everywhere." He smiled suddenly. "Mum went mad. She whopped him one with a saucepan, right on the back of his head. It didn't stop him drinking, though," he added sadly. "Sometimes he used to get so drunk that he'd lose whole days at a time. He'd just pass out somewhere, and when he woke up he'd think that it was still Tuesday and he'd be really amazed because it was, like, Friday. That's what this bloke might do. He might be like my dad. He might go and get so drunk that he might just forget me altogether." He sniffed and wiped his nose with the cuff of his parka. "He could just leave me here to starve to death and nobody would ever know. And then I'll get eaten by rats. They might not even wait till I'm dead. If there's enough of them, they wouldn't have to wait, they could just take me alive." Carlos stared up at the ceiling. "What do you reckon's worse, Aubrey, being killed by a gang of paedos and dumped in a forest, or being eaten alive by rats?"

It was a close call, thought Aubrey. It wasn't the sort of question that posed itself very often.

Carlos sighed. A great, weary sigh of resignation that rippled straight through his long, skinny frame. Aubrey put a paw gently on his arm. When Carlos had found Maria, when he had seen her poor dead body, cold and lifeless, stretched out on her bed, he had probably thought that the worst thing had happened. That was it. It just couldn't get any worse. How wrong he had been. The arrow on the wheel of Carlos's own particular fortune had merely quivered temporarily around the zone marked 'disaster' before plummeting straight down to the one marked 'destruction'. Aubrey knew that feeling well. It was the same one he'd had when they had banged the cage door shut on him at Sunny Banks.

He thought for a moment. It could have been worse, he supposed. At least Carlos was still in possession of all his limbs. He hadn't been battered to death or subjected to a hundred and one other indignities. Well, not yet anyway. Also, although he was stuck down here, at least the man hadn't tied him up or anything. On the less bright side, however, he was clearly still a prisoner.

The sound of that key turning had been pretty definite, and even from where Aubrey was sitting, he could see that, thin as he was, there was no way that Carlos could squeeze through the tiny window. He might, just about, manage his arms and legs but he'd never get his head through. And even if by some miracle he did manage it, there was the problem of reaching the ground. The ledge wasn't wide enough to take him, and there was no convenient drainpipe to shin down. The only option that Carlos had was to wait for the man to come back, if he did come back, and then plead with him to release him. Perhaps if he had time to think about things, he might be more open to reason. After all, he couldn't keep Carlos locked in here forever. Carlos might just be able to convince him that he didn't know anything and that he should let him go. On the other hand, if he carried on drinking, he might be like Carlos's father, he might fall asleep and completely forget about Carlos altogether.

Aubrey watched as Carlos dropped his head into his hands and hunched forward, rocking to and fro slightly for comfort.

"You know what, Aubrey? You're about the best mate I ever had." Carlos paused and then continued rocking and muttering through his fingers. "You're the only mate I ever had, really. At least you don't call me Pedro. At least you don't ask me to play football with you and then take the piss out of me for wearing crap trainers."

For a moment Carlos was silent, and then he straightened up and raised his head. He stared at the wall.

"Mr Goodman's a mate, too, in a way. Even though he's a teacher. All the kids like him. If you're in his tutor group, he sort of looks out for you. He got me out of a fight the other day. Jed Caparo told Liam Grainger that I'd been looking at his girlfriend. I didn't even know the great bonehead had a girlfriend. If Mr Goodman hadn't come along when he did, I reckon I'd be in a wheelchair by now."

At the mention of Caparo, Aubrey felt a sudden jolt of recognition. Of course. That was where he had seen the man's face before. Those same flinty grey eyes, that same sly grin. He was a dead ringer for that boy Jed Caparo that he'd seen hanging around the staff car park at the school. This bloke was exactly what Caparo would look like in ten or twelve years' time.

Carlos continued. "Mr Goodman, he's a good teacher, too. He was reading this book to us in class. It was really good. Even Jed Caparo liked it. It was all about this Big Brother bloke. We all thought it was going to be about the telly programme so we were disappointed at first, but it was about this Big Brother, and this bloke called Winston Smith and how everybody was being watched all the time. And it had these things in it called proles. Mr Goodman used to do all the different voices and that." He sighed. "I don't s'pose I'll ever hear the end of it now."

Carlos fell silent for a moment. Aubrey could hear the sound of his breathing.

"I reckon it won't be long before Mr and Mrs Goodman find out I've gone. One of them will call me for breakfast, and then when I don't come down they'll go upstairs and find out I'm not there. I put my pillow under the covers to stop them worrying, in case they looked round the door in the night. I wish I hadn't done that now. It makes it worse. It makes it look like I've run off again." He turned and stared miserably at Aubrey. "I know what they'll say. I know what they'll think of me."

Aubrey also knew what Molly and Jeremy would think of him. It didn't take a lot of working out; it was obvious. They would think that Carlos was an ungrateful little sod who had just done a runner at the first opportunity. They would think that he had taken them for a ride and that they had been foolish enough to fall for it. Probably even now they were looking around to see what he had nicked to take with him. He could hardly blame them for it. That was what everybody else would think as well. Probably that was what he would think, too, if he didn't know better. Because, when all was said and done, that was what kids like Carlos did. What else could you expect with a boy like that? He could almost hear the clamour of their voices – the police, the social workers, the friends and neighbours, and loudest of them all, baying for his blood in great clanging tones, would be big, horrible Rachel who had called him a murderer. Rachel, who had warned Molly and Jeremy about having anything to do with the likes of him. Rachel, who, they would think, had turned out to be right after all.

Carlos suddenly straightened his back and lifted his narrow shoulders. His face was scarlet and his eyes blazing. His mouth tightened into a thin hard line and his breath came hard and fast.

"You know what, Aubrey? Why should I just take all this shit? Why does it always have to be me? It ain't fair and I'm not doing it." He stared defiantly at Aubrey. "Why should I? Mum wouldn't, she wouldn't take it. She weren't afraid of nobody. She wouldn't just sit here waiting for them to come and get her. She'd do something."

A picture of Maria formed in Aubrey's mind, her hands on her hips, her chin thrust aggressively forward. Carlos was right. His mother would never have just submitted to all this. She would have screamed and fought and kicked until her captors would have either killed her on the spot or begged her to leave. But either way, at least she would have gone out fighting.

"There must be a way. There has to be. There has to be a way to get out of this room before he comes back." Carlos jumped up and started forward. He began to look wildly around him. "Or maybe I could get a message out somehow…"

Aubrey stared around the room with him. As far as he could see there was no exit from the room other than the door and the window, neither of which offered any possibilities, given that one was locked and the other was too small. Aubrey followed as Carlos ran over to the boxes that were piled on the table under which Aubrey had sat. He watched as Carlos pulled the lid from the top one. Inside lay a pile of old leaflets advertising the clubs and activities available at The Laurels for the elderly.

Carlos pulled out the top one, spilling the ones beneath to the floor in his excitement. He smoothed the leaflet out across the table and reached inside his parka pocket for his biro, which was the sum total of his school equipment. With trembling fingers he scribbled 'help' in big straggling letters underneath The Laurels logo bannered across the top, and then added, 'This is Carlos. I am here.' Flipping the leaflet over, he repeated the message on the blank space on the other side. Pulling out another, he wrote, 'Carlos is here. I am locked in. Please help me'.

He stuffed it in his pocket and rapidly wrote out five more. He folded them quickly, his nimble fingers turning the paper this way and that, and then ran to the window. Aubrey ran with him. Together they watched as a small squadron of paper aeroplanes lifted on the breeze and fluttered upwards, while at

161

the same time Carlos pushed his face against the gap and opened his mouth ready to let out a great angry roar.

Suddenly they both froze. Turning slowly, they saw the figure of the man filling the open doorway.

Chapter Twenty-Six

"What's that cat doing in here?"

Rick strode quickly towards the window but not quickly
enough. Aubrey was out and on the ledge in a flash. He
flattened himself against the side of the building and strained
his ears to hear what was happening inside. He didn't have to
strain very hard. The man's voice carried loud and clear.

"Stand up straight and do your parka up. We're going for a
walk."

From inside came the sound of a faint scuffle. The door
opened and then closed again, followed by silence. Aubrey
waited. If they really were going for a walk, that meant that
they would come outside of the building. If he stayed where he
was, he would have a clear view of where they went. Unless
they got in a car, of course.

He glanced down at the car park. The gate was still open
but there were no vehicles parked there. As he looked, Rick
emerged from round the side of the building, holding on to
Carlos with one hand and pushing him forward with the other.
Aubrey watched as they crossed the car park and disappeared
into the bushes. He winced as Carlos stumbled and turned his
ankle slightly as the man tightened his grip on his elbow.

Across the sky, a watery sun was beginning to break
through, and the faint thrumming sound of machinery starting
up began to filter across from the industrial estate. Aubrey
thought quickly. Whatever Rick was planning to do with
Carlos, he was unlikely to do it in the daytime. Apart from
anything else, there would be people around any minute now,
and presumably he would be required back at the house. Even
as the thought formed, a small minibus turned into the car park
and a group of elderly people began to clamber out. It must be
later than he had realised. He watched as one of them bent

down to pick up one of Carlos's scribbled messages. Without reading it, the woman screwed it into a ball and tossed it into the litter bin that stood by the gate post. So much for that.

He edged slowly along the ledge towards the fire escape steps. He had to do something. He couldn't just leave Carlos on his own, that was for sure. But what, realistically, could he do? It looked as though they were heading for the old barn, and if so, he could get in there, no problem. But there was a padlock on the door and Carlos wouldn't be able to get out. The end result would be that they would be no better off than they had been in the attic room. Maybe Vincent would have some idea.

Aubrey stretched his mouth into a great jaw-cracking yawn as he hurried round the corner towards home. He was desperate for a turbo round his food bowl and a good long kip in the airing cupboard, but it would have to wait. He had to find Vincent first. Across the road, Winston the milkman was swinging bottles down from the crates and striding swiftly up and down the garden paths. Aubrey hesitated for a moment but then continued. He was starving, but he had far too much to do to make a raid on the milk float this morning, tempting though it was.

He veered left along the path that led to Vincent's garden and jumped up onto the kitchen window sill. There was nobody there. He ran back down the path and towards his own garden. Vincent might be draped along the top of the back wall, it was one of his favourite places. There was no sign of him. He hesitated and looked around. Vincent's morning routine was pretty standard. If he wasn't on the wall, he was most likely to be either under the laburnum tree next door or on the shed roof. If he couldn't find Vincent, Moses might know where he was. There would be no trouble finding Moses; he would be either asleep in his little basket or watching the goldfish in the garden pond. Unless he was somewhere with Vincent, of course.

Aubrey jumped as the leaves on a nearby bush suddenly parted and a startled robin flew up into the air. The sound of

164

shouting broke through the morning calm.

"Shit. Shit, shit, shit."

Molly and Jeremy were standing facing one another in the kitchen. Aubrey crept up and watched them from the doorway of the utility room. Molly's face was tight with anxiety. Clearly they had discovered the pillow in Carlos's bed.

"Where do you think that he could have gone?"

Molly's voice was small. Jeremy shrugged. His expression was hard and set.

"Who knows? I haven't got a bloody clue. Your guess is as good as mine. We have no idea how long he's been missing. He could be anywhere by now. Bloody Australia, for all I know."

"He hasn't taken any of his things with him, he can't have gone far."

Jeremy snorted.

"We don't know that he hasn't taken anything with him, do we? I have no idea what he had in those black bin liners, I didn't stand over him while he packed them. He's probably just taken out the bits that he wanted and left the rest. Let's face it, he's not going to do a runner lugging two bloody great bin bags with him, is he?"

Jeremy's tone was grim. He sat down suddenly on a kitchen chair.

"His mother's handbag is still in his room," said Molly eagerly, "he wouldn't just go off and leave that. It's about all he's got left to remind him of her. He would never leave that behind him."

"Well, I doubt very much that he would take it with him," said Jeremy. "Even in the twenty-first century, boys carrying handbags tend to be just a little bit noticeable."

He stared glumly down at the table top, his shoulders slumped.

"You know what, Moll? It looks like Rachel was right after all. Oh, she's going to love this. I can just hear her, can't you?" He gave a sudden high falsetto laugh and tilted his head to one side. "Oh well, I did warn you, Jeremy, but you wouldn't listen, would you? You would insist that you knew better, but I

165

could have told you what would happen. You can't just take children in off the street, you know, especially children like that."

"Oh, who cares what Rachel thinks?" said Molly. "She'd have something to say whatever happened. Anyway, it's none of her business."

Jeremy rubbed at the worry line between his eyes with his forefinger.

"And what are we going to tell the police? How are we going to explain this to them? Oh sorry, officer, we seem to have lost him. He must have just slipped out when we weren't looking." He leaned forward and pressed the tips of his fingers hard against his forehead. "He was supposed to be in our care. We were supposed to be looking after him."

For a moment they were both silent, and then Molly said, "All that matters is that he's out there somewhere and we don't know where. I expect he got scared. After all, he's only fourteen and it's hardly surprising after everything that's happened." She paused. "He could be in some kind of danger, for all we know. Where," she repeated, "do you think that he could have gone?"

Jeremy sighed and raised his head again. "I don't know. We know that he used to live in Camden so that's the only place that I can think of, realistically, where he might go. I think, all things considered, that it's highly unlikely that he's gone back to The Meadows, and I don't know of any other place that he's associated with apart from Brazil, and I doubt that he's got that far. I assume he's got a passport, but whether he picked it up from the flat or not, I have no idea. I don't even know if he's got any money on him. I never thought to ask him."

"What about school?" asked Molly. "Did he have any special friends or anyone that he might have gone to? Could any of the other boys be hiding him somewhere?"

Jeremy shook his head.

"I shouldn't think so. The only friends that he made at school are the likes of Caparo, and he must have worked out by now that the only thing that Caparo is likely to give him is more grief. So unless he's much more stupid than I think he is,

166

he's unlikely to have gone there for help. Anyway, the only person that Caparo is ever tempted to help is himself." He paused and reflected for a moment, tapping down on the table with the tips of his fingers. "But maybe he has gone back to the flat. Maybe I'm wrong there. Maybe he's done a sort of instinctive run-for-home thing."

"Has he still got a key?"

"I don't know," Jeremy repeated. "I suppose so. I had a key, because the police gave it to me when I brought him back here. It never occurred to me to ask him if he still had his. And even if it had, I couldn't exactly demand that he gave it to me. It wasn't mine to ask for."

Molly chewed her bottom lip for a moment.

"I suppose that we are going to have to tell the police that he's gone missing?" She said slowly, "I mean, there isn't any way round it?"

Not unless Carlos managed some miraculous escape and turned up in the next five minutes, thought Aubrey. The police would be bound to find out anyway, and then Molly and Jeremy would be in it right up to their necks.

Jeremy stood up suddenly, his expression hard and angry. Aubrey tensed slightly and suppressed the slight feeling of panic that fluttered across his stomach. He had never seen Jeremy look like that before.

"Silly little sod. Silly, silly little sod. Why couldn't he just do as he was told and stay put? Things would have got sorted out eventually. As it is, he's just managed to make everything worse for himself. Wherever it is he's gone, the police are bound to find him sooner or later. He can't stay hidden forever, and then he'll have to go to Alderman Wenlock's whether he likes it or not."

Molly walked over to the window and stood for a moment staring out at the garden.

"Maybe," she said hopefully, keeping her back to the room, "he's just gone out for a walk. Maybe he's just gone out to get some fresh air or something. He might be back any minute now."

"I doubt it." Jeremy sounded suddenly weary. "He knows

that he's not allowed out on his own. We made that very clear to him. And anyway, if he's just popped out for a breath of fresh air, why would he put a pillow in his bed? He's obviously been gone all night." He paused. "This is all my fault. I was a fool to have ever trusted him."

He crossed the room and stood next to her. Feeling that a show of solidarity was necessary, Aubrey padded over to join them.

Jeremy put his arm around Molly's shoulder and softened his voice. "Oh, come on now, don't get upset, Moll. It's not the end of the world. Maybe he just wanted some time on his own and is planning to come back. But it might have helped if he'd left a note to tell us," he added. He leaned down and kissed the top of her head. "Try not to worry about it. I've got a free period first thing. We're going to have to tell the police, I don't think we've got a choice there, but I'll go and check the flat first. There's just an outside chance that he may have gone back. I think it's unlikely but you never know, it's worth a try. I'll ring school and tell the Head that I'll be in a bit late, I'll say I've got a flat tyre or something. We don't want this getting out before it has to, and if the Head gets wind of it she'll be on her broomstick and screeching it from the rooftops before we can blink. If Carlos is at the flat, I'll bring him straight back, and with a bit of luck nobody will be any the wiser. But you know, if we can't trust him, I don't see how he can stay here. We can't be watching him day and night."

He sighed, a deep exhausted sigh, and reached across to pick up his keys from the work surface.

"I'll ring and let you know if he's there or not."

Aubrey watched him leave and then ran back out into the garden. The morning was slipping away and he still had to find Vincent.

Chapter Twenty-Seven

"Got back all right, then?"

Aubrey jumped sideways. What was it about Vincent that enabled him to appear out of nowhere? He just never saw him coming. Aubrey wouldn't be surprised if he could melt through walls.

"Moses is missing."

"What?" Aubrey stood very still and his mouth went dry. His stomach lurched suddenly downwards in exactly the same way it had when he had once been foolish enough to investigate the inside of the lift in the multi-storey car park and the doors had shut on him. That plummeting feeling when the lift shot downwards was exactly what he was experiencing now. "When you say missing…"

"Not a whisker," said Vincent.

"I thought he was with you."

Vincent shook his head.

"No, mate, I thought he was with you."

Aubrey furrowed his brow and tried to think about the last time that he had definitely seen Moses. His last clear recollection was when he had seen him hanging on to a big white cat's back. The big white cat had shaken him off and then begun to swing him round by his tail. Aubrey had started to go over to help, but he'd been waylaid by a large, fluffy orange creature, and the next time he'd looked up both the white cat and Moses had disappeared. Perhaps Moses had got frightened and run off somewhere. After all, he was only little. He had probably been the littlest cat there. But he didn't really think it was very likely. Moses might not be very big and he certainly wasn't very bright, but he was a brave little soul. There was no way that he would have deserted, even if he had been terrified.

"He'll be ok, Vin." Even to his own ears, his voice sounded shaky. "He's always ok. Remember that time he was found in that empty bus at the bus station? And what about that time when he got locked in a garage for two days..." he trailed off, and looked at Vincent's serious face.

"Nobody's seen him this morning, I've asked around," said Vincent.

"We'd better go and look for him."

Vincent nodded.

They ran quickly and lightly across the top of the wall. He could tell Vincent about Carlos on the way. From the next door garden, Carstairs paused and looked up at them from where he was busy spraying a set of large terracotta flower pots. Aubrey wasn't altogether sure about Carstairs. He couldn't quite put his paw on what it was, but it was definitely something. He had been excused from the scrap last night on the basis that apparently he was delicate, or had a heart condition and was on special tablets or something, but Aubrey wasn't altogether convinced. Carstairs didn't look particularly feeble to him. It was something about his eyes, he thought, they were just that bit too close together.

As they reached number seven, they quickened their pace. All the cats knew about Duffy, even the name was enough to strike terror into a feline heart. A small, excitable, and extremely aggressive terrier, Duffy looked like a bunch of rags with teeth. He was owned by a cat-hating widower, and it was rumoured among the cat population that he enticed cats in for Duffy to play with. Whether or not it was true, nobody was quite sure, but what was true was that at least two cats had been hit by an airgun in the vicinity of number seven, although only Moses laboured under the misapprehension that it was Duffy who had actually fired the shots.

At the last but one garden, they stopped. Skirting swiftly around the flower beds, they crept quietly up to the house. Together, they leapt silently onto the kitchen window sill and stared in. In the corner was Moses' little wicker basket, and for a moment neither cat spoke. Not only was the little basket empty, but there was a full bowl of food next to it. As they watched, a large fly zoomed in and settled on the top of it. The food had obviously been there for some time. Aubrey felt a wave of anxiety ripple through him. He turned to Vincent, his mouth suddenly dry.

"It don't look good, Aubsie." Vincent's voice was low and concerned. "I've never yet known that boy leave a scrap of food, and that's a fact."

"What do you reckon we ought to do?"

"I reckon we better go looking for him. We can start at The Laurels and work our way back."

Aubrey nodded. Bad as this morning was turning out to be, at least they could be doing something instead of just waiting. If things worked out, they would not only find Moses safe and well but Vincent might also be able to think of a way to help Carlos.

They thumped heavily down from the window sill, no need for silence now; Duffy was sufficiently far away and the house in front of them was clearly empty. They made their way slowly back along the street, keeping close to the line of the privet hedges. They were both well aware of the risk they were taking. One cat walking along would probably escape attention, but two together looked very like a conspiracy and could easily attract attention from the wrong sort. There was something about cats being together that made people feel uncomfortable. Often, it had to be said, with entirely good reason. Nevertheless, danger notwithstanding, both Aubrey and Vincent felt an unspoken need to stick together this morning.

An uncomfortable tension hung between them, their combined guilt at not having checked the whereabouts of Moses the previous night weighed heavily on the morning air and pressed against them. The secret fear of seeing a small, stiff little blood-caked body squashed up against the kerb was more than either of them could bear to contemplate. They both knew that Moses couldn't find his way out of a paper bag, let alone navigate the byways of the industrial estate. And even if by some miracle he had found his way back to the high street, they both knew the risk of wandering on the highway. Neither of them wanted to voice it, but it was odds on that Moses had blundered about looking for his way home and been hit by an oncoming car. The wisest of cats was always at risk of being hit by a vehicle, and Moses wasn't the wisest of cats.

Moses, thought Aubrey savagely, when I find you, you little twit, I'm going to teach you how to find your own way home if it's the last thing I do. He knew that it was an irrational thought, given that Moses could be starting from anywhere, but it gave him some comfort. And then there was Carlos to worry about. How he was going to find out where he was and then bring him safely back home, he still didn't have a clue. All he could hope for was that Vincent would come up with something. How was it, he wondered, that his lovely comfortable life had suddenly got so complicated? He turned his head slightly as Vincent spoke.

"Of course, there's the high street to think about, but don't worry," he added, as a look of faint worry crossed Aubrey's face. "I know a back route."

Aubrey breathed a silent sigh of relief. Good old Vinnie, trust him, he always knew a back route. Going down the high street in the morning in full daylight on his own, with all the shoppers and workers milling about, was a risky enough enterprise. With two of them travelling together, the risks were multiplied a hundredfold. If they didn't find Moses at The Laurels, they would still have to work their way back along the main thoroughfares, but at least only having to make the journey once would halve the risk.

He fell in behind Vincent as he ran swiftly across the road and veered suddenly left through a wide gap which had been made by a bomb dropped during the last war, the pilot shedding the explosives randomly as he turned for home. The house that had stood there had taken a direct hit, and the plot had never been occupied by another building. The few parts of the house that had withstood the shock of the blast had crumbled over time, and now all that was left was rubble and waste ground. The thistle and weed wavered in the breeze high above their heads. Aubrey looked around him. He had heard Molly and Jeremy talk about the bombed house but he had never found the time to explore this patch before, although he had passed it often enough. It was one of those places that had been on his list, but he had always been on his way somewhere else and so he had never got round to it. He turned enquiringly to Vincent.

"It leads out from what used to be the back garden, down a sort of track, and then across a small field," explained Vincent. "It runs past the railway line and under the bridge, and then it goes right round to the back of the high street. There's cover almost all the way."

Aubrey thought for a moment. So far, so good. They were unlikely to be troubled by anybody on the industrial estate but they still had to get access to The Laurels, which might be a problem at this time of day. The place was full of elderly people who were quite likely to be looking out of the windows or even sitting on one of the benches which had been placed in what remained of the garden at the front. Two cats together would be bound to be noticed. He thought quickly. It would probably be all right, they probably wouldn't be bothered by anybody, but it was always better to err on the side of caution. The safest plan would be for them to go in under the gate separately, unless they went round the back and got over the wall. Except, of course, the tops of the surfaces were embedded with broken glass.

"Don't forget, Vin. We can't get into the car park over the wall. The top's covered in glass. We're going to have to go round to the front and slip in under the gate separately."

Vincent grinned.

"And that, Aubsie mate, is where you're wrong. Not all of the wall has got glass on it, I clocked it last night. There's a gap about halfway across." He paused and looked around him, scanning the surrounding view with narrowed eyes, and then turned back to Aubrey. "You see, Aubs, that's where they always get it wrong. In the detail. I mean, I ask you," he shook his head sadly, "what is the bleeding point of lining all the tops of the walls with broken glass and then leaving part of it blank? You might just as well throw a ladder over it."

Aubrey nodded, relieved. He hadn't noticed the gap himself

but he'd take Vincent's word for it.

They set off across the remains of the back garden and headed down towards the track. Aubrey looked sideways at Vincent. He still hadn't told him about Carlos.

"Vin, I was planning on going back to The Laurels this morning anyway. The boy that's been staying with us, Carlos. He's in trouble."

"What sort of trouble? What's he done?"

"Nothing really."

Vincent listened carefully as he explained about Carlos. He came to a halt and looked hopefully at Vincent.

"What do you reckon, Vin? My guess is that he's in the old barn."

Vincent nodded.

"Sounds like it. Those bushes don't lead nowhere else. Well, whatever the lad's done or not done, he didn't ought to be locked up and that's a fact."

Aubrey nodded. Being locked up, deserved or not, was a cat's idea of hell. At Sunny Banks, the best times had been the mornings when there had been a quick glimpse of the world outside when the food was brought in. When that door had opened, there had been a mad feline rush towards the wire mesh of the cages. The screws had thought it was because of the prospect of being fed and had made stupid little jokes about it, which just showed how little they knew about cat psychology. Aubrey knew better. He knew that there wasn't a cat in there who wouldn't have swapped five bowls of food for a chance to roll on his back in the sunlight and feel the breeze ruffle his fur.

***

The car park of The Laurels was half-full as the two cats scrambled over the wall and crept silently across the tarmac. Aubrey noticed with a sinking heart that among them was Dave's blue van, parked in the corner. He hoped to God that Rascal was safely locked in it and not running free somewhere around the grounds.

174

"You take that half, I'll take this." Vincent's tone was terse as he indicated the space in the car park to the left of him. "When we've found Moses, we'll go over and see what's happening in the barn."

Aubrey nodded. It made sense. He sped across to the far corner of the space that Vincent had indicated and began to track his way rapidly around the edges.

***

"It's no good, Aubsie, he's not here."

Aubrey looked around him. It was true. They had searched practically every inch of the car park, including round the back of the recycling bins, and found nothing. They had even investigated the inside of a pile of wooden crates stacked against the wall, just in case Moses had crept in there injured and been unable to get out. But there was no sign of him. Great tufts of fur lay scattered about on the ground, where they had been removed from their owners during the scrap last night, but of Moses there was not a whisker.

Aubrey glanced up at the fire escape steps. It was just possible that Moses had fled back up the steps and was still up there on one of the roof levels somewhere. Or perhaps he had managed to trap himself somehow in some of the guttering and was unable to climb out. He hoped to God that he hadn't fallen down one of the drain pipes and was stuck. They would never get him out.

He looked at Vincent and together they slipped quickly up the steps, glancing in at the windows as they passed each floor. Some of the rooms were occupied now. In one of them, someone was sitting at a piano and banging tunelessly on the keys. In the room next to it, a group of people were sitting around a table playing what looked like a game of cards. Aubrey was interested to see that one of them was sitting on what looked like some spare cards. He could just see the white edges poking out from under the woman's skirt.

They reached the top and ran quickly along the ledge, Vincent veering off to the right while Aubrey began to search the roof levels to his left. There was even more up here than he had realised last night. It was huge. The levels and chimneys seemed to go on for ever. Moses could be anywhere. He let out a low deep growl. If Moses was up here, he would surely hear and reply. He waited for a second. No response.

He hurried along the different levels, jumping from one to the next and keeping up a low, continuous growl. His heart beat fast as tiny little jet flames of panic began to shoot upwards in his brain and form silent pleadings. If the worst had happened, please don't let it have hurt him. And let it have been quick. Please don't let Moses have suffered. He reached the far side and began to make his way back just as the first few drops of rain began to fall. Coming round the other side and almost colliding with him, ran Vincent.

Vincent shook his head.

"He's not up here. I've searched every inch. Let's go and check the old barn and see what's happening, and then we'd better start making our way back."

Chapter Twenty-Eight

The two cats scrambled quickly up the side of the barn and peered down through the hole in the roof. In the corner, standing with his back against the wall and his head in his hands, was Carlos.

"What do you reckon, Vin?"

"I don't know. It's a tough one." Vincent frowned. "He could stand on something to reach the hole in the roof but he won't be able to get through it, it's too small."

Aubrey nodded.

"I reckon you're right. But there must be something that we can do. We can't just leave him here like this."

He stiffened suddenly. From down below came the faintest of snuffling sounds. Together, the two cats crept back to the edge of the roof and looked over. There beneath them, nose to the ground, his wiry little body trotting happily in and out of the bushes, was Rascal. Aubrey's heart sank. That was all they needed. If he spotted them up there on the roof, they'd be trapped for hours. He stared down in despair.

"Don't worry, Aubsie." Vincent gave a wry smile. "I know his sort. He'll get bored in a minute and go away. We'll just have to wait him out."

Aubrey nodded gloomily. It didn't look like they had much choice. He opened his mouth to speak and then stopped. Coming into view was one trainer-clad foot, followed immediately by the rest of Rick. From below came the sound of the padlock being taken from the door. Aubrey and Vincent looked at each other and moved swiftly back towards the hole in the roof.

"Still here then?"

Rick laughed, a mirthless barking noise that sounded slightly rusty, as if he didn't make it very often. Even from where they were standing on the roof, Aubrey and Vincent could smell the pungent odour that wafted upwards. A stifling tangle of cheap aftershave, stale body odour, and alcohol seeped into the atmosphere and collided head-on with the stench that was already present. They watched as Carlos dropped to the floor and hunched defensively into himself.

Aubrey and Vincent crouched low. The rain that had been no more than a slight spit earlier now began to spatter against their backs and drum on the corrugated metal of the roof. The two cats peered down the hole. Had the man looked upwards, he would have seen four feline eyes watching him intently.

Carlos remained in his sitting position. He made an almost imperceptible move in order to push his back slightly straighter against the wall and bring his knees up closer to his chest. Aubrey could see the whites on the knobs of his knuckles as he locked his hands tightly around his shins.

"What's up? Cat got your tongue?"

Vincent nudged Aubrey in the ribs and they grinned at each other. From below came the sound of a short, excited yelp. Rascal had obviously found something interesting among the bushes.

The man crouched down and sat on his haunches. Pulling a small, flat half bottle of whisky from his pocket, he unscrewed the cap and took a huge gulp. Giving a long, slow sigh of satisfaction, he ran the tip of his tongue around his lips as if to savour every last drop. Aubrey and Vincent watched as Carlos shrank away from him. The man straightened up again and stared down into Carlos's eyes, his head slightly to one side as though considering.

"I expect your mum and dad are getting worried about you by now, Dan. They're probably wondering where you are."

He looked thoughtful and tipped his head to the other side while he waited for Carlos to answer.

Carlos spoke, his voice low.

"I ain't got no mum and dad."

"Who do you live with then?"

"Nobody. I don't live with nobody."

The man crouched down again and took another swig from the bottle in his pocket. He stared intently into Carlos's face.

Even from the roof, Aubrey and Vincent could feel the sudden cold tension that had crept into the atmosphere. Aubrey looked at Vincent in alarm. Whatever was happening now, they were into new territory. As if to echo his fears, a sudden clap of thunder shook the barn and a streak of lightning cracked across the sky, turning the light from a dull, pearl grey to a livid, purple-tinged yellow. From outside, the intensity of Rascal's barking increased.

Vincent turned to Aubrey, his voice low and concerned.

"I don't like the look of this, Aubsie mate. This bloke don't look like the full ticket to me."

Aubrey nodded. He agreed. He was starting to think that this bloke was like the human equivalent of Rupert, except that he was worse. Rupert didn't drink, or not as far as he was aware, anyway. Tough as it was being stuck up here on the roof with Rascal just below them waiting to rip their innards out the second he noticed them, he'd rather be up here than in there with that man. He stared down, transfixed by the scene that was unfolding in front of them. He felt his body tense and shiver slightly as the man continued speaking, lowering his voice and dropping his tone to a calm, almost conversational level. To Aubrey's ears, it sounded more threatening than if he'd been shouting. He watched the man's face. His skin had become pale and glistened with sweat, and his eyes were like glass.

"Liars must be beaten. That's what my grandma used to say."

His voice was flat and hard. He paused and stared straight upwards for a moment. Aubrey stiffened and held his breath. He was looking right at them. His glance swung away back to Carlos, seemingly unaware that he had just made eye contact with two cats on the roof. Aubrey slowly let his breath out again.

"I lived with my grandma when I was young, Dan. We all did. Me and my brothers. Our mum didn't want us. She went off with some bloke to Manchester. We didn't have anywhere else to go, so Social Services put us in with Grandma." He looked thoughtful, as though he was trying to remember. "All of us boys, four of us together, packed into Grandma's little house like human sardines. Cosy. You like sardines?"

Carlos shook his head.

"No," Rick agreed. "Me neither."

He paused and drew a packet of cigarettes from his pocket. "Smoke?"

Carlos nodded, his eyes never leaving the man's face. Rick lit a cigarette for himself and then passed one to Carlos and flicked his lighter across the end of it.

For several moments, they sat and smoked together in silence and then Rick said, "She didn't mind anyway, she liked it."

"What?" Carlos looked confused.

"Grandma. She liked us all living with her, because she got the money off Social Services for looking after us. She said she'd never been so well off. But you know what?"

Carlos shook his head. Rick's eyes narrowed.

"I hated her. We all did. We were glad when she died. I wouldn't tell most people that, Dan, but I can tell you because we're mates."

Carlos nodded enthusiastically.

"We were planning to kill her anyway," he continued casually. He paused and stared up at the plume of blue smoke curling from his cigarette, a faraway look in his eyes. "It was my idea. I wrote it up in an exercise book that I nicked from school. It was a proper plan, with times and what we were all going to say when the police came, and everything. I watched a lot of those cop shows on the telly, I knew what sort of things they'd ask us. We were going to break the kitchen window and then kill her with the bread knife. We were going to take her purse and chuck some things around, and then pretend that the house got broken into and we found her like that when we came home from school. We wouldn't even have to wear gloves in case of fingerprints or anything. We didn't need to, we lived there. But we didn't have to kill her in the end." He sounded almost regretful. "She dropped dead of a heart attack."

He jumped up suddenly and began to stride about the barn.

Three pairs of eyes watched him in alarm as he set off first in one direction and then veered off sharply in another, as though he'd just forgotten something.

"I burnt the exercise book, just in case someone found it." He pulled up sharply and turned to face Carlos. He laughed. "It was a good plan, though. I tried it out later," he added. "Some bloke who had a shop. I wanted to see what it felt like. It was good."

Aubrey felt his heart jolt. Raj. So that was what it had all been about. Target practice for this mad bloke. And as a result, Raj had died and his own life had changed forever.

"I never got caught for it. They never even questioned me. He was only some old paki anyway."

Aubrey stared down at his paws. As it was in life, so it was in death. Raj hadn't mattered to anyone then and he didn't matter to anyone now. Except to Aubrey. He had mattered to Aubrey.

Chapter Twenty-Nine

Aubrey and Vincent remained crouched, mesmerised by the scene unfolding below. Below them, Rascal continued to snuffle around the bushes.

"We all got split up after Grandma died. First off, we got sent to that children's home, that Alderman Wenlock place, and then they put us into separate foster homes and tried to get us adopted. Well, not me, they said nobody would want me because I was too old, but my brothers, they tried to get families for them. I tried to keep in touch with them afterwards. I tried to check and see if they were all right and that, but they kept moving them around so it was difficult to keep track of them. Leon, he got sent to Derby. I don't know why." The man stared mournfully at Carlos. "Maybe it was because he was a different colour to the rest of us."

He paused and stared into the middle distance. Aubrey watched as Carlos surreptitiously dropped his hand down to scratch his leg. He was obviously trying as hard as he could not to break the man's train of thought. As long as the man was talking, he wasn't thinking about performing acts of violence.

"After I left school, I used to go back in my lunch hours from work sometimes and wait outside the school gate to see if any of them came out. That's how I found Jed again. That caretaker, though, he used to come out and tell me to clear off. He threatened to get the police on me once. Like I was some kind of pervert or something." The man looked affronted. "Anyway, he's on my list."

Aubrey watched as Carlos smiled slightly and nodded sympathetically. Clever lad. He was trying to make a relationship with the man. Under the circumstances, it was about the only option he had, but he was smart to have worked it out. The bloke was clearly crazy, but then Carlos had some experience with lunatics. He'd lived with Maria for the first fourteen years of his life.

"My grandma, she was a dear old lady. She used to get the tea and cakes out when the social workers came visiting. And then she used to beat us."

Rick smiled suddenly, a wide split of a smile that showed the strange gaps in his teeth and lit up his eyes.

"She had this old school cane that used to hang over the arm of her chair, and we all had to take our pyjamas off and line up for it every morning. All of us, even Jed. He wasn't even old enough to be at school. She used to do it in the sitting room with all the curtains closed before we got dressed. And then we had to say, 'Thank you, Grandma.' She said it was to stop us being bad. She said that we'd be grateful later on."

He laughed again, the same rough barking noise that Aubrey and Vincent had heard earlier, and dropped the end of his cigarette to the floor, grinding it hard under his trainer. He moved across the room towards Carlos and dropped down beside him again. He put an arm around his shoulder.

"I like The Laurels. It's good here." He pulled the bottle from his pocket with his free hand and took another swig. "I don't even have to do anything much, just open and close the place and generally keep an eye on things. See to some of the maintenance and that. You know what, Dan? It's the first proper home I've had really." He swayed slightly and put out a hand to steady himself. "After I left Alderman Wenlock and started working, they got me a bedsit. Just a room in this big house. It had a sink and a gas ring in it, and a bathroom along the corridor that I had to share with everyone else. At The Laurels, I've got a proper flat with a kitchen and a shower and everything." Aubrey heard the sudden note of pride in his voice. "I couldn't believe it when they gave me the job. That was down to Dave, really. I would never have got it if it hadn't been for him. He's got contacts on the Council." He snorted. "He's got contacts everywhere. Do you know Dave?" he added conversationally.

Carlos shook his head.

"I met him in the Coach and Horses one night. He

183

remembered my mum. She'd done him a couple of favours in the past. So when I told him that I was fed up with where I was working at the factory, he got me the job here. There's only one thing that I don't like about The Laurels, only one thing that spoils it." The man leaned closer to Carlos and lowered his voice slightly. Aubrey could see that Carlos was trying not to recoil from the whisky-laden breath. "It's the old people. I don't like them, Dan. If it wasn't for them, this place would be perfect."

Had it ever occurred to him, Aubrey wondered, that he might be in the wrong job?

"One of them threatened me, you know." The tone of injured innocence was unmistakeable. "Honestly. Can you believe it?"

Aubrey watched Carlos's expression as he opened his mouth to speak and then closed it again. The question had clearly been rhetorical. Rick pulled out his bottle of whisky again and took another huge gulp before continuing.

"She said that she knew I was up to something. She said that she'd come across the likes of me before. Which was quite rude really, when you think about it." He paused and frowned down at Carlos, waiting for confirmation. Carlos nodded back at him. "Anyway," he continued, "she'd been poking around in the attic rooms. Which she shouldn't have been," he added, the righteous tone back in his voice. "They know very well that some places are out of bounds so she didn't have no business up there. No business at all. Well," he shrugged his shoulders and spread his hands in front of him. "I had to do something, didn't I?"

Carlos nodded in agreement again, his face passive.

"She came up to me one day when I was cleaning the ground floor windows and said that they knew all about what was going on, her and those old bitches Bradshaw and Lomax that she used to hang about with. She said that she'd actually spoken to one of them through the door. She knew Swahili or something." He fell silent for a moment as though thinking. "She said that her dad used to be some sort of vicar in one of those places. Trust her," he added bitterly. "If we'd had giant pandas in there, she would have spoken giant panda as well. She was that sort. Annoying, if you know what I mean. Anyway, I tried to explain it to her. I told her that what me and Dave were doing was actually a good thing. I said that it was their choice. Nobody was forcing them. They wanted to do it so that they could get a better life, better than the one that they had in their own country anyway. I said that what we were doing was helping them. We were bringing them over here and helping them to make a future for themselves. We were doing them a service. Obviously we couldn't do it for free, could we? I mean, we had to cover our costs."

Aubrey watched as Carlos started to shake his head and then changed his mind and nodded instead. It was obviously the right reaction. Rick smiled down at him.

"You know what she said, Dan? She said, 'Tell that to the judge.' And then she stuck her hand out, literally, stuck it out right under my nose, and asked me for money. She said that they wanted it for a coach trip to Margate. I was shocked," he added. "I mean, she used to be a school teacher."

At last Carlos found his voice.

"Did you give it to her?"

"Oh yeah, I gave it to her all right." Rick smiled his frightening wide smile again. "And the other two. I was going to leave them alone at first. I reckoned they'd be frightened enough, but then when I thought about it later, well, I had to really, didn't I?" Aubrey heard the chilling tone of reason in his tone. "The thing is, I didn't really have much choice, Dan. I couldn't just leave them, could I? Not after they knew and everything. And it weren't like they mattered or anything. They were practically dead anyway."

And then suddenly the man laughed again, but it was a different laugh this time, a terrifyingly high-pitched squealing noise that seemed to gurgle up in his throat and bounce out across the walls. It reminded Aubrey of some of the noises that he'd heard from the abattoir on the edge of town. He shivered and watched as a trickle of sweat slid down the side of Carlos's forehead.

Rick suddenly dropped his arm from Carlos's shoulder and

straightened up again. He reached into his pocket for the bottle and stared at it. It was nearly empty.

"Did you tell Dave?"

Carlos was keeping his tone deliberately even, Aubrey realised. He was trying to keep the man talking. The man shook his head.

"No. He's a funny bloke, Dave. He might not have liked it. Even though," he added, "I was doing it for the business." He rubbed at his eyes as though he was tired. "I waited a while to see what would happen about Jenkins. But you know what? Nothing. Nothing happened. I waited for the police to come calling, but when they did, they just asked a few questions about when she used to come to The Laurels, what days she was here, and what clubs she joined. They wanted to know who her friends were and stuff like that. Even when they found Lomax and Bradshaw, they just came and asked the same questions and then they went away again."

For a moment he was silent, and then he continued, a slight note of regret in his voice.

"One thing that worried me, though, one thing that I was a bit bothered about, was old Telling. I didn't really mean to hurt him, it was just an accident. I felt a bit bad about that."

Aubrey caught his breath.

"He wasn't mates with that old cow Jenkins and her crew, but he looked like he knew something. I could tell. It was the way he looked at me, sort of sideways. And then once, I saw him standing near the bottom of the stairs and he had this sort of funny look on his face. And I thought, what if he's just been up to the attics? I couldn't take the chance, so I went round to his place one day to see if I could reason with him. I thought I could get him to understand. The funny thing was," he paused as though puzzled and then continued, "he kept acting like he didn't know what I was talking about. I got a bit annoyed. But it wasn't my fault that he hit his head. He shouldn't have wound me up by pretending not to know what I was on about. I only sort of shoved him a bit, and he fell backwards..." He sighed and sniffed. "Actually, I've still got the key to his place. I keep meaning to go round and see if there's anything worth having."

Carlos nodded back at him, as if understanding his viewpoint entirely. The man stopped and looked at him closely, as if he was seeing him properly for the first time. He frowned.

"I need to go back up to the house for a couple of minutes and check that everything's running ok this morning. I won't be long. Stay here till I get back."

Like Carlos had a choice, thought Aubrey.

Rick suddenly reached forward and gripped Carlos by the front of his parka with one hand while he felt into his inside pocket with the other. The air of companionship evaporated instantly and was replaced by a chill that descended into the atmosphere like the first fall of snow. Aubrey shuddered. This bloke's moods came and went more quickly than Rupert's. He watched, appalled, as he caught the glint of metal in Rick's hand as he pulled out a long knife. Leaning over Carlos, he ran the tip gently along his cheek.

"Missing you already."

The two cats watched as the man let go of Carlos and strode over to the door. From outside came the sound of the padlock being locked back into place. Without hesitating, Aubrey dropped down noiselessly through the hole in the roof, followed immediately by Vincent. They had to think of a way to get Carlos out of there, and they had to think quick. Carlos looked up, startled at the two cats sitting silently in front of him.

"Aubrey. Oh, mate."

Carlos reached forward and clutched Aubrey to his narrow chest. Aubrey waited for a moment and then gently pulled away. Carlos stared into Aubrey's golden green eyes. Aubrey stared back. He sat quietly as Carlos leaned over and stroked his fingertips across his head. He turned and stroked Vincent with his other hand, running his palm across the top of Vincent's sleek head and down under his chin. He dipped his head slightly to read the name on Vincent's collar, and then stopped suddenly and reached into his pocket. With a trembling hand, he pulled out the leaflet which he'd stuffed in there earlier and on which he'd written a message. Aubrey tensed slightly. He hoped that Carlos wasn't having any silly ideas about trying to put it into one of their mouths to carry home. That sort of thing was dogs' work. You couldn't ask a cat to do it.

Carlos stared around the barn, clearly looking for inspiration. The cats watched him unblinking as his hand strayed, as it always did in moments of uncertainty, to his earring. He twisted it slowly round, a glittering fake diamond stud that he'd bought for three pounds on the market. As they watched, a slow small smile spread across his face. With fumbling fingers, he pulled his earring from his ear and pushed the post through the leaflet. He stretched his hand towards Vincent.

"Vincent, Vincent. Come here."

Vincent looked sideways at Aubrey who nodded back at him. Vincent moved an inch closer. Carlos reached across and pushed the post of the earring through one of the holes in Vincent's collar, fastening it with the fake diamond on the other side.

Vincent opened his mouth to speak and then stiffened. From outside came the very faintest rustle of a tread on the grass.

"Quick, Aubs, move it. It sounds like he's coming back."

Together Vincent and Aubrey flew back up the wall and out through the hole in the roof. Aubrey paused for a moment to get his breath.

"That was close."

Vincent nodded. The note attached to his collar fluttered in the cold wind. He lifted his face to the air and then turned to Aubrey.

"Notice something?"

Aubrey pricked his ears and grinned.

"Rascal's gone."

As soon as he'd said it, he knew that they had spoken too soon. From below came the sudden sound of hysterical yapping. Leaping and snarling at the barn wall, trying to reach the cats that he had just spotted on the roof, was Rascal. And just behind him were Dave and Rick.

Chapter Thirty

"What the merry bloody Ellen's going on here, Rick?"

Dave's voice soared upwards and crashed out through the hole in the roof as he strode across the barn floor towards Carlos.

Up on the roof, Aubrey and Vincent looked at each other.

"That's done it," said Vincent. "We should have made a run for it while we had the chance."

He stared down at Rascal who had re-doubled his efforts to fling himself onto the roof, his short, wiry body leaping high into the air and twisting upwards in half-hoops. Aubrey nodded, his brow furrowed.

"Do you reckon we could chance it, take a risk? What do you think? As long as Dave's here, the lad will be safe. He wouldn't dare do anything while he's in there. If we jump down the other side and then just make a run for it, we could be halfway home before Rascal's worked out what's happened."

"Yeah, but if he catches up with us…"

They both turned back to the hole in the roof as Dave's voice continued to crash through the morning air.

"What's that boy doing in here? What's going on?"

They watched as Dave reached suddenly into his jeans pocket and pulled out a grubby handkerchief.

"Christ, that smell." He stuffed the handkerchief across his nose. "Who's the kid?"

"It's all right," said Rick. "He's my little brother."

Carlos, Aubrey, and Vincent looked at the man in astonishment.

"I didn't know you had a little brother living round here," said Dave suspiciously. "You've never mentioned him before."

"I don't have to tell you everything." Rick's tone was

belligerent.

"Actually, mate," said Dave, "you do. Anyway, he'd better keep his mouth shut."

"Course he will, won't you, Dan? He's family."

Carlos swallowed and nodded. Dave looked doubtful.

"Have you been drinking again?"

Rick shook his head.

"Anyway, I've been thinking," continued Dave. "The first thing we've got to do is sort out this mess in here." He nodded towards the rolled-up carpet. "And then I reckon we should wind up the business altogether and quit while we're ahead. We've had a good run. We've only got a few left to sort out. I can make some phone calls and then we can get them moved on quick. That just leaves the greenhouse to sort out before the police come snouting around again."

"I told you before. They've been round already asking their questions. Why should they come back?"

Dave snorted.

"Get real, mate. There's a body count of five and rising. Think about it. The Laurels is one of the things that all those people had in common. At the very least, the police are going to be back to ask more questions from the rest of the crumblies. Christ, it's just our luck. We get the perfect set-up going here and then some crumbly-hating psycho starts running loose." He wiped a large, fat hand across his brow, which had started to sweat. "Anyway, you know as well as I do what the Old Bill are like. They're like damp. Once they're in, you can't get rid of them. They could turn up again at any minute. We were just lucky the last time they came that we'd moved a set on the night before."

"They didn't all use The Laurels. That Brazilian woman that got herself killed over at The Meadows, she didn't use The Laurels, did she? She didn't have anything to do with this place."

Aubrey tensed. He hoped that Carlos wasn't about to hear something that he didn't need to.

"No, mate. But there's still a connection. She was old Telling's cleaner. More to the point, she was one of my bloody

190

tenants." He pulled his jacket off and sat down heavily on a large oil drum, which buckled dangerously beneath him. Aubrey stared with interest at the large wet patches that had started spreading across the underarms of his plaid shirt, turning the faded red into a deep crimson. "Christ, if the police pick up on The Meadows racket, I've had it. But I tell you what." Dave's mouth set in a grim line. "If they do get on to it, I'll take the rest of them down with me, I swear. There'll be a few less Councillors and Officers at the next housing committee meeting, that's for sure," he added.

For a moment neither man spoke, and then Dave said slowly, "Swear to me that you had nothing to do with any of this. Swear on your life."

"I told you before. I swear. It's got nothing to do with me. Don't keep saying it. Anyway, why would I? What reason have I got?"

"You tell me." Dave narrowed his eyes and sucked on his teeth. "You know what, Rick? I'm beginning to think that you were one of my less good ideas."

"You didn't say that when you wanted me to work at The Laurels. I seem to think that you thought then it was a very good idea. In fact, if I recall correctly, you said that running into me was a golden opportunity."

Dave stared at him with his small blue eyes, and chewed thoughtfully on the side of his thumb.

"And then there's the small matter of that," he said, changing tack. He dabbed at his sweating face with his grubby handkerchief and nodded towards the rolled-up carpet which was still pushed up against the wall.

"That's all right. I'll take care of that." Rick smiled his bright, alarming smile. "Me and Dan will put it in your van, won't we, Dan?"

Carlos smiled, a small sickly smile, and nodded.

"Oh, really. You're going to put it in my van, are you? And then what are you going to do with it, take it for a drive?" Dave demanded.

"The canal, maybe…"

"Oh yeah, right, of course. Obviously. And how long do

you think it would be before it went floating past all the sodding anglers on the bank?"

"All right then, I'll take it somewhere else. I'll take Dan with me in the van," he repeated.

Aubrey watched nervously as Rick's hand slid into his inside pocket.

"Just shut up and listen," said Dave. "We've got to think quickly and we've got to make a plan. There's the greenhouse to sort out, too, don't forget."

From outside, Rascal's barking reached frenzy point.

"Can't you stop that bloody mutt barking? It's getting on my nerves."

The two cats on the roof tensed as Dave strode across the barn and pulled the door open. Reaching out with one hand, he dragged the protesting Rascal backwards into the barn by his collar.

Vincent nudged Aubrey.

"Quick, mate. Before they come out again."

In the time it took for Dave to kick the barn door shut again, the two cats streamed down the side of the barn. To their left, Carlos's scarf still lay where it had fallen, the cheerful blue and yellow stripes draped among the bushes.

Chapter Thirty-One

Aubrey and Vincent ran lightly down the street, their paws hitting the pavement in perfect unison. Ahead of them, parked outside Molly and Jeremy's house, sat a police squad car. Aubrey drew to a standstill and turned to Vincent.

Vincent narrowed his eyes. "Looks like the Old Bill's here again."

Turning down the garden path, they sidled round the open kitchen door and then paused on the threshold, hesitating for a moment in the shadows. Neither cat liked entering a room in which there were quite so many people, especially when one of them was Rachel. In the kitchen, chaos seemed to be reigning supreme. Molly was crying and trying not to, while Jeremy was shouting. All the available light appeared to be blocked by big people in uniform. In the background, being supremely unhelpful, hovered the large presence of Rachel.

"I'm telling you, if I had any idea where he's gone, I'd tell you." Jeremy's voice crashed into the little available space that remained, and he thumped on the table with a closed fist to emphasise his point. "Why wouldn't I tell you? What reason would I have? For God's sake, I don't know any more about the boy than you do."

"He was in your care," murmured Rachel, and helped herself to another biscuit from the tin.

Jeremy turned to her furiously. His normally cheerful face was bright red and his eyes were as close to a bulge as Aubrey had ever seen.

"I know that, thank you," he spat through gritted teeth.

"So," said the largest officer, lowering his bulk down onto one of the kitchen chairs and flicking open a small notebook, "let's just run through this again, shall we, sir?"

Jeremy collapsed onto the chair next to him and ran his

hand across his forehead.

"I've told you. We've been through all this before. Molly and I were having breakfast. Carlos hadn't come down. At first we thought that he'd overslept, and then we called him and he wasn't there. That's it. There's nothing else to say."

"But you didn't think to inform us for at least another hour?"

"No," said Jeremy flatly. "I didn't inform you for at least another hour."

"And why would that be, sir? I mean," he added helpfully, as though further explanation was needed, "was there a particular reason why you didn't feel that it was necessary to notify us immediately?"

"Because…" Jeremy exhaled a great lungful of air and then almost visibly wilted down.

"Yes, sir?" said the officer, pen poised eagerly over his notebook.

"Because…" Jeremy looked across at Molly and shrugged his shoulders. "Because, I don't know, I suppose I thought that Carlos might have just gone out for some fresh air, or maybe he had gone back to the flat where he lived, perhaps just to be to be on his own for a while. The boy has just lost his mother, you know, and in particularly horrible circumstances. Everybody seems to be forgetting that."

The officer nodded and then added thoughtfully, "He also happens to be an important witness in relation to her murder, if not an actual suspect."

"If he's a suspect, then it's only because you can't find anyone else," snapped Jeremy.

"Possibly." The officer smiled sadly.

"If you really thought he was such a danger to the public, then he should have been placed in custody and not just left free to roam the streets."

"Not free to roam the streets, Jeremy," said Rachel, through a mouthful of biscuit. "He was supposed to be here with you and Molly."

"Anyway, all his things are still here, they're still in his room, so he can't have gone far," said Molly. Aubrey watched as she twisted and squeezed the crumpled tissue in her hand. "You can go up and have a look, if you like."

The police officer tipped his head and gave a slight nod to a young policewoman who had been standing unobtrusively by the door to the hall. Aubrey turned his head to look as she slipped out and ran lightly up the stairs.

"Would you like some more tea, Officer?"

Rachel, who had clearly designated herself as Only Person Present With Any Common Sense, lifted the kettle and waved it slightly in the air. Molly stood up and walked purposefully towards her.

"Thank you, Rachel." Grabbing the kettle from Rachel with rather more force than Aubrey thought was strictly necessary, Molly smiled sweetly at her. "It was so good of you to come and see if there was anything that you could do to help, but you mustn't let us keep you. I'm sure that a busy person like you has lots of important things to do this morning."

Torn between maintaining her position as incredibly busy person with lots of important things to do and wanting to stay and see the fun, the latter won.

"Actually, I was calling round to leave some more tickets for our fund-raising for Bishop's. I thought that you might take some into work, Molly. It's the Bishop Caulfield Gala Fun evening next Friday," she added, turning to the police officer. "Would you like some tickets, Officer?"

The policeman shook his head. Rachel continued, unabashed.

"But of course, as soon as I saw the police car outside, I knew that there must be something wrong."

"Nothing gets past you, eh, Rachel?" said Jeremy, flatly. Aubrey suppressed a snigger.

Rachel turned to the police officer and raised her eyebrows and then turned back to Molly, composing her face into a sweetly patient smile and laying her rather alarmingly large hand over Molly's small one.

At his side, Aubrey felt Vincent nudge him.

"Come on, Aubsie mate. The sooner we get this over with, the sooner we can carry on looking for Moses. We've wasted half the morning as it is."

Aubrey emerged from the shadow of the door and walked towards Jeremy, tail in the air. Vincent followed.

"Aubrey!" Molly leaned down and gave him an affectionate stroke across his back. "Have you brought your friend in with you?"

The police officer looked over at Vincent and frowned.

"She seems to have something stuck on her collar." He bent down as he spoke and lifted Vincent on to his lap. "Come on, puss, there's a good girl."

Vincent narrowed his eyes and glared down at Aubrey, who looked quickly away to hide the grin that was threatening to break out.

The police officer twisted his head sideways to look at Vincent's collar.

"It's probably a note from its owners, asking people not to feed it. It's probably been begging at people's doors," said Rachel. Vincent transferred his glare and stared at her in outrage.

"Well, I'll be buggered." The police officer stood up, still holding Vincent round the middle, and stared down at Jeremy.

"What?"

"It looks like a note, a note from the lad. From Carlos."

At that moment, the young female police officer slipped back into the kitchen.

"Most of his things are still here, sir. Including his mobile phone."

She held it out as she spoke, the small cheap pay-as-you-go lying flat on the palm of her hand.

Chapter Thirty-Two

Aubrey sat up suddenly at the sound of the front door opening and the murmur of voices in the hall. Jeremy must be back. He listened for a moment to the tread on the stairs, and then jumped off the quilt on which he'd been preparing to curl up asleep. He slipped underneath the bed just as Molly and Jeremy came into the room. He was exhausted. He had only just got back himself.

While Jeremy had gone with the police to find Carlos, he had been out searching, too. He and Vincent had scoured the neighbourhood for Moses, but to no avail. There had been neither sight nor sound of him. They had scanned every kerbside, peered down every alleyway, and checked under every parked car en route, but they had found nothing. Short of rounding up all the other cats and mounting a full search party – and he was half-thinking that it was looking as though that was what it would come to – he couldn't think what else they could do. Still, as Raj used to say when Bitch didn't turn up asking for money, no news is good news. Actually Raj used to say no Bitch is good news, but it meant the same thing. So while they weren't entirely certain that Moses was alive, they weren't entirely certain that he was dead either, and that had to be a good thing.

He lay quietly and listened to the sound of the running water from the shower room and the faint burr of the electric toothbrush as Jeremy began to clean his teeth. It was far too early for Molly and Jeremy to be going to bed, it was still light outside. Perhaps Jeremy felt the need to clean himself after everything that had been happening. He knew that feeling. After getting sprung from Sunny Banks, he had felt exactly the same himself.

Jeremy walked back into the bedroom, toothbrush still in

hand. From his hiding place beneath the bed, Aubrey watched the restless movement of Jeremy's legs as he shifted from one foot to the other. Little drips from his toothbrush began to fall and soak into the carpet. Molly sat down on the edge of the bed, the bottom of her cotton dress forming a curtain in front of his line of vision. He shrank further into the shadow as she reached down and straightened the edge of the quilt that he'd rumpled when he'd jumped off the bed.

There was silence for a moment and then Molly said, "So what's been happening? Is Carlos all right? Did you find him? I've been waiting all day for you to ring."

"Sorry. I did try a couple of times but you didn't pick up."

"I couldn't. I was on the phone at work. I tried to ring you back but you didn't answer. Why didn't you leave a message or text me?"

"I thought in the end that it would be better to wait until I got home."

Aubrey's mouth went suddenly dry. Jeremy's voice sounded really serious. What had happened? Why couldn't Jeremy leave a message? He braced himself in readiness for whatever was coming next.

"Anyway, there wasn't much time. Everything seemed to happen quite fast," said Jeremy. "When we got in the police car, one of the officers radioed for assistance in case there was trouble and then we drove straight to The Laurels. When we got there, they told me to stay in the car. I didn't, obviously," he added. "But we couldn't find Carlos anyway. He wasn't anywhere in the house. We searched in every room."

Molly was silent for a moment and then she said, "So where was he?"

"In the end, someone thought of the old barn, and there he was." Jeremy paused for a moment. "I used to play in there when I was a kid. We all did. The old man that lived there used to come out and chase us off. That was half the fun, waiting for him to come out and start shouting."

"And?"

There was a strained silence and then Jeremy said, "There was blood everywhere. I've never seen anything like it."

"Oh, my God."

Aubrey crept out from under the bed. What did it matter now that he shouldn't be in the bedroom? He sat in stunned silence at Molly's feet. This was all his fault. He and Vincent should have stayed on the roof. They wouldn't have been able to do anything, but at least the last image that Carlos had seen would have been two friendly faces. He would have known that they were there. He wouldn't have died alone. Aubrey stared at the carpet. He had let Raj down and now he had let Carlos down, too.

He looked up miserably as Jeremy continued talking.

"It wasn't Carlos's blood, it was Dave's."

Molly and Aubrey stared at him in astonishment.

"Dave? Dave the builder?"

Jeremy nodded.

"The same."

"What on earth was Dave doing in the barn?"

"It appears that, in addition to his building business, he's the driving force, literally, behind a little racket along the lines of immigration-r-us. When Dave was supposedly off in his caravan at the seaside or visiting his elderly mother, he was actually taking his van across the Channel and bringing illegal immigrants back here to The Laurels. He was in it right up to his fat, little armpits. There were three men hidden up in the attics. The police found them when they were searching for Carlos.

"Dave and his partner had a regular thing going. Dave would pick the men up, bring them back, and then after a couple of days he would move them on to another address somewhere in the Midlands. It was the perfect set-up. Only the ground and first floor of The Laurels are ever used, and it's deserted at night. Plus the fact that it is right in the middle of the industrial estate, so there are no nosey neighbours to notice any comings and goings. Once all the old folk had gone home for the day, Dave and his partner could come and go as they liked."

"His partner?"

"Dave's new best friend. Rick Caparo, older brother of Jed,

and the soon-to-be former caretaker of The Laurels. The pair of them were also doing a nice little line in growing cannabis in the derelict greenhouse."

"Caparo? Isn't that the boy who got Carlos into all the trouble in the first place? The boy who was..."

"Waving a gun around in the newsagents." Jeremy finished the sentence for her. "The same. It's funny, I haven't seen the older Caparo since the day he left school, but I would have recognised him anywhere. He hasn't changed much."

"What about Carlos? Is he all right?"

"He's fine. Well, as fine as you can be when you've just been held hostage by a complete nutter. When we burst in, he was just sitting on the floor. He looked dazed. He didn't say a word. He just sort of kept looking at me and blinking. A bit like Aubrey when we brought him home from the rescue centre, do you remember?"

Aubrey remembered all right. From the time that they'd helped him into the cat basket that they'd brought with them, right through to the next morning when he'd woken up and found himself parked next to a warm radiator with a bowl of food beside him, he'd been in a kind of daze. He had half-suspected that Molly and Jeremy would suddenly sweep in and say that it was all a mistake, that they'd got the wrong cat, and then they would bundle him back into the cat basket and cart him off to Sunny Banks again, where they'd swap him for one of the cute kittens.

"So, is Dave... is he..."

"No." Jeremy shook his head. "He's alive, but only just. According to the statement that Carlos gave later, Dave and Caparo started arguing and Caparo just reached into his jacket and pulled a knife on him. I think that we got there just about in the nick of time. Dave's lost a lot of blood and they've taken him off to the hospital, but they think that he'll probably survive. According to one of the ambulance men, it was only having so much lard around his middle that saved him. Otherwise, he'd have been a goner. He had his little dog with him. It was just sitting next to him. They've taken it to the rescue centre."

200

Molly stood up suddenly.

"I need a drink."

Aubrey lay across Jeremy's lap, his chin resting on Jeremy's forearm. He looked across at Molly as she sipped carefully at her wine. She looked very pale. He wasn't surprised. He was probably pale himself, under all his fur.

"So how did Carlos end up in there with them?"

"According to Carlos, he was over at The Laurels and Caparo thought that he was spying on him or following him or something, so he decided to lock him in the barn."

"But what was Carlos doing over there in the first place? Obviously it's where he went when he left here last night, but why?"

Jeremy shrugged.

"God knows. He said that he just felt like a walk and he ended up there."

Carlos, thought Aubrey, was a mate. He could easily have said that he was following Aubrey, but he hadn't. Just in case it got Aubrey into some kind of trouble.

Molly nodded and took another careful sip of wine.

"So, this Rick Caparo character, is it him? Is he the one that's been doing all the murders?"

Jeremy nodded.

"It looks like it. The police aren't saying too much, but one of them told me that they had their eye on him anyway. They were getting ready to bring him in for questioning."

"Why? What put them on to him?"

"Well, apart from the fact that he works at The Laurels and The Laurels is one thing that connects most of the victims, this same officer said that there was a witness who saw him hanging about near Mr Telling's house not long before he died, and then saw him there again on the day that he actually died. The same witness also saw him over at The Meadows on the day that Carlos's mother died, so he thought that it was probably worth reporting it."

"Who was it?"

Jeremy smiled.

"Winston. The milkman. He's got a round over at The Meadows as well as the one he does here. He was in the same year as Rick Caparo at school. He recognised him."

Aubrey smiled to himself. Good old Winston. So that was what he had been doing that day when Aubrey had seen him talking to the police officer.

"Why do you think Caparo did it? What motive could he possibly have had?" asked Molly.

Jeremy shrugged his shoulders.

"I really don't know, although he was always a strange boy," he mused. "I never really knew much about him. As far as I can remember, his mother only ever came to one parents' evening, and to be honest I couldn't get much sense out of her. She seemed half-cut. But Rick Caparo was one of those kids where you always suspected that there was more to him than met the eye, although not in a good way, if you know what I mean. He never actually did anything, but somehow, if ever there was trouble, he was always the first kid you thought of. He was always a bit of an outsider as well. Usually kids like that have a hard time at Sir Frank's, but he didn't. None of the other kids ever picked on him, not even the bullies. I think that they were afraid of him. I didn't really like being alone with him myself, although I could never quite put my finger on what it was about him. The younger brother is just the same."

He hesitated for a moment and then he said, "There was someone else in the barn with them, too, in a sense."

"What do you mean, in a sense?"

Aubrey could feel that Molly was holding her breath.

"One of the immigrants that they'd brought across in Dave's van. He was dead, poor soul. According to Caparo, he fell ill in the middle of one night and they didn't dare get a doctor out to him, so he died. They wrapped him in a roll of old carpet and stored him in the barn while they were trying to work out what to do with him. From the smell of the place, I'd say that he'd been in there for quite a while."

"Why on earth didn't they bury him? Nobody ever goes over there. They would probably have got away with it, and at least it would have given the poor man some sort of final resting place."

"Carlos said that was what Dave and Caparo started arguing about. Dave told Caparo to go and get a shovel or something, and the next thing that happened was Dave was on the ground."

"So, was Dave involved in all the other murders as well?" asked Molly. She shivered suddenly. "To think that he's been in our house. Drinking our tea."

And eating your biscuits, added Aubrey silently.

"No, I don't think that he was involved in the other killings," said Jeremy. "And to his credit, when they were carrying him out to the ambulance, he did say that he was sorry about the body in the barn."

"Sorry that the man was dead, or sorry that he'd been caught?"

"Both probably," admitted Jeremy.

"Will the police count that as murder, too?" asked Molly.

"I don't know. I don't think so. It might be gross negligence manslaughter for failing to get a doctor or something like that. Not that it will make much difference to Rick Caparo. One more on the sheet is going to be neither here nor there."

"What do you think is going to happen to him now?" Molly said.

"I'm not sure that he'll be fit to plead. When the police burst in, he just stood there. He didn't even look surprised. Dave was lying on the floor groaning, the blood was pouring out of him, but Caparo just looked as though he was wondering what to make himself for dinner. One of the officers called an ambulance while the others cuffed Caparo, and he just let himself be led away. He didn't even raise an eyebrow, let alone a fist. Mind you, he was reeking of alcohol. There was one strange thing, though," he added.

"What?"

Aubrey felt Jeremy shift slightly beneath him.

"Just as they were leading him away, he turned back and leaned over."

"And?"

"He kissed Carlos on the cheek and stroked his face. Very

gently."

They were both silent for a moment and then Molly said, "So where is Carlos now? Not still at the police station, surely?"

"No, they carted him off to the children's home eventually, but how long they'll keep him there and whether he can come back to Sir Frank's or not, is anyone's guess. I expect the Head will do her best to keep him out."

He sighed and ran a hand over Aubrey's back.

"Did the Social Services send anyone in the end?" asked Molly.

"Eventually they sent some kid. He was wearing jeans and trainers, and he sweated a lot. In fact, he didn't look much older than Carlos himself. He seemed more concerned about protecting his own back than offering anything constructive. He kept muttering to himself and putting little ticks on a sheet."

"What for?"

"God knows."

Molly thought for a moment and then said, "When will we know what they decide to do about Carlos?"

"I haven't got a clue. Nobody's really obliged to tell us anything anyway. I mean, we're not official foster parents or anything. In a sense, none of this has got anything to do with us."

They both fell silent for a moment, and then Molly said, "Rachel rang earlier. She wanted to know what was happening. She also wanted us to know that Clive may be up for an OBE, but we're sworn to secrecy."

"What?"

Aubrey didn't know what an OBE was, but from Jeremy's outraged reaction it was clearly something big. He listened with interest.

"According to Rachel, they've had the nod. Whatever that's supposed to mean."

"Ye Gods and Bloody Great Big Fishes. What's he getting it for? Services to hypocrisy?"

Molly smiled.

"Probably. Anyway, Rachel's full of it. She's already planning her outfit."

"Do you know what really depresses me?" Jeremy tucked his chin down into his chest and stared across the room.

"What?"

"I doubt if Clive has ever done one single thing in the whole of his self-centred little life that didn't have some benefit to him attached." He sighed. "Ah well."

He paused and then turned to face Molly.

"Moll, about Carlos…"

"Yes?"

"One thing that the sweaty kid from Social Services did say…"

"What?"

"Well, he did mention that there was a possibility of Carlos being fostered. If they could find anybody local prepared to take him, that is."

"And can they?"

"Can they what?"

"Find anybody local prepared to take him."

"Probably not. Apparently foster parents aren't keen on teenaged boys. If they do manage to find somewhere for him, it's likely that they'll have to move him out of the district. Either that, or leave him at Alderman Wenlock's."

Molly was silent for a moment and then she said slowly, "I know what you're thinking, Jeremy, but don't go getting your hopes up. It's not as simple as you might think. It's not like just turning up at a rescue centre and picking a cat. You have to apply and go through a whole process. There's all sorts of checks, and probably training and stuff that you have to go through. It's not something that can just happen overnight."

"But if it could…" Jeremy's tone sounded hopeful.

"Well, I suppose that we have got a spare room…"

Jeremy hugged Aubrey closer.

"I knew you'd say that. To be honest, I did sort of mention it to the sweaty kid. Like, how we might go about it and that sort of thing."

"And what did he say?"

"Nothing very helpful, really, although he did say that he would find out for us and gave me the number of someone to contact. I don't know." He paused and thought for a moment. "I just feel that we've come this far with Carlos, we can't just abandon him now. He's got nobody else. And of course," he added, " there is one huge advantage."

Molly smiled.

"What's that?"

"It will piss Rachel off no end."

Chapter Thirty-Three

A quiet hush lay over the neighbourhood. For once, all the cats were indoors. Even Bernard the tortoiseshell from number sixteen, who was an outdoors type of cat if ever there was one, had spent the evening draped quietly across one of the work surfaces in the kitchen while his owners were out. Outside, the computer-generated missing posters adorned the lampposts and the bus shelters. None of the cats could read but they all knew the word 'missing', especially when it was printed in great big letters with a picture of Moses underneath it. Aubrey had barely been able to look at it. The bright-eyed little cat with the sticking-up fur and tiny little paws staring straight and trustingly into the camera, had been more than he could take.

He wandered through to the kitchen and took a sniff at his food bowl. It was no good, he just didn't fancy anything. Upstairs, Molly and Jeremy were still fast asleep, oblivious to the fact that Aubrey had been under their bed for most of the night. He hadn't been able to sleep. Every time he'd drifted off, he'd been startled awake again, images of Moses still hanging in the air in front of him. Moses holding on for dear life to that big cat's back in the fight, Moses skipping up the garden with a message from Vincent; and worst of all, Moses lying stiff and cold and alone somewhere. Dead. He leapt onto the kitchen window sill and stared gloomily out into the dark garden, waiting for the dawn to break.

Moses was an annoying little twerp, it was true. He was as thick as the proverbial two short planks. He needed everything explained to him at least twice, and he had a tendency to forget even that before he'd taken three steps. In terms of brain revving power, Moses went from nought to five in about twenty minutes. On the other hand, he had a heart as big as a lion's and was always as happy as the day was long. As long as Moses had something to eat and the odd kind word, he was fine, all was right in his little world.

Aubrey's heart smote him. He hadn't always been kind to Moses, he knew. Many a time he had been irritable and short-tempered, often when it wasn't even Moses' fault, like when he'd just been delivering a message or something. He squeezed his eyes shut. What he'd give to have Moses delivering a message to him now. He opened his eyes again to see a big, dark shape staring back at him through the window on the other side. Vincent.

He hurried out through the cat flap as Vincent jumped down onto the gravel path.

"Any news?"

Aubrey tried to keep the pleading out of his voice. Vincent shook his head.

"It's what I came to ask you."

Together, they sauntered slowly round the side of the house and out onto the front path. The very faintest sound of bird song began to break through the silence. In the distance they could hear the electric hum and whine of Winston's milk float.

"Fancy a pint?"

Vincent nodded his head. At the bottom of the street, Winston's float turned the corner and began to creep slowly towards them.

"Come on then."

They ran swiftly across the road and leapt lightly onto the back of the float as Winston parked it outside number twelve.

"All right, Aubrey?"

Aubrey froze, paw mid-air suspended above a strawberry yoghurt pot. Surely there couldn't be two cats with a little squeaky voice like that? He turned in confusion to Vincent, who had also stopped in his tracks. For a moment, they stared at each other.

"Moses!"

"All right, Vin?"

From underneath an upturned crate, a small bright-eyed cat emerged, wriggling his way free, little pink nose and the tips of tiny paws first.

"Moses…"

It was no good, words failed him. He gulped hard. He was torn between the desire to give the little cat a good clump round the ear and holding him as close to his chest as he could.

"Moses." Vincent's voice sounded strange, and Aubrey suddenly realised that it was because he was as choked as he was. "You do realise, don't you, that everybody's been looking for you? Where have you been all this time?"

Moses looked from one to the other, confused.

"I got lost after the scrap and then I saw Winston, so I jumped on the float."

"Do you mean," Aubrey asked incredulously, "that you've spent the last twenty-four hours touring the neighbourhood with Winston?"

Moses nodded, eyes shining.

"Does Winston know that you're here?" demanded Vincent.

Moses shook his head. "I fell asleep under his seat."

Aubrey opened his mouth to speak, and then closed it again as Winston jumped back into the driving seat and started the engine.

"Might as well stay for the ride while we're here," said Vincent. He steadied himself as the float jolted forward, and turned to grin at Aubrey and Moses. The three cats sat side-by-side and gazed out at the breaking day as the milk float glided forward.

Fantastic Books
Great Authors

CROOKED
CAT

Meet our authors and discover
our exciting range:

- Gripping Thrillers
- Cosy Mysteries
- Romantic Chick-Lit
- Fascinating Historicals
- Exciting Fantasy
- Young Adult and Children's
  Adventures
- Non-Fiction

17835879R00127

Printed in Great Britain
by Amazon